A Christmas
Mystery
in
Provence

To Phyllis

A Christmas Mystery
in Provence

Mary-Jane Deeb

My guardian
angel in
friendship &
gratitude

Mary-Jane Deeb
October 2004

PARACLETE PRESS
BREWSTER, MASSACHUSETTS

Library of Congress Cataloging–in–Publication Data

Deeb, Mary-Jane.
    A Christmas mystery in Provence / by Mary-Jane Deeb.
        p.   cm.
    ISBN 1–55725–410–9
    1. Women detectives—France—Provence—Fiction. 2. Newspaper
publishing—Fiction. 3. Americans—France—Fiction.
4. Provence (France)—Fiction I. Title.
PS3554.E3433C48 2004
813' .54—dc22

                                                                2004016772

10 9 8 7 6 5 4 3 2 1

© 2004 by Mary-Jane Deeb

ISBN 1-55725-410-9

Published by Paraclete Press
Brewster, Massachusetts
www.paracletepress.com

Printed in the United States of America.

To

Marius and Hadi

AUTHOR'S NOTE

The ancient town of Grasse in Provence is set on a hill overlooking the French Riviera and the Mediterranean Sea. It is built around a twelfth-century cathedral, Notre Dame du Puy, which very much resembles my own fictional Cathedral of Notre Dame des Fleurs. In fact, the two could be mistaken for each other were it not for the little chapel with a beautiful stained glass window of the nativity scene which exists only in my novel. Even before the Cathedral was built, Grasse was a free city, allied to Pisa and Genoa, and only incorporated into France in 1482. I write this in case, dear reader, you wondered why my fictional heroines, though French, have an Italian surname.

The glimpses you get in the novel of the history of Grasse are in general quite accurate. I have to admit, however, that I have no way of knowing for sure if the Duke of Berry ever gave Louis d'Anjou, the Count of Provence, the Book of Hours which brought such havoc into the de Medici household. But the *Trés Riches Heures du Duc de Berry* and the *Belles Heures du Duc de Berry* really do exist, and are among the most beautiful Books of Hours of late medieval Europe. The former is presently located in the Condé Museum in Chantilly, in France, while a perfect nineteenth-century copy of the latter is in the Cloisters at the Metropolitan Museum in New York. The illustrations described in this novel are also real in every detail. If you are ever tempted to, you can see these for yourself by visiting the museums. To see reproductions of these works, I suggest you consult the *Trés Riches Heures of Jean, Duke of Berry*, first published by George Brazillier in 1969 in New York and reprinted in 1989; and

Millard Meiss, *French Painting in the Time of Jean de Berry: The Limbourgs and Their Contemporaries,* published in London in 1974 by Thames and Hudson.

Mary-Jane Deeb

CAST OF CHARACTERS

GRAND-MÈRE (or Madame de Medici): the French matriarch who lives in an eighteenth-century villa in Grasse. She has gathered her family together to celebrate Christmas in an old-fashioned Provençal manner, but little does she know what she has set into motion.

MARIE-CHRISTINE (or Chrissy): Grand-mère's half-American granddaughter has returned to Grasse to take over the reins of *Le Loup-Garou*, the local paper she owns. She never counted on a family scandal to put her paper back on a sound financial footing.

PRISCILLA ABERCROMBIE: Marie-Christine's mother. She worries, and with good reason, that her only daughter will get into trouble every time Chrissy visits her grandmother in Grasse.

JEAN-PIERRE de MEDICI: Marie-Christine's father and Grand-mère's eldest son. As head of the family, he is called upon to restore the social order when it is disrupted by murder.

VALÉRIE: Grand-mère's unrivaled cook and housekeeper. She is quite unprepared for what Christmas will bring to the de Medici household.

JEAN (or Gros-Jean): Valérie's husband, and Grand-mère's butler, driver, gamekeeper. He takes note of the inaccuracies in people's statements to the police.

CLAUDE BIZZARD: Inspector of the *Police Judiciaire* at the *Quai des Orfèvres* in Paris and Grand-mère's favorite policeman. She has invited him to spend Christmas with the family, but murder and mayhem follow him even to Grasse.

XAVIER de la ROCHEREAU: Grand-mère's son-in-law and head of a large auction house that specializes in the sale of paintings, sculptures, and antiques. He hates leaving Paris, so why has he come to spend Christmas in Grasse?

GENEVIÈVE de la ROCHEREAU: Grand-mère's middle child and Chrissy's aunt. Elegant and smart, she runs her own consultancy to rescue failing businesses. But is she as successful as she appears to be?

HELÈNE de MEDICI: Grand-mère's youngest daughter and Chrissy's aunt. She is a divorcée, an unpublished poet, and blurts out truths that embarrass some and frighten others.

PHILLIPE BOUSQUET: the charming ex-husband of Helène. He does not like to work, and trouble seems to follow him wherever he goes.

GERARD BOUSQUET: Helène and Phillipe's twenty-two-year-old son. He is clever but not always the angel he appears to be.

SISTER FELICITY: from Scholastica Abbey on Cape Cod, an expert on medieval manuscripts. She brings to Grasse the *Belles Heures du Duc de Berry*, a famous French Book of Hours. She is not aware of the dangers that lurk behind the peaceful facade of that small Provençal town.

MONSEIGNEUR BERNARD d'EPINAY: Bishop of the Cathedral of Notre Dame des Fleurs. He wants to bring two rare French manuscripts to Grasse. But will he be able to do so on time to celebrate his cathedral's eight-hundredth anniversary?

ALAIN LEMOINE: a librarian from Strasbourg, who knows a great deal about medieval manuscripts. Chrissy wonders how a librarian could be so young and handsome.

FRANÇOIS MARTEL: the hen-pecked mayor of Grasse, who loves dining at Grand-mère's. He tells the story of a five-hundred-year-old mystery that was never solved.

MATHILDE MARTEL: the mayor's wife. She writes recipes for *Le Loup-Garou* and has a new hat for every occasion.

LEON BAUDE: the managing editor of *Le Loup-Garou*. He and his small staff, including Vivianne and Paul, worry about rumors of people with nefarious intentions who are spending Christmas in Grasse.

DOMINIQUE PASTEUR: Grasse's police inspector. He is not too happy sharing the investigation with his colleague from Paris.

FRANÇOIS GUERRIER: Assistant to the police inspector. He keeps an eye on the de Medici household, but fails to prevent a break-in.

PROLOGUE

Ms. Catherine E. Stuart
Associate Publisher
MacPherson Publishing Group
Palm Beach, Florida

Dear Catherine,

February in Paris is just toooo dreary! You're lucky you're in Palm Beach. At least there's sun and sea there. Paris is so . . . cold . . . and gray! After all the excitement at Christmas at my grandmother's house in the south of France, this city seems pretty dull. Am bored to tears! Mother says that Coco Chanel lived at the Ritz for thirty years. Boredom must have driven her to haute couture. I mean one *must do* something for entertainment. Don't get me wrong, this place is gorgeous, but give me Grand-mère's house in Grasse any day! So much is always going on there, and the food is scrumptious. But I had to come. After all that happened in Grasse at Christmas, I had to pacify Mother and agree to spend a mother-daughter week with her in Paris.

Let me tell you: the story I've been involved in made all the papers in France last month! You won't believe what I've been through. Have written it all up and will send you the manuscript under separate cover. For now, I am using excerpts for my paper *Le Loup-Garou* (Did you know I am the owner and editor-in-chief of a local paper in Grasse?).

The story begins when Papa and Mother decide to join me in France to spend a nice peaceful Christmas holiday *en famille* with my grandmother who is getting on in years. The family includes my two aunts, their husbands and ex-husbands, a cousin and his friend, and others including an incredible nun from Scholastica Abbey on Cape Cod.

Within a couple of days we have a five-hundred-year-old mystery on our hands, followed shortly thereafter by grand theft and murder. But I won't tell you more, as I want you to read my manuscript. I know that you're very busy with your new job at MacPherson Publishing, but do a classmate a favor and tell me what you think. The story is absolutely true (you can check the facts in *Le Figaro* and *Le Monde*, for January 2nd). My manuscript has an insider's view of what really happened, and who the true heroes are. Perhaps your company would be interested in publishing it?

You will receive the manuscript early next week. If you want to discuss it over a glass of *vin maison*, and a little *tapenade* of capers and black olives, why don't you come and spend a few days with me in Grasse this spring? Grand-mère loves company, and I know she'll love to have you come and stay at her house. Hope to see you soon. Big hug!

Chrissy
Le Ritz, Paris

A Christmas
Mystery
in
Provence

I

It is dark and cold when I arrive at the house. The icy drizzle has not stopped since we left the airport at Nice. Grand-mère sent Jean to pick us up in her old Citroën, but I alone took it. Mother absolutely refuses to ride in this car.

"You cannot believe the contraptions they call cars over there. Death traps—that's what they are," she complains to her friends in Scarsdale.

Wrapping herself in her sable fur coat, Mother makes a last attempt to dissuade me outside the first-class lounge of the airport.

"Why you want to ride in this clanging wreck, Chrissy, I just cannot understand."

"You and Papa take the limo to the Carlton. Jean will drive me to Grasse. Don't worry, Mother, I'll be all right."

Sighing in resignation, she picks up her jewel case and gives me a peck on the cheek. Papa hugs me and says, "Tell your grandmother that we'll be coming over for tea early next week, and that I am expecting Valérie's *vert-vert.*"

By a miracle the Citroën has made it to the door of the eighteenth-century villa. Valérie, Grand-mère's housekeeper-cum-lady-in-waiting, and Jean's wife, must have been praying to St. Marguerite. They are all waiting in the hallway. Lavender shawl crossed on her ample bosom, Grand-mère enfolds me in her arms the way she has always done as far back as I can remember.

"Ah, *mon enfant!* I have really missed you!"

"Me, too, Grand-mère!" I say, giving her soft cheek a big kiss. "Me, too!"

Pulling me away from her, she inspects me with her bright blue eyes.

1

"Let me look at you. Ha! Just as I expected! You have lost weight, and look emaciated. It is all those raw vegetables and skinless chickens that your mother feeds you!"

The moment I land on French soil the battle resumes between my American mother, Priscilla Abercrombie (of the Abercrombies of New York, as she likes to point out) and my French grandmother on my father's side, Eleanore de Medici of Grasse (as she never ceases to remind me). It is a battle that began when Grand-mère's only son, my father, decided not to run the *parfumerie* in Grasse that had been in the de Medici family for over 350 years, and instead went to live in the United States and married an American. It was only my birth, a couple of years later, and Papa's promise that I would spend my summers in France with my grandmother, that brought a truce between mother and son. Grand-mère, however, never quite forgave her son for his betrayal of the de Medici name and patrimony. When I turned one, she announced that I would be her sole heir, and on my twenty-fifth birthday she proceeded to transfer ten million dollars to my bank account!

If Grand-mère had stopped at that, family relations might not have been too badly strained. Father is in the oil business, as are the Abercrombies. So my legacy does not make a big dent in the family fortune. But Grand-mère had to listen to me and indulge my whims. When I told her last summer that my secret wish was to become a writer, she bought me a newspaper (with part of my inheritance, of course). Well, not exactly the *Wall Street Journal*, but a small provincial paper that was going belly up: Grasse's *Le Loup-Garou*. The former publisher then got himself murdered, my life was threatened a couple of times, and I almost joined the ancient shipwrecks at the bottom of the Mediterranean when someone threw me overboard from his yacht.[1]

---

[1] See M. J. Deeb, *Murder on the Riviera* (Brewster, MA: Paraclete Press, 2004).

My adventures did nothing to smooth family relations. However, they did convince me that I could do more than while away my summers on the French Riviera, playing tennis, swimming, and dancing. I could run a paper, solve a mystery, and take care of myself under rather trying circumstances. It also became clear that since I now owned a paper in Grasse, I had to be physically there to run it. I would have to spend more than just my summers in southern France. I would have to live and work there.

So here I am in Grasse, ready to spend Christmas and the rest of the winter season with my grandmother. My parents have decided that, for once, they too will spend Christmas on the Riviera. Not at Grand-mère's, however, but at their usual haunt—the Carlton, one of the most luxurious hotels in Cannes.

"If Queen Victoria could spend part of the winter season in the South of France, my dear, so can I," Mother told one of her bridge partners last week, as she was preparing to leave New York. I think she was trying to convince herself.

Back to the present. Grand-mère is observing me with a critical eye.

"Valérie, you will exert every effort to make sure that Mademoiselle Marie-Christine puts some flesh on these unsightly bones."

Valérie is standing behind Grand-mère with a big grin on her weathered face. She is wiping her hands on her apron. Must have been exerting precisely such an effort back in the kitchen just before I arrived.

"*Mais bien sûr, Madame.* How are you, Mademoiselle? We are so glad to have you with us, especially for Christmas. You just wait and see what I have prepared for you. It will be the happiest

Christmas we have had in this house, since . . . since your father and your aunts were young."

"Valérie! How are you?" I give her a big hug. She smells of rosemary, and warm bread.

Jean takes my bags up to my room, where a fire is burning in the fireplace. There is no central heating in the villa, nor air-conditioning.

"My ancestors did not need central heating, so why should I?" argues Grand-mère when the subject is brought up. Mother cannot understand.

"Our ancestors lived in caves! Is it necessary to freeze to death because they did?"

My room in summer is cool, and smells of lemon, jasmine, and wax. In winter it is filled with the smell of pinewood and of the oranges on the table next to the fireplace. The billowing goose down comforter with tiny pink flowers, and the down pillows are soooo inviting! But I cannot flop down there and go to sleep. Must first go down and have a little chat with Grand-mère and try at least one of Valérie's cookies, her *madeleines au citron*. If I don't, tomorrow Valérie will sulk, and Grand-mère will give me a lecture on good behavior!

◆

"Slept like a *marmotte,* have you?" asks Valérie, referring to the traditional woodchuck.

She has entered my room at 9 AM sharp, drawn the curtains and opened the wooden shutters. A big tray with fresh coffee, croissants, strawberry and apricot jams, little curled balls of homemade butter, and a plate of cheeses, have been placed on the table next to the oranges.

When I wake up in Grand-mère's house, I always know where I am. No confusion, no jet lag. The coffee's aroma gets me out of bed and into my slippers and woolen dressing gown in a jiffy.

"Thank you, Valérie," I say as I settle next to the fireplace and bite into my croissant.

"Your bath will be ready in fifteen minutes, and then Madame wants to see you in *le petit salon*." Valérie has a big smile as she points downstairs.

"Your grandmother is so happy you are back. She woke up this morning and was downstairs all dressed up before I could prepare her morning tisane.*"

Le petit salon is Grand-mère's personal living room on the first floor. That is where she reads, prays in the morning, has her tisane, and retires at night before going to bed. I have rarely been in there and only on solemn occasions. Childhood memories of this room are linked to the loss of my dog Asterix, the cancellation of a birthday party, and the breaking of a precious vase that I had knocked over while playing. I therefore approach *le petit salon* with some trepidation.

"Ah, there you are, *ma chérie*! You look better already. I see some color in your cheeks. Come and sit next to me. I have a lot of things to tell you."

Grand-mère pats the cushion on the sofa next to her. The room is as I remember it: furnished with overstuffed sofas and armchairs in pale green velvet. The tables, a desk, and a large bookshelf are all in polished dark oak. The heavy velvet curtains with gold tassels have been pulled to let the gray winter light filter into the room. A cheery fire is crackling in the fireplace.

"First, young lady, your paper: *Le Loup-Garou* has been run most efficiently, in your absence, by Sister Angela and that friend of *Inspecteur* Bizzard, Leon Baude. He did the reporting, Sister

Angela did everything else. However, Sister Angela had to return to Cape Cod, and Scholastica Abbey, yesterday. She asked me to tell you good-bye—and *à bientôt*. She also left a little gift for you that you can open only on Christmas day."

Sister Angela, Claude Bizzard—the names bring back last summer's adventures. When I was nursing a great big lump on my head, Sister Angela took care of me, and when I sank to the very bottom of the Mediterranean, Claude saved my life. Wish they could be here now! But Grand-mère is looking stern. Peering over her glasses, she frowns:

"Marie-Christine, you are not listening!"

"Yes I am, Grand-mère. I was just remembering last summer."

Her face softens.

"I hope you have recovered now. *Hein*? Because you have work to do. Leon Baude will also leave next week. He is expected to return to his job in Paris. You must now take the reins of your paper and hire new people, or else. . . ." Here Grand-mère's voice drops to a hoarse whisper, "*Le Loup-Garou* is dead."

Le Loup-Garou, the "Big Bad Wolf" or "Werewolf" of children's tales, my newspaper, dead?!

"Never, Grand-mère. I will not let it die."

Although indignation has the upper hand at the moment, I must confess to my shortcomings.

"It's true that I did not have much editorial experience when I took over the paper last summer. I needed Claude's help and I learned a great deal from him. But now I really do mean to run *Le Loup-Garou*. Did you know that I even enrolled in a journalism class at Columbia University this fall?"

Rather a long speech from yours truly, but it seems to work. After a searching look into my very soul, Grand-mère relaxes. She draws her shawl closer to her chest, and clears her throat.

"Marie-Christine, will you please call Valérie and tell her to bring me my tisane."

Just as I get up from the sofa, the door opens and Valérie appears with a steaming cup of camomile and a little plate of madeleines.

"What took you so long? I was beginning to freeze in here. Can you do something with this anemic fire? Marie-Christine will change her mind and return to New York if this house feels like an icebox!"

Valérie mutters, *"Bien Madame,"* and sets the cup and cookies on a small table next to Grand-mère. How she puts up with my grandmother I'll never know, but the two of them have managed to live together in this house for the past fifty years!

She places a new log in the fireplace and scuttles wood and ashes noisily. Before shutting the door as she exits, Valérie winks at me and points to the madeleines.

"I made these for *you*, not for *her*!"

Grand-mère selects the largest madeleine from the plate and grimaces after biting into it.

"Last month's batch tasted better. Too much sugar."

"Well, Grand-mère, what is it that you wanted to tell me that could not wait?"

Grand-mère picks up her tisane, inhales deeply the steam of the camomile tea, and then takes a noisy gulp from the cup.

"Marie-Christine, I have an *exclusif* for next week's issue of *Le Loup-Garou!*"

Am stunned. Grand-mère has a scoop for my paper?! This is sooo not Grand-mère. I mean it's like the French President skateboarding! Or Mother eating frog legs!

"What exactly do you mean by an *exclusif*, Grand-mère?" I ask cautiously.

Grand-mère chuckles. She is looking very pleased with herself.

"Ha, ha! You are shocked! You think your old Grand-mère does not know what an *exclusif* is. Let me tell you, *mon enfant*, in 1941 during the war. . . ."

Definitely do not want to hear (again) any war stories. I lay my hand firmly on her arm, and bring her back to this millennium.

"I know, I know, Grand-mère. You helped the *Resistance,* and *Le Monde* later wrote about you. But please tell me what scoop do you have for *Le Loup-Garou*?"

Heaving a big sigh and turning her eyes upward, Grand-mère asks *le Bon Dieu* to have mercy on her impatient granddaughter. She then resumes, in a conspiratorial tone, "I have it on the best authority that some extremely rare and valuable objects will be arriving in Grasse next week."

She stops and takes another sip from the tisane. Suspense is killing me.

"What objects?" I ask impatiently.

Grand-mère frowns. She disapproves of even the slightest sign of disrespect.

"Sorry, Grand-mère, but what rare and valuable objects are we talking about here?"

"The *Trés Riches Heures de Jean, Duc de Berry*, my dear.[2]

I am not quite sure that we are on the same wavelength here. Were we not just talking about a "scoop"? Sort of like . . . a sex scandal? A crime in high society? I look at Grand-mère. She seems all right. It was only this past summer that she (and I) helped the police solve a dastardly crime. Is it possible that age has begun to tell?

Grand-mère is shaking her head in disbelief.

___

[2] See *The Trés Riches Heures of Jean, Duke of Berry*, Introduction and Legends by Jean Longnon and Raymond Cazelles (New York: George Brazillier, Inc., 1969).

"You do not know what I am talking about, Marie-Christine? Shame on you! Once *everyone* knew what the *Trés Riches Heures* was. Today your generation knows little of the history and culture of this great country. The *Trés Riches Heures* is the single most famous illuminated manuscript of medieval Europe. It was commissioned in the early fifteenth century by the French Duke of Berry who invited the de Limbourg brothers to illustrate a Book of Hours. The Duke, and eventually the illustrators, died before the manuscript was completed. It was only toward the end of the fifteenth century, under the patronage of the Duke of Savoie, that the work was finished by a different artist. It is a masterpiece! Magnificent! Unique!"

I get up and poke the fire. How can I tell Grand-mère that her illuminated manuscript does not exactly fall under the category of a "scoop"? With my back to her I mumble, "I'll be sure to inform the readers of *Le Loup-Garou* that the manuscript is coming to Grasse next week."

"*Mais non, mais non*, Marie-Christine, you do not understand. This is a very special event."

Grand-mère knocks her cane to the floor in her agitation. I turn back and pick it up. Have resigned myself to receiving a lecture on a subject I know (and care) "diddly-squat" about. So I grab a madeleine for comfort and settle on the plump sofa next to Grand-mère.

"Let me tell you what this is all about," resumes Grand-mère, breathing heavily in her excitement. "For the past year Monseigneur d'Epinay has been working very hard to put together a unique exhibit at the Cathedral."

(A note here: Monseigneur Bernard d'Epinay is the bishop of Grasse's twelfth-century Cathedral of Notre Dame des Fleurs. We first met when he held me over the baptismal font some twenty-five years ago. At the ripe age of three I decided he needed a nickname, and "Pepy" is what I still call him when we are *en famille*. He and Grand-mère have been friends forever, and he often seeks her advice on delicate matters concerning the community).

"As you know, Marie-Christine, Monseigneur d'Epinay is a very influential man. He knows many people in high places in Paris, London, Washington, and elsewhere. They consult him when they need his assistance, and his opinions are highly valued because they are always based on sound judgment. In the past three years relations between the United States and France have deteriorated significantly. Americans are visiting France less often than before. Although I personally do not think this is a great loss, the airlines and the tourism industry do not share my opinion. Your countrymen are also boycotting French wine and French perfume. I have to admit that this is hurting the wine and perfume industries, as well as the growers of grapes and flowers in Provence, and in Grasse in particular. Do you see what I'm getting at, Marie-Christine?"

Not really. Always knew that Grand-mère was well-informed, but was not aware that she was an expert on international affairs as well.

"I'm afraid I'm at a loss, Grand-mère. What do precious manuscripts have to do with Grasse's perfume industry, Provençal wine, Monseigneur d'Epinay, and American relations with France? But most important what do all those things have to do with *Le Loup-Garou?*"

There I said it. Got it off my chest. Must be all the memories linked to this room that are bubbling up, 'cause I am feeling definitely irritable.

"But everything, *mon enfant*, everything," says Grand-mère, waving her hands and dropping her cane again.

"You see, Monseigneur d'Epinay is always very concerned about the problems of his flock. . . ."

"You mean the people of Grasse?"

"*Mais bien sûr*, the people of Grasse. Who else? Therefore, anything that upsets this community, upsets him, *évidemment*."

That is not at all self-evident. Lots of people don't care a hoot about what happens in their community as long as their own turf is secure. Lots of self-serving politicians, for example, . . . but Grand-mère is continuing.

"So, when American tourists stopped buying our perfumes and our wines, many of our Grassois farmers, wine vendors, and others lost their jobs and savings. Marie-Christine, you do not realize the state the economy of Grasse is in."

Frankly, I have not given it much thought. Grand-mère has a point here. As a professional editor and owner of Grasse's leading paper, I really should be paying more attention to the economy.

"So the good bishop has thought of a way of promoting better Franco-American relations and attracting tourists back to Grasse."

The wood is crackling in the fireplace. The room smells of burnt leaves, and camomile tea. Grand-mère is telling me a story, just like when I was a kid!

"He got the idea when he was visiting Scholastica Abbey in America last year. You know how he loves the place, and how close his relations are to the Sisters and Brothers there."

(Scholastica Abbey, located on Cape Cod, is Monseigneur d'Epinay's home away from home. It is an ecumenical Christian community of married members and celibate Brothers and Sisters who live according to a Benedictine monastic tradition. Last summer Sister Angela, one of his protégés and a member of the Abbey, came and stayed with Grand-mère while she was studying fresco art at the Notre Dame des Fleurs Cathedral.) Grand-mère clears her throat and rearranges the cushion behind her back.

"It was Sister Felicity at Scholastica Abbey who gave him the idea. She is an expert on medieval illuminated manuscripts, and worked in a big library in New York before joining the Abbey. Apparently Sister Felicity mentioned to the bishop that, while at the library, she had worked on the conservation of a beautiful early fifteenth-century French manuscript called *Les Belles Heures de Jean Duc de Berry*. Well, Monseigneur d'Epinay was very familiar with the other Book of Hours of that same Duke, which is now in the Condé Museum in Chantilly. Those two prayer books, illuminated by the same artists, had not been seen together in over four hundred years.

"What better tribute then, to the historical relations between France and the United States, than to display the two manuscripts together, in Grasse, on the eight-hundredth anniversary of the Cathedral of Notre Dame des Fleurs, on New Year's Day?"

Have to admit that this is not such a bad idea after all.

"Grand-mère, do you mean this New Year's Day? In two weeks' time?"

"Yes, yes, of course, Marie-Christine." Ha! Who is impatient now?

"But the manuscripts are not here yet, are they?"

"No, they'll be here in a day or two. There were so many formalities and papers to sign, and permissions to ask! When all that was done, the New York Library asked who was going to insure the manuscript? Monseigneur d'Epinay was shocked. It had not even occurred to him that the manuscripts needed to be insured. The deal was going to collapse until I reminded Monseigneur that your uncle, Xavier de la Rochereau, was the head of this big auction house that deals with art, paintings, sculpture, antiques, etc., and would know what to do. To make a long story short, Xavier found an insurance company that was willing to insure the manuscripts for the week that they will be on exhibit."

Grand-mère looks very pleased with herself. She is a very shrewd business woman. After all it was she, and not my grandfather, who ran the family *parfumerie* for almost fifty years, and turned it into a very profitable business.

"So you have seen Uncle Xavier and Aunt Geneviève?"

Geneviève has taken after her mother. She is Papa's sister, the middle child, and definitely intimidating. A graduate of the *Ecole Nationale d'Administration*, the French equivalent of Harvard's John F. Kennedy School of Government, she has her own consultancy and helps put faltering businesses back on their feet. Xavier, whom she met in Paris a zillion years ago, is very aristocratic in pedigree and manner. Tall, slim, and pale, he projects the image of a consumptive nineteenth-century poet.

"Oh yes, *chérie*, of course. They are coming tomorrow and spending a few days here until the eight-hundredth anniversary celebrations on New Year's Day!"

Am not quite enthused by the news. My aunt and uncle never had any children of their own and do not warm up easily to my generation's views on life. Smile wanly, "It is Christmas, I suppose." I try to sound cheerful.

Grand-mère looks at me suspiciously.

"What do you mean, Marie-Christine? Of course it is Christmas, and the whole family will be coming here for dinner on the twenty-fourth, and lunch on Christmas day! It has been years since we've had a proper Christmas *en famille* with all the members of the de Medici clan together under one roof. But this year, thanks to you, *ma chérie*, we will have a wonderful Provençal Christmas as in the good old days when your grandfather was alive!"

Grand-mère's face has lit up with joy at the prospect. My spirits are sinking by the minute.

"*All* the family, Grand-mère?"

"*Mais bien sûr!* Your poor aunt Helène is coming too. At least, she is well rid of that husband of hers, although, *entre nous,* I believe she still cares about him! I did warn her that Philippe was a skirt-chaser and a *fainéant,* who would never do an honest day's work in his life, but she would not listen. Stubborn like her father! Despite the large dowry I gave her, Philippe managed to waste all her money on horses and women and then abandon her, and your cousin, Gerard was only five at the time."

I had heard the story of "poor Helène" many times before. From the time I was twelve Grand-mère would warn me not to turn out like her youngest daughter. Aunt Helène has the beauty that Renaissance painters liked: fulsome with long red hair. Claiming to be a poet (as yet unpublished), she believes she has a license to say what she thinks when she thinks it. Can be quite embarrassing sometimes.

Grand-mère is mentally organizing the dinner. Can see her counting the people around the table, and making a mental note of whom she will seat next to whom.

"Your parents will be here as well. I suggest you invite a friend for Christmas—perhaps that nice Inspector Bizzard. You know he has no family and might enjoy spending his Christmas holidays in Grasse. Monseigneur d'Epinay will come with Sister Felicity from Scholastica Abbey. I believe they will bring the manuscripts here for safekeeping until they are displayed in public on New Year's Day. No one is supposed to know about this."

"I won't say a word," I promise. Although I wonder how this is going to be a scoop for *Le Loup-Garou* if I cannot even reveal the whereabouts of the manuscripts.

"Then Gerard is also coming. He must be what, twenty-two, now?"

"Yes, Grand-mère, he's twenty-two and very smart. Papa told me that he has just graduated from the University of Strasbourg with a law degree."

"I'm glad I have two intelligent grandchildren! But only you, *ma chérie,* bear the de Medici name. *He* will always be the son of Philippe Bousquet."

Have always felt a bit uncomfortable with Grand-mère's often expressed preference for me over my cousin Gerard. I try to compensate by defending him, whatever he does. And he is no angel, mind you.

Grand-mère struggles with her cane and pulls herself up from the sofa.

"There are so many preparations ahead. I want to make this an unforgettable Christmas for you, Marie-Christine."

And unforgettable it would be. But on that chilly morning in December, with the wind blowing outside and the fire crackling in the grate, Grand-mère and I had no idea what was awaiting us.

II

After this conversation with Grand-mère it is time to tackle the pressing issue of what to do with *Le Loup-Garou.*

So I call Leon Baude, the managing editor who is leaving for Paris next week. Leon is a personal friend of Inspector Bizzard (he of the sea rescue), and with Sister Angela has run the paper for the past three months. Invite him to one of Grasse's very chic eating spots to express, in so many dishes, my deep appreciation for his efforts on behalf of this city and more specifically its local paper.

The *Restaurant La Bastide St. François*'s chef, Jacques Dubois, has been compared to the great chefs of Europe. His restaurant is an old, Provençal, stone country house set on a hill just outside Grasse, with a breathtaking view of the Bay of Théoule. We meet at 1 PM. I know Leon Baude only through e-mail. He is waiting at the door of the restaurant: short, red-haired, and stocky with a brown overcoat and a red muffler. He grins and holds out a gloved hand, "Recognized you immediately from the pictures in last summer's *Le Loup-Garou.* Congratulations on solving the case of the murder of Monsieur Rondin!"

The maître d' finds us a corner table with an outside view. The fire is blazing in the chimney and the room is already quite full. Jacques Dubois (a friend of Grand-mère, of course) comes to our table, "Ah! Mademoiselle de Medici, how great to see you! Back from America? And how is your extraordinary Grandmother? I have not seen her since last spring. Please give her my warmest regards and tell her that she has an open invitation for lunch or dinner whenever she chooses to visit us at *La Bastide.*

"And now for lunch. May I recommend the crayfish with asparagus served on a purée of chick peas? Or the duck liver served with artichoke hearts and finely chopped black truffles? You can start with the *amuse-gueules*, little palate teasers for which we are quite famous. For dessert a dish of wild wood strawberries in a spiced wine sauce and fresh Chantilly cream. What do you think?"

Leon and I look at each other.

"I will take the crayfish." My mouth is watering at the description.

"And I will have the duck liver," Leon jumps in as if the duck might fly away if he does not order immediately.

"While we're waiting, why don't you bring us some of your *amuse-gueules*," I add as an after thought.

I have taken off my mink jacket and stretch my legs towards the fireplace. I just love my new patent high-heel boots. Chef Jacques Dubois is choosing the wines. Holding the list close to his nose, and squinting a bit, he decides:

"For you, Mademoiselle, I suggest a half-bottle of the local *Chateau Sainte Marguerite* of 1992. And for Monsieur, the *Domaine des Quatres Vents* of 1995. An exceptionally good year. They will highlight the flavors of your respective dishes."

When the *amuse-gueules* are served and the wine poured, it is time to get acquainted. Conversation does not exactly flow. Leon is shy and the chic restaurant seems to overwhelm him. Although he has removed his coat, the red muffler seems to be securely attached to his neck, for comfort?

"So, did you enjoy running *Le Loup-Garou?*" I ask conversationally.

Answer "Yes," accompanied by a tug to the muffler.

"Wasn't Sister Angela a great help to you?"

More tugging, "Yes."

"Will you be leaving for Paris next week?"

"Yes." Begins to look rather red in the face. I think Leon is slowly strangling himself.

"Leon, don't you think it is quite warm in here? Perhaps you should take your muffler off?"

"Yes, yes, of course." With a bit of a struggle he manages to extricate his neck from the muffler. Looks flustered but his color is returning to normal.

I raise my glass, "Here's to getting to know you!"

Get him to drink to recover and unwind. He swallows half his glass.

I raise my glass again, barely touching it with my lips.

"Here's to *Le Loup-Garou.*"

This time Leon gulps the whole glass. He definitely looks much happier. Removes his jacket and reveals a bright red sweater that has seen better days. I wave to the waiter to get Leon another half-bottle of the *Domaine des Quatres Vents.*

"So now, Leon, tell me how *Le Loup-Garou* is *really* doing."

The wine, I very much hope, will remove his inhibitions, because I need to get a complete picture of the situation.

A couple of hiccups and a glassful later, Leon's tongue loosens up.

"Well, Marie-Christine (is it all right if I call you Marie-Chris . . . Marie-Chrissss . . . tine?)

I nod, patiently awaiting the report.

"Well, Marie-Christine, the paper is *not* doing well."

I reckoned as much, and am preparing for the worse.

"*Le Loup* is booo . . . bobooo. . . . "

I guess, "Boring?"

"*C'est ça!*" Seems relieved that I said it and not he.

Need him to explain.

"Who says it's boring?"

Leon puts his hand to his neck in search of the muffler, then looks regretfully at the chair where it is rumpled up.

"Everyone."

I eye him suspiciously. Don't like blanket statements. He reaches for the bottle and pours himself another glass.

"*Le Loup* needs to be overhauled: new ideas and new people. We can't just pick up stories from other papers and rehash them. Your board of directors has not done much to help. The one exception is the mayor's wife, who sends us recipes for Provençal dishes every week. Hic! Hic! In fact, this is turning out to be the most popular column of *Le Loup*, and Madame Martel is fast becoming a local celebrity in her own right, apart from being the mayor's wife. People have started writing to the paper asking for advice on how to cook certain traditional dishes, and she answers them. Could become an 'Ask Mathilde' column."

Shrewd man! Leon has given me a sense of the direness of the situation. If Madame Martel's dishes are the most exciting part of the paper, we are in big trouble. The rest of my board? Well . . . they were all suspects in the murder of the previous owner of *Le Loup-Garou* last summer, so I guess they are not too fond of the paper now.

Leon is watching me warily. Not sure if the blame is going to be laid at his door. The problem is I have to come up with something. Am the editor-in-chief, am I not?

"So, do you have any ideas about new content and new staff?"

He smiles, relieved at the turn of the conversation.

"Yes, I have two people. They are interning on the paper. You could meet them this afternoon, if you want to."

"Good idea. Let's go to the office after lunch."

Just then two waiters sail in with our lunch. Amid a lot of flourishes, trays, and white napkins to highlight the incomparable cuisine of Chef Dubois, we are served. Leon searches in vain for his missing muffler and starts tugging at his sweater instead. Despite the theatrics, the food is excellent. The chef's crayfish with asparagus would make Valérie's lower lip tremble with jealousy. When I get back home, she will ask me what I had for lunch and then surreptitiously try to find the recipe and prepare the dish for Grand-mère.

"How is your duck liver?" I ask Leon. He has closed his eyes to better savor his first bite.

"Awesome! One should add this recipe to those of Madame Martel's in *Le Loup*. Will definitely increase the sales of the paper," he answers in a reverent tone.

Ditto for the wild wood strawberries smothered in whipped cream. By the time we have sipped our expresso and I've paid the bill, Leon and I are great friends.

"Leon, do you think you could stay another couple of months with *Le Loup?*" (I am also shortening the title of my paper—sounds better.) Before he can answer, I continue, "I will double your salary. I just need you to help me change it into something people will want to read. You could also train the two new staff members."

He hesitates. I knew that Jacques Dubois' food could work miracles!

"I don't know if you are aware, Marie-Christine, but your paper is in the red. How will you be able to afford to double my salary?"

I had not realized it had come to this.

"Leon, I have inherited some money. The paper can be saved if you stay on and we figure out together what needs to be done. If not, I'm afraid I'll just have to close it down and fire the staff."

Leon frowns. Bites his nails. Fiddles with his scarf. Finally he makes up his mind.

"I think you will have to talk to Claude Bizzard about this."

My face feels very warm suddenly. I haven't seen Claude in more than three months, not since . . . since . . . he left for Paris after saving my life.

"Why should I call Claude? Why won't you?"

"Well, because he'll listen to you." Squints as he looks at me. "He thinks very highly of you."

We are standing outside *La Bastide* and it is getting cold.

"Get into my car, Leon, and we'll talk about this as we drive back to the paper."

I have parked my two-seater red Ferrari in the parking lot of the restaurant. Leon is overwhelmed.

"*Quelle fichu voiture!*" Leon's eyes are shining. He caresses the hood reverently. Walks slowly around it. Blows on the glass and wipes it with his scarf. Peers inside and whistles.

"How did you get a car like this?"

"A gift," I shrug as I click open the doors.

Papa gave me that car last summer after I was almost drowned and my lavender Bug was stolen. Left it at Grand-mère's when I was in New York, and now enjoy zooming about in it.

Leon finally gets into the car, afraid to touch anything.

"So who are the two interns?" I ask, hoping he won't get back to tugging his scarf.

"Vivianne is a history of art student—she's very bright. She's the photographer and our graphics designer. Paul graduated from journalism school this summer, and needs the experience of working on a paper. He is our main reporter for Grasse."

21

We park on the *Boulevard du Jeu de Ballon*, one of the city's major business districts. The office of *Le Loup-Garou* occupies a three-room apartment on the second floor of a turn-of-the-century building. As usual the elevator is not working, so we climb the stairs. Mother visited me once when the elevator was actually working. She swore she would never set foot again in my office until they changed the elevator. Later that day I overheard her talking on the phone to a friend in Scarsdale: "What the French call an *ascenseur* is nothing more than a bird cage where you hang in there for dear life until it finally shakes you off on the next floor!"

The heavy wooden door is closed. Leon knocks, using the bronze knocker with the embossed wolfhead which I found in an antique shop in Nice last summer. Thought it appropriate for *Le Loup-Garou's* headquarters.

Vivianne opens the door. She is a little woman with thick glasses and a brisk manner.

Leon introduces us.

"Of course, of course. I recognized you immediately from the photographs in *Le Loup* taken last summer. Come in, I was just making some coffee."

She bustles to the kitchenette, calling out: "Paul! Paul! Mademoiselle de Medici is here!"

Paul strides in from the other room. Tall, strawblond hair, navy sweater, big grin.

"Hi, I'm Paul. Reporter . . . sort of . . . well, trying to be."

He pulls up some chairs, relieves them of papers, magazines, which he drops in a corner, and we sit down. Vivianne returns carrying an assorted set of mugs with steaming coffee.

"To warm you up. It's rather cold in here."

Very soon they are talking about the paper, the stories, the problems. They joke about the popularity of the recipes of Madame Martel. Then Vivianne asks, "So what's the story of the *Trés Riches Heures du Duc de Berry?*"

Surprised, shocked. I thought Grand-mère had said it was going to be a scoop and that no one knew about the manuscripts.

"How do you know about the *Trés Riches Heures?*"

Paul looks up from his mug.

"Everyone in Grasse is talking about it. The story goes that your grandmother and Monseigneur d'Epinay talked to some important people in Paris and New York and convinced them to bring the two famous manuscripts, the *Trés Riches Heures* and the *Belles Heures* together for the first time in our cathedral at Christmas."

"New Year's," I correct him.

"So it's true!" exclaims Leon jumping up from his seat and spilling coffee on his red sweater.

What can I say? If everyone is talking about it, why make a big deal of it?

"Yes, it is true. It was supposed to be this big secret. But since it isn't I'll try to get all the details out of Grand-mère, so that *Le Loup* will have a good story. Do you think it will prop up the sales?"

Am still not quite convinced. But *Le Loup's* staff is unanimous. Paul is excited.

"It will be my first really big story!"

Vivianne nods, while cleaning her glasses that have been steamed up by the coffee.

"We'll take great pictures!"

Wiping his sweater with a paper napkin, Leon adds "Lots of people will come to Grasse to see the manuscripts—that will be good for the tourist business."

"It won't be only tourists who will be visiting Grasse," says Vivianne, lowering her voice. "I've heard rumors. . . ." She stops as if afraid to continue.

"What rumors?" I ask.

"Well, I'm not sure I should be repeating what I was told in confidence." Vivianne gets up and takes the empty mugs back to the kitchenette. Leon follows her, "Vivianne, we are all part of *Le Loup-Garou* here. You can tell us." It is not a request; it is an order.

She returns and sits down. She leans forward and whispers:

"I heard that there are some parties who are *very* interested in the manuscripts."

Am getting a bit irritated at all this secrecy when everyone seems to know everything except me.

"What parties?" I ask, trying to appear indifferent.

In a conspiratorial tone Vivianne proceeds, "I will not name names, but a friend of a friend heard that three well-known European antique book dealers are going to spend Christmas and New Year in Grasse."

She stops and looks up at us, eyes shining with expectation. Reminds me of one of Mother's Irish terriers who'd drop a ball at our feet so that we would play with him. Frankly, I don't understand what she's getting at.

Paul jumps in.

"Vivianne is trying to tell you that these dealers may be very interested in the manuscripts."

Vivianne frowns, annoyed at the interruption, "Well, of course, Paul, antique book dealers would be interested. That's not the point."

"What *is* the point, Vivianne?" Am losing patience here.

She sits back on her chair, rearranges her skirt, and then smiles triumphantly, "The point is that they might want to steal the *Trés Riches Heures*."

There, she has dropped the ball. Leon looks at her as if she's gone slightly batty.

"Vivianne, you know very well that these manuscripts are unique. Even if the dealers stole them, they would never be able to sell them because they are instantly recognizable."

Still smiling, she wags her finger at Leon, "That's where you are mistaken. Some collectors would pay tens of millions of euros just to own these manuscripts. They would never come up on the market. The manuscripts would just disappear in someone's chateau, and would never be heard of again for another four hundred years!"

I've heard of that kind of collector, the obsessive kind who wants to own the *Mona Lisa*. Possessing that which they cannot buy becomes irresistible to some who have everything. And the *Trés Riches Heures du Duc de Berry* is so unique that a jaded spirit with tons of money just might want to acquire it.

Leon, however, is not impressed. In the tone of a school teacher reprimanding his pupil, he says, "Vivianne, I am surprised at you. Are you telling us that the book dealers are crooks? Don't you think that viewing these two extraordinary manuscripts is reason enough for them to want to come to Grasse? Come, come. You should know better than to believe the gossip in this town."

The young woman blushes. She glances at me furtively to see what I think. Have to come to her rescue.

"I am sure that there will be a great deal of security around these manuscripts. Grand-mère did mention something about insurance, so I suppose they will be insured against theft, and probably every other disaster: flood, fire . . . I don't know. . . . "

But I am curious, "What makes you that think that the manuscripts could be stolen?"

Vivianne has regained her composure, and straightens herself on the chair before answering, "The person who told me this knows what he is talking about. He works for an insurance firm and has come across all kinds of fraudulent crimes. He said that the bringing together of these two unique manuscripts is such a rare event that it may trigger an attempt to steal them. He said he knew of some ruthless collectors around the world who would pay fortunes to have one or both of these manuscripts in their possession."

We have fallen silent. What if Vivianne were right? What if someone were going to try to steal those manuscripts? What would Grand-mère do? Or Monseigneur d'Epinay for that matter? It would be a disaster!

Leon looks unconvinced. He scratches his chin where some red fuzz seems to have appeared in the last few minutes. Crosses his legs, pointing his boot towards Vivianne. She moves her chair slightly closer to me.

"Wouldn't it be a rather obvious crime if the manuscripts disappeared while the book dealers were in Grasse?" he argues. "The least bit of suspicion that they were in any way involved in such a theft could ruin their reputation permanently."

"You mean the thing about Caesar's wife being above suspicion . . . ?" interjects Paul, who has been silent all this time. He must have already heard Vivianne's story.

"Yes, yes . . . I mean that would be the crime of the century in the manuscript world. I don't think any book dealer would want to be on the same continent, let alone the same town, when such a theft is perpetrated."

Leon has a point there. I am really beginning to appreciate the man. Must call Claude tomorrow and see if he will let Leon stay on for a little while longer to help with *Le Loup*.

But Vivianne will have the last word.

"Think of the money involved."

III

Back *chez* Grand-mère. I find her settled comfortably in a big armchair before a roaring fire in the *grand salon*. With her is Madame Martel, the mayor's wife, sporting a bright red hat in the shape of a bell and decorated with miniature Christmas trees and snowmen.

"Aaaah," she bellows when I appear at the door. "There's your granddaughter! Doesn't she look well after her misadventures this summer!"

Sounds as if she were expecting me to be still covered with sea-weed. My first instinct is to flee, but Grand-mère waves me in.

"Marie-Christine, why don't you tell Valérie to bring another cup and a fresh pot of coffee. Then come and join us. Madame Martel was just telling me about her latest recipes for *Le Loup-Garou.*"

A few minutes later, Valérie brings a pot of coffee which she sets on a little table between Madame Martel and Grand-mère. Next to the coffee pot is a tray with a tea-cake and some of Valérie's savory *tartelettes aux noix*. Pick up three and settle down on the sofa. Those little walnut pastries with whipped cream can make one almost forget that Madame Martel is in the room. But not for long.

"I must tell you that I receive dozens of letters daily praising my recipes and asking me how to prepare this or that dish. My dear, Madame de Medici, you just cannot imagine how my public keeps me busy."

Melodramatically, she raises her hand to her hat and brushes back a couple of snowmen and Christmas trees. Meant to express how overwhelmed she is with her fans' adoring attentions. She drones on for what seems hours, but is only fifteen minutes.

Finally, it's time to say good-bye. Madame Martel rearranges her hat which now seems poised to ring in the new year. Grand-mère and I accompany her to the front door.

"I am looking forward to seeing your daughters at dinner tomorrow. It has been years. . . ."

And with that she departs in a whirlwind of shawls and scarves.

Holding a half-eaten *tartelette* in my hand, I look at Grand-mère in disbelief.

"Grand-mère, you're *not* inviting the Martels over for dinner tomorrow. Are you?"

Grand-mère heaves a big sigh.

"She practically invited herself over when I said your aunts were arriving tomorrow. Anyway, Marie-Christine, remember that were it not for Madame Martel's culinary column, your paper would not be doing too well."

I put my arm through the arm of the old matriarch and we walk slowly back to the living room. Valérie has cleared the cups and cakes but left me one little walnut pastry on a plate. Grand-mère settles back in her armchair, and I take the place just vacated by Madame Martel.

Leaning over towards the flickering fire I rub my hands to warm them up. The moment one moves away from the fire one freezes. I then tell Grand-mère about my encounter with Leon and the staff of *Le Loup-Garou.*

"I am going to have to put more money in the paper. It is in the red, you know."

Grand-mère nods her head absentmindedly.

"I'm calling Claude Bizzard tomorrow to ask him to let me keep Leon for another couple of months to run *Le Loup.* Do you think it's a good idea, Grand-mère?"

She suddenly becomes alert.

"Claude Bizzard? Yes, yes. That's a very good idea. Call him and tell him to come down for Christmas Eve dinner."

◆

Whenever Grand-mère entertains, even her nearest and dearest, she insists on a *grand nettoyage*—a major housecleaning. No speck of dust is allowed to rest anywhere. The silver turns into mirrors, and the floors must reflect the chandeliers. Work begins at the crack of dawn when Valérie, with the help of women from a nearby village, prepares to wage war against *la poussière*—dust visible and invisible. For me this activity holds none of the delights that it does for Valérie and her crew. I just bury my head under my comforter and try to sleep for another couple of hours. That is until Valérie arrives with a cup of coffee and croissants and insists on opening the shutters, lighting the fire in the fireplace, and informing me of what is taking place in the rest of the house.

"Now, Mademoiselle, you must dress and come down. You know your aunts are coming in this afternoon. Your grandmother will need your help."

Reluctantly I struggle out of bed, shivering. Valérie has set my red woolen dressing gown and slippers at the bottom of the bed. I put them on, then curl up on the big armchair next to the fire. Munching on my croissants, I ruminate.

"But Valérie, what can *I* do?"

"Well, Mademoiselle, you know as well as I do, how difficult the relations are between your grandmother and her daughters. Your aunt Geneviève is so very much like Madame, her mother, quite stubborn if I may say so, that they will disagree on everything, of course."

It does not make any sense but Valérie has put it in a nutshell. My aunt Geneviève will always find a reason to contradict her mother, and Grand-mère will never acknowledge that her daughter may be right sometimes.

"So you, Mademoiselle, with your tact and diplomacy, must help smooth things between them, at least until after Christmas."

Valérie moves briskly about. She has started the bath water running and placed some Fragonard rose and lavender soap and body lotion on the table next to the tub. Holding two large white towels, she continues to talk.

"And your poor aunt Helène—well, you know she has been such a disappointment to Madame. Married the wrong man, and lost all her money. And the art and poetry, well, your grandmother does not quite appreciate her talents. So Mademoiselle, it will be you who will have to be talking to your aunts."

I definitely need a second cup of coffee. This is shaping up to be a rather trying Christmas holiday.

"Valérie, I don't think I'll be able to survive these holidays, let alone be an ambassador of cheer and goodwill!"

"Don't worry, Mademoiselle. You are a de Medici too. You will know what to do when the time comes."

With these enigmatic words, Valérie leaves the room. Nothing better left to do than to prepare to face *la famille* this afternoon.

◆

Tante Geneviève and her husband, Xavier de la Rochereau, are the first to arrive. Jean, Valérie's husband, opens the door and goes out to the car to pick up their suitcases. I come down from my room to receive them. In a silver gray suit with a silver gray fox trailing from her shoulder, my aunt extends both her hands towards me.

"Marie-Christine, how are you, my dear? It has been ages since I last saw you!" She brushes my cheek with her lips. Smells like an expensive salon. "Xavier, don't you think Marie-Christine has grown up?"

"It was only two years ago, Tante Geneviève," I protest. Grown up, really! Sounds as if I had been a toddler when she last saw me.

My uncle Xavier is struggling with a miniature white poodle named Pushkin. The yapping dog has managed to entangle himself and his leash between my uncle's legs.

"Get that animal back in its cage!" roars my uncle, trying not to take a nosedive into Grand-mère's porcelain vase on the table across from the door.

My aunt, blithely ignoring her husband's plight, moves toward the living room. She is tall, dark, slim, and has worn a classical chignon for as long as I can remember.

"*Maman!*" She calls out to Grand-mère, who is sitting straight as a rod in her armchair next to the fire. She is dressed in black with her pearl necklace, ready to receive company.

"Ah, Geneviève. Have you had a good trip?" Mother and daughter dutifully embrace.

"Oh, yes. Quite agreeable, thank you. Xavier is having some problems with the dog, but otherwise everything went well."

At that moment Jean returns with an elegant Hermès suitcase under each arm.

"Jean," calls out Grand-mère, "please put Monsieur and Madame de la Rochereau in Madame's *chambre de jeune fille.*"

Uncle Xavier, slightly disheveled, and with his tie pointing in the direction of the porcelain vase, enters into the living room holding Pushkin tightly on its leash. Tante Geneviève follows Jean to her old bedroom.

Xavier bows and kisses Grand-mère's hand. Quite a feat as he still manages to keep a firm grip on Pushkin. Like his wife, he is also tall, slim, and stylish.

"*Bonsoir,* Maman. You look ten years younger than when I last saw you. It must be the good weather of Grasse," he says smiling. But the gray eyes show little pleasure at being in Grasse. Wonder what it took Tante Geneviève to get him here.

"*Bonsoir,* Xavier. Thank you for the compliment. I hope you will enjoy your stay among us. I know it is not Paris, but Provence can be a very enjoyable place, even in winter."

Somewhat discomfited by Grand-mère's clear reading of his thoughts, he picks up Pushkin and moves towards the door.

"I am sure it will be most enjoyable," he answers hurriedly. "Now, will you excuse me? I will join Geneviève upstairs and help her unpack. Dinner at eight?"

"Yes, but do come down a bit earlier. We will have an apéritif with the other guests."

Just then, the doorbell rings again. There is a great deal of commotion at the door. Valérie opens and exclaims enthusiastically,

"Ah! Mademoiselle Helène! Pardon, Madame. I am so happy to see you!"

I move towards the door to welcome the new arrivals.

It's my aunt Helène, Grand-mère's youngest daughter. She was a hippie when she was young and never quite realized that times had changed. Lots and lots of frizzly red henna-dyed hair cascading on her face, shoulders. Quite a few pounds heavier than I remembered. She is framed in a billowing cape, and is adorned with scarves and beads of varied colors and lengths.

"Good old Valérie!" Helène hugs Valérie, then pushes her away and looks at her. "You have aged! Has Maman been working you too hard?"

Before Valérie can find the appropriate words to answer, my aunt Helène continues:

"Give me a hand with those bags. And where is Jean? There are more boxes in the cab."

She sees me standing in the hallway.

"Marie-Christine! How are you, *ma chérie?* Heard that someone tried to murder you this summer! Is that true? That must have been very exciting! You will have to tell me all about it."

Helène will blurt out anything that comes into her head. Can be quite embarrassing sometimes. Right now, I understand what she means so I will not quibble with her choice of words.

Jean has rolled up his sleeves and is bringing into the house an ill-assorted set of suitcases, boxes, carpetbags, and packages wrapped in brown paper with bows on them. Guess those must be Tante Helène's Christmas gifts for the family.

"By the way, Marie-Christine, do you have fifty euros for the cab? I don't know where I put my purse. I'll pay you later. That's a good girl."

I climb upstairs to my room to find the fifty euros. I know I will never get them back. My aunt Helène does not have a clear sense of the mine and thine. She can be extraordinarily generous one moment, and take something that doesn't belong to her the next.

By the time I return, Valérie and Jean have managed to move everything out of the taxicab. The hallway meanwhile has acquired the appearance of a caravanserai.

"Here you are, Tante Helène. The fifty euros for the cab." I hand her the money.

"They're not for me, they're for the driver. Do go and pay *him!*" She exclaims, irritated at my lack of initiative. Not even a thank you! Reluctantly I step outside and pay the harried-looking driver who has been standing in the cold rubbing his hands.

Having waited more than fifteen minutes in the sitting room for her daughter to appear, Grand-mère decides to get up and see what is happening in the hallway. (Grand-mère can be very formal sometimes. She expects her children, and grandchildren, to come and pay their respects when they first arrive.) Decidedly unimpressed by the state of things, she greets my aunt Helène rather coldly.

"Ah there you are, Helène!" Looking disparagingly at her daughter's scattered belongings, "What in the world are all these bags for? Jean, Valérie, please remove these things and put them in Madame's old room. We are having guests tonight and cannot have the hallway looking like this!"

Helène, having extricated herself from her cape and dropping it on the floor, beams at Grand-mère. She does not seem to have heard one word that was said about the state of her belongings.

"Maman, I got you the most fabulous gift! You'll never guess what it is. I'm keeping it hidden in my room until Christmas Eve!"

She comes up to Grand-mère and wraps her arms around her. The old matriarch is moved. She pats her daughter on the back.

"I'm glad you came. How is the boy?"

"Gerard? He should be here anytime. He is driving from Strasbourg with a friend."

"I'm glad my twenty-two-year-old cousin, Gerard, is coming. We'll have fun!"

The words are barely out of her mouth when the bell rings again.

It's Gerard in a black polo shirt and blue jeans. He grins at me, "Hi, Marie-Christine! Where do we park?"

I walk into the garden and point out to him where the cars are parked.

"You forgot? It's in the old stables, down there by the olive trees."

"Guess I haven't been here in a while. But first, let me introduce you to a friend."

Out of an old BMW sedan emerges this great-looking guy. I mean really, really good-looking: Greek god type of fellow. Great body, wavy black hair, smile to dazzle any Hollywood producer into offering him a contract on the spot. Odd friend for Gerard though. He must be at least ten years older than my cousin.

We shake hands. He has big, powerful hands.

"Alain LeMoine," he smiles.

"Marie-Christine de Medici," I smile back. Hope I look good in my winter white cashmere sweater and pants. I wish I had not pulled my hair back into a ponytail this morning. Would have looked much more attractive with copper-red hair loose on my white sweater.

"I hope you can stay for dinner tonight," I suggest.

Alain hesitates.

"Well, I'm not sure. . . ."

But Gerard jumps in immediately.

"Of course you must stay. You know, Marie-Christine, he drove most of the way and did not even stop once so that I would not be late for dinner. He hasn't eaten a thing since breakfast this morning."

"That's settled then," I say. "You are staying. There will be plenty to eat and I'm sure Grand-mère won't mind another person."

He shrugs nonchalantly.

"Very well, then. I'll stay."

Gerard slaps him on the back.

"Great! You'll enjoy the food here. Grand-mère has a wonderful cook. Grab one of my bags and let's go in. Marie-Christine is freezing out here."

I am shivering. Did not realize how cold it was. The sun sets by 5 PM in the winter and the temperature drops rapidly after that.

"Race you to the house," I call out to Gerard, and start running.

He bounces after me, but Alain manages to get to the door before either of us. Out of breath and laughing, we rush inside with Gerard's bags. Grand-mère and Tante Helène are still in the hallway chatting, although my aunt's bags have been cleared.

"Hi Mom! Hi Grand-mère!" Gerard goes up to his mother and hugs her, then kisses Grand-mère on both cheeks.

"And *who* is that?" asks my aunt, turning towards Alain and examining him from head to foot as if he were an expensive fur coat.

Not in the least discomfitted by my aunt's odd behavior, Alain bows his head, "Alain LeMoine, a friend of Gerard."

"Mother, Grand-mère, I hope you don't mind, we asked Alain to stay over for dinner."

Grand-mère extends her hand to Alain.

"Welcome to the de Medici residence. Any friend of my grandson is welcome here. Why don't you both go to Gerard's room and freshen up? You must be tired from your drive. The aperitifs will be served at seven-thirty. Dinner is at eight." Turning to Gerard she adds, "And do take your bags to your room please. Valérie and Jean have had too much to do already."

◆

Am a bit late: come down for the aperitifs at 7:40. The living room is already full of people chatting and a big fire is crackling merrily in the grate. Just love the smell of wood burning. Valérie always adds some dry olive twigs, a bit of lavender, and some mysterious herbs from a potpourri she keeps under lock and key in a cupboard in the pantry. Jean, all dressed up in his old dinner jacket, is serving a warm, aromatic wine spiced with cinnamon. One of Valérie's nieces, in a plain black dress with a little white collar, is carrying around a tray with a homemade duck paté. Little yellow ceramic bowls filled with green wheat and lentil shoots traditionally grown during the Christmas season decorate the mantelpiece.

"These plants portend luck and prosperity for the family if they grow well," insists Valérie. The oracle of Grasse brooks no rational objection on my part.

The mayor and his wife are in deep conversation with Tante Geneviève and her husband as I enter the room.

"Aaah! There she is! The beauuutiful granddaughter of Madame de Medici!" Mathilde Martel's voice sounds like the starting of engines at the "Indy 500."

"Good evening, Madame Martel," I say as we shake hands. Can't help looking at her hat—a stiff rectangular affair shaped like the Queen Mary, pointing southeast. She beams at me.

"Yes, quite elegant, don't you agree?" She waves her forefinger at me. "And it cost a pretty penny. But then I am a working woman, and I can afford to pamper myself sometimes!"

No doubt she is referring to the recipes she writes for *Le Loup-Garou.*

Grand-mère waves to me from the other side of the room. She is standing, leaning on her cane, and talking to Monseigneur "Pepy" and a woman in a loose beige outfit and a white sweater. Recognize her immediately by her habit as being one of the sisters of Scholastica Abbey of Cape Cod.

I excuse myself and leave Madame Martel to explain to my aunt Geneviève where she found that mini-battleship she is sporting on her head.

"*Bonsoir,* Monseigneur," I smile and shake hands with my favorite bishop.

"Good evening, young lady. I trust you found your paper thriving? Sister Angela worked very hard to keep it going, you know." His gray eyes twinkling, he turns and introduces me, "Sister Felicity, this is Marie-Christine de Medici, the granddaughter of Madame de Medici."

Fiftyish, I would guess. Tall, thin with thick glasses. Looks like one of my college professors. She is definitely uncomfortable in this crowd. Guess she'd rather be alone with her books. Warm smile though.

"Of course, Chrissy! Sister Angela told us all about your adventures last summer! You were very brave!"

"Not really, I guess I was just lucky." I am dying to ask her a question before everyone starts talking again.

Clearing my throat that has become dry, I jump in.

"Sister Felicity, is it true that you brought with you the manuscript of *Les Belles Heures* from the States?"

Must have spoken very loudly in my attempt to get her attention. Suddenly the room is completely silent. Everyone is looking at us.

Startled, she looks at Monseigneur d'Epinay. He frowns, and rubs his chin.

"I am supposed to make the announcement on Christmas Eve at the Cathedral. This is to be my Christmas gift to the people of Grasse. So please let it go no further than this room. You are all part of the de Medici family so I can tell you this. Yes, Sister Felicity has brought the famous Book of Hours of the Duke of Berry from the United States with her to Grasse."

"Where is it?" calls out Madame Martel from the other side of the room.

An embarrassed silence follows. I see Grand-mère waving to Jean, who is standing at the door of the dining room.

"*Mesdames et Messieurs, le diner est servi!*" he announces.

IV

Monseigneur d'Epinay is visiting, so the table is set with Grand-mère's antique damask tablecloth. The gold-bordered Limoges china and crystal wine glasses sparkle by candlelight. Two candlesticks, with six candles, stand guard at each side of the table. Valérie insists there should always be twelve candles at formal dinners, "For the twelve disciples," she nods piously. Whenever I propose less light at the table and more on the ceiling, Valérie wags her finger at me, "You do not want to incur their wrath, little one." And raising her eyes to the heavens, she leaves it entirely to my imagination what the terrible consequences would be were I to remove a candle or switch on the electric lights.

Grand-mère has arranged everyone in a hierarchical order. Seated at the head of the table, she has placed Monseigneur d'Epinay on her right and the mayor on her left. Madame Martel is next to the bishop, while Sister Felicity is escorted by Jean to the chair next to the mayor. Xavier de la Rochereau, looking like a medieval martyr, slides into his chair next to Madame Martel. Gerard jumps happily into his. Turning towards Sister Felicity, he grins. I am seated next to Gerard, while Tante Geneviève, in a silver and lavender sheath, presides at the other end of the table. To her left is Alain LeMoine looking quite dashing in a black blazer and black polo shirt. My aunt Helène, in some kind of striped orange and purple turban, has settled between Alain and her brother-in-law, Xavier.

"From Bukhara," she responds to the curious glances.

Monseigneur "Pepy" looks at Grand-mère, who nods, then he lowers his head and prays.

"Thank you, God, for the food we are about to consume. And thank you for bringing the de Medici family together under this roof." Wish that I could be as confident as the bishop!

Jean, who has been standing by the door holding a large tureen, begins serving.

"Madame de Medici! I have not had a purée of chestnut soup in years!" exclaims the mayor. He raises his glass, which Jean has filled with wine, "To the best hostess in Grasse!"

Everyone follows suit with murmurs of *"à votre santé."*

I think Valérie has added a touch of cognac to the soup to enhance its subtle flavor. It seems to warm up the conversation. Tante Helène looks across the table to Sister Felicity, "So what is the story of this manuscript you have brought with you, *ma soeur*? Where did you find it, and why did you bring it to Grasse?"

Sister Felicity has been sitting quietly eating her soup. She looks up somewhat startled by the abrupt question. Takes off her glasses and wipes the steam from the soup with her napkin before answering. In very precise French she begins, "The *Belles Heures*, or the Book of Hours, was commissioned by Jean, Duke of Berry, sometime in the beginning of the fifteenth century. The Duke loved beautiful books, as did his brother King Charles the Fifth, who as you know had assembled a large library in the Louvre."

Gerard has swallowed all his soup and has begun to fidget on his chair.

"What is a Book of Hours?" he asks. Grand-mère glares at him. But Sister Felicity turns to him and answers quickly, "It's an illustrated private prayer book divided according to the times of the day and the seasons of the year."

Gerard is still not quite clear about the whole matter. "So, what's so special about this prayer book?"

"Young man . . . ," begins Grand-mère, frowning menacingly. But it is my uncle Xavier who answers—pale skin flushed and pale eyes glittering.

"*Les Belles Heures* and especially *Les Trés Riches Heures* of the Duke of Berry are some of the most beautiful illuminated French manuscripts. Three artists, de Limbourg brothers, and their assistants, worked for years to paint the miniatures in these manuscripts which resemble panel paintings. No other Book of Hours can compare to these."

"I am not sure I would agree with you on this point," all eyes turn towards Alain LeMoine. A friend of Gerard is actually challenging my uncle Xavier, the head of de la Rochereau auction house?

Eyes still glittering, and voice as cold as the ice in the ice-bucket in which Jean has placed the wine, my uncle Xavier asks, "Would you mind explaining yourself, Monsieur LeMoine?"

Alain, looking supremely confident and at ease (and gorgeous), responds, "What about the *Grandes Heures* or the *Heures de Bruxelles?*"

Jean is removing the soup plates, while everyone is staring at Alain. Uncle Xavier nods with definite interest at Alain, "Jacquemart de Hesdin? Of course, he was the master painter of the Duke of Berry in the 1380s. The de Limbourg brothers were influenced by his style, but developed their own."

My aunt Helène, seated between the two men, is fast losing interest in the conversation.

"How do you know so much about medieval manuscripts, Monsieur LeMoine?"

"I am a preservation specialist of rare manuscripts at the *Bibliotheque Municipale de Strasbourg.*"

Alain a librarian? Am quite bowled over by this revelation. I had no idea that there were any young, let alone good-looking librarians! I mean . . . aren't librarians supposed to be old, shy, and bespectacled?

Jean wheels in a small table with a large baking dish. Grand-mère announces, "Valérie has prepared this Cod *Brandade* à *la Bénédictine* especially for Geneviève, who loved it when she was a child."

Tante Geneviève smiles for the first time this evening. On her left cheek a small dimple appears that makes her look impossibly young, although I cannot quite imagine my aunt ever being a child. She looks definitely pleased, and addressing Jean she calls out, "Jean, please thank Valérie for the *Brandade*."

"Very well, Madam." Jean continues serving.

"Why is the *Brandade* called *à la Bénédictine*?" pipes in Gerard.

Grand-mère again glares at him.

"Gerard, I don't know what they teach in school these days, but. . . . "

"It's all right, Maman," says Tante Geneviève. "I'll tell him the story you used to tell us." After taking a bite from the piece of *Brandade* that Jean has placed on her plate, and closing her eyes to savor it better, she turns to Gerard, "Legend has it that a few hundred years ago, a monastery in Marseilles received the unexpected visit of Benedictine monks from a nearby town. Not having enough salt cod to feed everyone, the cook created this dish by adding potatoes, milk, puréed garlic, and chopped truffles to the fish and baking it in the oven. It was so good that the Benedictine monks took the recipe with them and it later became a staple dish of the region."

Madame Martel, who has been unusually silent, adjusts her hat. The tip of the battleship hits the back of my uncle Xavier's head. He spins around to see who is behind him.

44

"What the . . . ?" When he realizes there is no one there, he turns back looking puzzled and rubs his head. Madame Martel appears quite unaware of the incident.

Addressing Sister Felicity across the table, she asks, "I understand that you are from an abbey in the United States, *ma soeur.* Is that where the *Belles Heures* now resides?" Something in her tone seems to imply that that abbey may somehow have pirated the manuscript.

"No, it is part of the collections of the Cloisters, the branch of the Metropolitan Museum in New York that is entirely devoted to European medieval art and architecture," answers Sister Felicity quietly, as she finishes her *Brandade.*

Monseigneur "Pepy" clears his throat quite loudly to attract attention.

"With your permission, Sister, I will share with you all the story of these manuscripts."

Jean clears the plates of the *Brandade.* Valérie has slipped in and placed a silver tray on the sideboard next to the door leading to the pantry. Jean carries the tray and begins serving the ladies.

"Quails!" exclaims Madame Martel, forgetting all about the manuscripts. In her excitement to look at the next dish she turns her head towards Jean, and the hat again hits the back of my uncle Xavier's head. This time his hand moves rapidly to catch the offending attacker, resulting in a tug-of-war between Madame Martel and Xavier de la Rochereau, each pulling at the hat from behind their backs, not realizing what is happening.

Gerard kicks me under the table, and I take my napkin and pretend to wipe my mouth to hide my giggles. Grand-mère does not seem to think this is funny at all, "But what are you doing, Xavier, Mathilde? *Voyons!* You are behaving like children. Take off that hat of yours, Mathilde. Can't you see that it is getting in the way?"

Madame Martel, apologizing profusely, removes her hat, which Jean places on a chair next to the sideboard. My uncle Xavier has resumed the martyred look, resigned it seems to having a miserable time for the rest of the evening if not the rest of the week in Grasse.

The quails on a bed of rice, smelling of an aromatic *bouquet garni* of Provençal herbs, create a much-needed diversion.

"Do tell us the story of these manuscripts, Monseigneur," I ask to get the conversation going. A hum of assent sounds from around the table.

Laying his fork and knife to the side of his plate, and leaning forward to look at all of us, the bishop begins, "The Duke, Jean de Berry, ordered the painting of the *Belles Heures* sometime between 1410 and 1412, and the *Trés Riches Heures* immediately after in 1413. This, however, was a turbulent period in the history of France, and the Duke found himself embroiled in the battles between the Burgundians and the Armignacs. Suffice it to say that about the time the illumination of these manuscripts began, the Duke of Berry's residence in Paris, the *Hotel de Nesle*, was ransacked, and his *Chateau de Bicetre* was pillaged and burned. In 1413, he was besieged by the Burgundians in Bourges, the capital of Berry. War with England followed, resulting in the defeat of France in Agincourt in 1415 and the death of a large number of French noblemen, including two of his grandsons. In June 1416, the Duke died brokenhearted. That same year the three de Limbourg brothers, Jean, Paul, and Herman, also died without finishing the *Trés Riches Heures.*"

"Were they murdered?" asks Gerard, who loves detective stories of the hard-boiled type.

The bishop rubs his chin, "We really don't know the circumstances of their deaths. But given the fact that they occurred after a period of prolonged military conflict, we can assume that some kind of epidemic may have been responsible. However, foul play cannot be completely ruled out."

"What happened to the manuscripts?" I ask. Want to have as many details as possible for *Le Loup-Garou*.

"Well, that's the interesting thing. The manuscripts disappear for almost seventy years between 1416 and 1485, when they reappear in the collections of the Duke Charles I of Savoie. The Duke then asks a painter whom we believe to be Jean Colombe to complete the *Trés Riches Heures*, which he does in the style of his day, not bothering to imitate that of the de Limbourg brothers. Then the Duke dies in 1491 and the *Trés Riches Heures* disappears again. There are many theories as to its whereabouts during that time but no solid proof."

Alain LeMoine pitches in, "Monseigneur, you are not eating. Your quail is getting cold. Permit me to continue the saga of these manuscripts."

"By all means," answers the bishop, looking relieved. "I will interrupt though, if I think you have left something out."

"Of course," answers Alain. Am really impressed by this guy. Looks *and* brains do not go together often in the men I meet on the Riviera.

Calmly and deliberately, Alain picks up his glass and looks around the table. Monseigneur d'Epinay has resumed eating. My aunt Helène is fidgeting with her turban, and Gerard her son is waving to Jean to give him a second helping of quail. The rest of us have put our forks and knives down and are waiting to hear the rest of the story. Alain drinks from the wine Jean has served, and then in a deep well-modulated voice picks up the tale from where the bishop left off.

47

"The Duke of Savoie died without an heir. His widow, Margaret of Austria and daughter of the Emperor Maximilian, is believed to have transferred the manuscript to the Netherlands. We are not sure of this, except for the mention of a large Book of Hours in Margaret of Austria's private chapel in Mechlin in 1523. At her death in 1530 it appears that this Book of Hours went to Jean Ruffaut, one of the executors of her will and paymaster of Charles V of Germany. Thereafter, the manuscript disappears once again."

"Not for very long since we have it here," interrupts Tante Helène impatiently. She looks bored with this talk of manuscripts. Alain frowns, but continues as if he had not heard her remark.

"Well, it reappears throughout the eighteenth century in the possession of different Genoese families, first the Spinola family, then the Serra family, and later the Baron Felix de Margherita of Turin. It is finally located by the Duke d'Aumale in the second half of the nineteenth century, and is identified as the famous *Trés Riches Heures* of the Duke of Berry. By whom? I forget. . . ." Alain turns towards the bishop, but it is Sister Felicity who answers.

"The eminent scholar, Leopold Delisle, in 1881."

"Right you are, *ma soeur*. Yes, it was Delisle who was able to establish that this was indeed the missing manuscript." Alain seems pleased with his performance. Smiles as if he expects applause.

Cough and a loud "Hum, Hum" from the direction of the mayor, François Martel.

"Madame," bows his head in the direction of Grand-mère, "dear friends." The mayor is obviously preparing to speak and wants all attention to be directed his way.

"May I first say that it is always a great honor and pleasure to be in such valued company as that of the de Medici family. But this evening has been particularly delightful because of the erudite conversation at the dinner table." He adjusts his pince-nez, and brushes his thin mustache delicately with his forefinger.

"I am also very grateful to Monseigneur d'Epinay for having brought to our attention the importance of those manuscripts for the city of Grasse. As you are all aware by now, these two manuscripts will be shown together at the Cathedral of Notre Dame des Fleurs on New Year's Day on the occasion of its eight-hundredth anniversary, something that has not happened since the death of the Duke of Berry in 1416.

"However, what you may not be aware of is the story behind the disappearance of the *Trés Riches Heures* from the collection of the Duke of Berry. Monseigneur d'Epinay, and the young gentleman here, Monsieur . . . ?"

"LeMoine," answers Alain quickly.

"Yes, d'Epinay and LeMoine have told you part of the recorded history of the manuscripts. We in the mayor's office, which like the Cathedral was part of the church's holdings in this city since the twelfth century, also have documents that refer to a Book of Hours that once belonged to an Armignac Duke. The document states, quite ambiguously I must admit, that this manuscript may hold the secret of a hidden treasure!"

Sister Felicity is sitting quite upright and looks directly at François Martel, "But I thought this was just a legend!" she exclaims.

My aunt Helène, who is on her third or fourth glass of wine, and whose turban is gradually unraveling, wags her finger at Sister Felicity, "What is legend for some, is truth for others. Monsieur *le maire,* tell us the story—the legend of the buried treasure."

"But Madame, I never said the treasure was buried!" says the mayor, looking confused.

Jean sets two large bowls of green salad at each side of the table. Everyone begins serving themselves in a clatter of plates and silver.

Monseigneur d'Epinay intervenes, "Sister Felicity is right. There is a legend about a hidden treasure linked to those manuscripts. Jean Duke of Berry was an avid collector not only of beautiful manuscripts and works of art, but also of jewels. He had a rare collection of chalices, crosses, frames, and caskets in solid gold, encrusted with precious gems which he bequeathed to the *Sainte Chapelle* in Bourges. He also had an invaluable set of twenty rubies thought to be unique in Europe, one of which was said to weigh 240 carats! Those rubies were never found after his death."

"The legend has it, that after the attack on his residence in Paris in 1411, the Duke realized that the Burgundians were after him, and that all he owned was at risk. So he called upon the services of the three de Limbourg brothers, who were not French but Dutch in today's parlance, and commissioned the two works. In those works the Duke instructed them to include encoded information about where those rubies were hidden. To find the rubies the two manuscripts needed to be viewed together, according to the legend. So before he died, in order to protect the secret of the location of the rubies, the Duke ordered that one of the two manuscripts, the *Trés Riches Heures* be smuggled out of France for safety."

More hum-humming from the corner of the mayor.

"But, Monseigneur d'Epinay, our dear friends need to be told how the *Trés Riches Heures* was taken out of France—would you permit me?"

Monseigneur d'Epinay, with a sweeping gesture of his hand and a bow of his head, accedes to the mayor's request, "By all means, Monsieur *le maire,* by all means."

The mayor puts his right elbow on the table and extends his left arm halfway across—a position no doubt he adopts when he addresses Grasse's municipal council.

"As was mentioned earlier, the *Trés Riches Heures,* after disappearing for seventy years, is found in the possession of the Duke of Savoie in 1485, who orders the painter Jean Colombe to complete the work of the Limbourg brothers.

"The curious story is: how did the manuscript get to the Duke of Savoie?"

At this critical juncture of the discourse, Jean arrives with a tray of eight different cheeses. Valérie surreptitiously puts three baskets of bread on the side board. Everyone begins talking. Alain has found a bottle of wine half-full in the ice bucket, and pours some in my aunt Geneviève's glass and then in his. Tante Helène holds out her glass for a refill. Gerard yawns loudly, then apologizes. Grand-mère is beginning to nod. No one seems particularly curious about how the manuscript got to the Duke of Savoie. But I need to get that story for *Le Loup-Garou,* so I ask the question the mayor wants asked, "So how did the *Trés Riches Heures* get to the Duke of Savoie?"

Ouch! Get a kick under the table from Gerard. I glare at him. Really tempted to kick back.

"Through Louis III d'Anjou of course!" exclaims the mayor triumphantly.

Silence follows. Everyone at the table looks at him as if he has gone off his rocker. With my pointed heel on Gerard's foot as a warning, I follow up with the inevitable question, "Why Louis d'Anjou, Monsieur *le maire?*"

The mayor looks around the table and realizes that no one has grasped his astounding revelation. Clearing his throat, and addressing us no longer as members of his municipal council but as children of Grasse's elementary school, "Because in 1417 Louis d'Anjou was Comte de Provence and married to Marguerite de Savoie. He is the man Jean Duke of Berry trusted to take the *Trés Riches Heures* to a safe place, and he brought it to Grasse!"

Light is beginning to dawn.

"And that's why we have this document in the *mairie*, about an Armignac duke and his Book of Hours with the secret of the treasure!" This could be a really good story for *Le Loup-Garou* after all. Needs a bit of research, but I think Leon can go to the *mairie* and find out more. It will get us some new subscribers.

"And what was the relationship of Marguerite de Savoie to the Duke of Savoie?" asks my aunt Geneviève, holding her wine glass delicately with small finger extended.

"I believe she was the grand-aunt of the Duke, but I am not sure. She had no children of her own. The House of Savoie in the fifteenth century was very powerful and ruled Provence as well as parts of Italy such as Naples. The royal family of Italy today belongs to the House of Savoie."

"And that is why the manuscript was eventually found in Italy, I suppose?" asks Tante Geneviève.

"Monsieur Martel, while I find your theory most interesting, I am afraid I am not quite convinced"—a professorial comment from Sister Felicity.

"And why not, *ma soeur?*" The mayor's voice has gone up a couple of decibels, a sure sign that he is irritated by the contrary remark.

"Well, because Jean de Berry's daughter, Bonne, married Amedee VII de Savoie. Therefore, it would be quite natural for the *Trés Riches Heures* to have passed directly through that line to the Duke Charles de Savoie in 1485."

Monseigneur d'Epinay raises his hands as if he wishes to stop the discussion.

"Sister Felicity, Monsieur *le maire*, permit me to intervene in this discussion. I must take the side of Monsieur Martel on this issue. You see, when Jean Duke of Berry died, an inventory of his possessions that would naturally have gone to his two daughters, (he had no son), was made. The document, however, does not mention the existence of the *Très Riches Heures*. If that manuscript had gone to Bonne and her husband, it should have first appeared in the inventory like the rest of the Duke's property. Furthermore, we know that the mother of Louis III d'Anjou, Yolande d'Aragon, upon the death of Jean Duc de Berry asked to examine the *Belles Heures*. She then bought that manuscript, and paid less than half its value. The point is, why did she want the *Belles Heures*? She must have had a number of beautiful Books of Hours of her own."

Alain jumps in excitedly, "You mean because the family already had the *Très Riches Heures?*"

The mayor cackles, "He, he, he. That's right, Monsieur LeMoine, that's right. Louis d'Anjou had been given the *Très Riches Heures* by the Duke of Berry for safekeeping, and had then learned about the secret it held. However, he needed both manuscripts to find the treasure. So he had his mother purchase the *Belles Heures.*"

Gerard, who did not seem to have paid any attention (except to kick me), suddenly jumps into the conversation, "So now that we have both manuscripts we can look for the treasure. What do you say, Monsieur *le maire*? Finders keepers?"

"Not quite, young man, not quite," smiles the mayor. "Even if, theoretically speaking of course, the rubies were ever found they would belong to the estate of the Duke of Berry."

"What if there were no more descendants in that family?" chimes in Tante Helène. Her orange and purple turban is now sitting on her shoulders like the large Cheshire cat of Alice in Wonderland.

"Then it would go to the French state," maintains the mayor, squinting over his pince-nez.

"How boring," remarks my aunt Geneviève, addressing no one in particular.

At that moment Jean comes in with a *savarin au kirsch* on a Limoges serving dish. It is smothered with a *crème Chantilly*, and decorated with Valérie's preserved cherries which are soaked in kirsch.

Treasures and medieval manuscripts are quickly forgotten as we ooh and aah over this blissful dessert. A peaceful silence follows, with only the sound of forks on plates. Outside the wind is howling. The ambers are dying in the fireplace. A feeling of contentment and well-being reigns over the household.

Suddenly the flame of the candles begin to flicker. There is a draft . . . a shutter bangs upstairs. And then . . . a scream! A crash! . . .

V

Silence follows the crash. Everyone sits frozen at the table. Then Alain jumps up, followed by Gerard, and moves quickly towards the door leading to the pantry. I rush behind them. Alain opens the door, then stops suddenly. I bump into Gerard, who steps on Alain's foot.

"Idiot, watch where you're going," Alain whispers.

"The lights are out in the house," whispers Gerard.

It is very dark in the pantry. Some faint light is coming in from the open kitchen door. The rain is coming down heavily outside. Great gusts of wind blow into the room. It feels icy. Alain walks into the pantry and steps on broken glass.

"There's food on the floor."

Gerard calls out, "Jean! Valérie! Where are you?"

Some noise is coming from the kitchen. Footsteps, then a small wavering light. It seems to be growing bigger by the second. We stand afraid to breathe.

A big shadow enters the pantry from the kitchen holding a petrol lamp.

"Jean! What in the blazes is happening?" Am so relieved to see him!

"It's the storm, Mademoiselle. The electricity went off a few minutes ago. I thought it was a short circuit so I went down to the basement to see if I could fix it. But the whole neighborhood is without light. So I brought up the petrol lamp."

"A few minutes ago, you say? But why didn't we notice anything?" asks Alain frowning. His eyes look huge in the dark.

"Well, Monsieur, that's because the lights were not on in the dining room. You only had candlelight."

"But you served us the *savarin*." Alain persists.

"I did not want to interrupt your dinner, Monsieur."

My uncle Xavier comes in looking like a ghost.

"What in the name of . . . is going on in here? Who screamed?"

Had forgotten the scream. It sounded like . . . like . . .

"Where is Valérie?" I shout, suddenly realizing that it must have been her.

We look around the kitchen as Jean holds the petrol lamp above our heads.

"What a mess!" exclaims Uncle Xavier.

Behind him are my two aunts and Grand-mère. Everyone seems to be talking at the same time, "What happened? Who screamed? Why is it dark in here? Where's Valérie? Why is it so cold in the kitchen?"

The floor is littered with shattered china. Different cheeses are spread on the floor. My uncle Xavier seems to have stepped into the brie and is cursing under his breath.

Just then we hear Valérie's voice from the garden, "I am sure it will be all right, Monsieur."

Holding an umbrella and what appears to be a small suitcase, Valérie enters through the kitchen door. She is followed by a tall man wearing a dark raincoat and a floppy hat. Both are dripping wet. We all stand there staring at them, in silence.

Tante Helène's voice suddenly pierces the silence.

"Phillipe! What are you doing here?"

◆

Half an hour later we are back in the sitting room. My aunt Geneviève and my uncle Xavier have excused themselves and have gone up to their room. She has complained of a headache, and he obviously has had enough excitement for one evening. The electricity is not back yet, so Valérie is arranging candleholders on tables around the room. Jean is stoking the fire and adding wood, while Alain is taking orders for Cointreaux and cognacs. Steaming cups of coffee are brought in on a tray by Valérie's niece. A little square of thin, dark chocolate has been placed on each saucer.

Grand-mère has settled in her favorite armchair next to the fire and is holding court.

"So, Phillipe, tell us what you were doing up here tonight?"

Phillipe, first identified, by Tante Helène in the pantry, is indeed none other than Phillipe Bousquet my erstwhile uncle, who spent on wine, women (other than his wife), and horses, the entire dowry Grand-mère gave her daughter when they got married. A real charmer even at fifty, he has curly gray hair and an impish smile. Apparently women of all ages have fallen for that smile. He is now trying it on Grand-mère, but it is not working. She did not approve of him when my Tante Helène married him, and even less when they finally divorced. There is a glint in her eye that indicates she will show him no mercy whatever his hard-luck story is. He has tried too often to beg and borrow from the de Medici estate for Grand-mère to feel any pity towards him.

"Well, Maman," Grand-mère winces (but it is customary in France to call your mother-in-law, Maman), "you see I wanted to come up to Grasse to surprise Helène and Gerard. I knew from Gerard that you were all planning to spend Christmas at the villa, and so I came up tonight to be with them." He is seated opposite Grand-mère to be better examined by her. Looking quite pleased with himself, he asks Alain for another cognac.

Holding his tulip-shaped cognac glass with both hands to warm it up, he inhales the aroma—a real connoisseur of wines and eaux-de-vie.

"So I came up tonight, as I was saying. The weather was horrible, and the traffic just impossible. Everyone apparently has had the same idea of driving up here to visit the family for Christmas."

Phillipe surveys his family (or should I say ex-family?) and meets only sullen stares.

Undeterred he continues, "There was an accident on the road. So anyone even thinking of going down to Cannes or Nice better think twice." He looks at Alain and Sister Felicity. "The road is completely blocked. No one can come up or go down the *autoroute* tonight. The forecast is for snow later this evening and early tomorrow morning, which means that the side roads in the hills will be impassable as well. I had thought of staying in a hotel, but unfortunately all of Grasse's hotels are full until the day after Christmas. So here I am!" Phillipe beams at everyone and finishes his cognac.

"Why did you come through the kitchen door, Phillipe? Why didn't you ring the bell at the front door, instead?" asks Tante Helène, who seems unsure whether to be happy or unhappy that her ex-husband has turned up.

"I did. But no one came to the door," he answers, sounding annoyed.

Valérie, who has finished lighting the candles, addresses Phillipe, "If you would permit me, Monsieur. The electricity was off, that is why the front bell did not ring."

"Well, there you are," he turns to Grand-mère. "I could see lights in the dining room, so I went around to the kitchen door and found it unlocked and walked in."

Valérie is still standing in the sitting room, rubbing her hands together with a pained expression on her face. She too turns towards Grand-mère, "It was such a shock, Madame, seeing a man enter my kitchen. I could have sworn I had locked that door. And what with the storm, and the electricity gone, and Jean down in the basement—I just screamed and dropped the plate with the cheese. I was so scared, Madame, and I didn't recognize Monsieur Bousquet."

Grand-mère is frowning. "That's all right, Valérie, that's all right. Calm yourself. Now what are we going to do with you all tonight? If the roads are blocked, as Phillipe is saying," she eyes him suspiciously. Guess she's not sure whether or not to believe his story. "Then you must spend the night in my house. No point in getting out there on a night like this and being killed in a traffic accident."

Monseigneur d'Epinay walks up to Grand-mère, "Thank you for your hospitality, Madame de Medici. But the Cathedral and the nunnery, where Sister Felicity is staying, are close by. So we will drive back. The snow has not started yet, and if we leave now we will be there in less than fifteen minutes."

"Very well, then, Monseigneur," says Grand-mère, picking up her stick and getting up.

"Valérie, please bring the coats of Monseigneur and Sister Felicity."

As Valérie leaves the room to get the coats, Grand-mère says to the bishop, "Good-bye and Godspeed!" Then dropping her voice, "I'll take good care of them."

The mayor and his wife come up to Grand-mère. Monsieur Martel bows and kisses Grand-mère's hand, "Thank you for a most enjoyable dinner, Madame de Medici. We too live close by and do not want to abuse your hospitality any longer. So we also will leave now."

"What a wooooonderful evening! So much excitement! So much fun! What is a little snow? Monsieur Martel and I are not afraid of the elements!" exclaims Madame Martel as she shakes Grand-mère's hand, her hat positioned north-south ready to battle the snows of the Himalayas.

After they leave, Grand-mère, who walked them to the door returns to the sitting room. Gerard and Alain have been arguing in a corner, and Tante Helène has pulled up a chair and is consulting with Phillipe.

Gerard rushes up to Grand-mère, "Grand-mère, please tell Alain that he must not try to drive back to Strasbourg tonight. I've got a sofa-bed in my room that he could use."

Grand-mère waves her hand in Alain's direction, and then sits back in her armchair. "Yes, of course he must stay. Young man, you will not go out on those treacherous roads tonight."

Gerard hugs his grandmother. I too am glad Alain is staying. The Christmas holidays may not be that boring after all. Alain smiles, "Thank you, Madame de Medici. You are most kind."

Grand-mère then turns towards Phillipe.

"I suppose you are staying too?"

Tante Helène intercedes on his behalf, "Well, maman, you cannot very well throw him out in this weather!"

A momentary flash in Grand-mère's eyes reveals that she can and gladly would, but reason and kindness prevail.

"Very well then, he can stay in the room downstairs. Valérie will make up the spare bed there. As you brought your bags with you, I presume you have everything you need?"

◆

Next morning I awake at the sound of a house cheerfully humming with people. From my window I can see that all of Grasse and the hills around are covered with snow. Shower, dress, and run downstairs. Valérie has prepared breakfast in the dining room and placed croissants, cheeses, jams, a tray of cold cuts, and hard-boiled eggs on the sideboard. The coffee pot is half full. Family members are coming in and serving themselves, while others are moving out, having finished. In the kitchen Valérie is arguing with the delivery man who has driven up with today's groceries. I can hear Jean talking to the woodcutter who brought wood for the fireplaces.

Gerard pops in and grabs some croissants.

"Alain and I are driving to town to buy newspapers. Need anything, Marie-Christine?"

Shake my head as my mouth is full of croissant and home-made strawberry jam.

I decide to consult Grand-mère about the family situation. The house has filled up with unexpected guests, especially my uncle Phillipe, and am worried about possible disturbances in the overall harmony of this family gathering. Knock on the door of *le petit salon,* but get no answer. As I am about to leave, I hear the opening and closing of drawers. Perhaps Grand-mère has not heard my knock, so I open the door and enter. Sure enough she is sitting at her heavy wooden desk apparently searching for something in an open drawer.

"Good-morning, Grand-mère," I chirp, dropping a kiss on top of her head.

Grand-mère starts. She looks up and I can see big, dark circles under her eyes.

"You startled me, Marie-Christine. I did not hear you come in," she says.

"Is everything all right, Grand-mère?" I ask, concerned, putting my arm round her shoulders.

She slumps in her chair and puts her face in her hands. .

"What's the matter, Grand-mère?" Am really getting worried. Have never seen Grand-mère like this. It cannot be the family. Can it?

"What have they done to you?" I ask fiercely. Am ready to throw the whole lot out of the house if they are upsetting my grandmother!

She looks up at me, puzzled, "Who? Done what?"

"Grand-mère tell me, please, what is bothering you?" Cannot bear to see Grand-mère in that state. She is the traditional rock of this family. If that rock is shaken, then nothing can be quite right with the world anymore.

Grand-mère shakes her head, then pointing to the chair next to her, asks me to sit down.

"I suppose it will have to come out sooner or later . . . ," she hesitates. Pulls a handkerchief from her pocket and blows her nose.

"What has to come out, Grand-mère?" A vision flashes before my eyes: the de Medici fortune is gone and we are all bankrupt!

"What happened last night." More blowing of the nose.

"Last night?" Cast my mind back to last night. A number of unusual occurrences come to mind, such as Gerard's father turning up in the middle of a storm. Would that be enough to upset Grand-mère this much?

Grand-mère stuffs her handkerchief back in her pocket and rubs her left knee (rheumatism back again?). She then makes up her mind.

"Marie-Christine, you are going to be the first to know. Last night I organized this dinner *en famille* so that Monseigneur d'Epinay could come over to the house without drawing too much attention."

I find myself completely at sea. Why would Grand-mère need to camouflage the visit of Monseigneur d'Epinay to her house under the guise of a "family" affair?

"But Grand-mère, the bishop has come regularly for years to your house for dinner! Why the subterfuge?"

"Well, because last night he was bringing with him something very important."

Beginning to see the light, I lean forward, excited, "You mean he brought with him *Les Trés Riches Heures?*"

Grand-mère lowers her head and resumes rubbing her knee. She seems to be in pain.

"Yes, Marie-Christine. Monseigneur d'Epinay brought this unique manuscript here for safekeeping. He was worried about security at the Cathedral because word had leaked out that the manuscript was in Grasse."

"Yes, I know," I nod. Take her hand in mine and caress it. Her hand is cold. "A Leon Baude told me. Everyone in Grasse knows about the two illuminated manuscripts."

"Apparently. I had not realized that there would be so much interest. But Monseigneur d'Epinay heard rumors of people who wanted to acquire the manuscript."

"Yes, Leon told me that too. Apparently there are antique book dealers from all over Europe who have come to Grasse to view the manuscripts."

Grand-mère looks at me. There is real distress in her voice as she whispers, "That's what the bishop was afraid of."

A really awful idea is beginning to take shape in my mind, "Grand-mère, you mean that . . . that. . . ."

She nods, unable to articulate the words. "Grand-mère, are you saying that the *Trés Riches Heures* was stolen last night?" I shout, as the reason for her distress suddenly hits me.

VI

"Shh . . . ," she puts her finger to her lips to get me to lower my voice.

"But when, last night?" I can't think clearly.

"Sometime between the time the bishop brought the manuscript at around 7 PM and this morning around 6 AM, when I found it missing."

It takes a few seconds for what Grand-mère is saying to sink in.

"Grand-mère, what are you saying? You mean someone . . . someone in *this* house stole *Les Trés Riches Heures?*"

Grand-mère shakes her head.

"I don't know what to think, Marie-Christine. I really don't know anymore. But who else could it be?"

That's just not possible.

"Grand-mère, have you looked everywhere? Perhaps you hid the manuscript somewhere else and you forgot. I mean, it happens to everyone."

"*Non, non, ma chérie.* I am quite sure I put the manuscript right here, in this drawer. Last night Monseigneur d'Epinay and Sister Felicity arrived at seven, before the others came for drinks, and we sat in this room, chatting. Both the bishop and the sister witnessed where I hid the manuscript."

"Why did you put it there?" I ask, looking at the now empty drawer.

"Because that was the only place I could think of that had a solid lock. I was planning to move the manuscript to a private box in my bank today or tomorrow."

"Was the lock broken?" I am staring at the desk but can see nothing amiss.

"No, Marie-Christine. Nothing was broken. The thief must have had a key." Grand-mère sits back in her chair and looks down at her keys which are lying on her lap.

"Grand-mère, did you carry the keys with you at all times since yesterday?" Am trying to think of different possibilities.

Grand-mère shakes her head.

"I have asked myself the same question a hundred times since this morning. I don't remember. When you move around the house with keys all your life, everyday is like any other day. I could have left them on a table, temporarily. But was it yesterday I did this, or the day before, or even last week? I just don't know."

I get up and walk to the window. Check the handle on the windowpane to see if the window is locked. Grand-mère nods.

"Yes, Marie-Christine, the window was locked."

"But it must have been someone who knew that the manuscripts were in that drawer, Grand-mère." Am thinking out loud.

"That's exactly my thought, *chérie*." Grand-mère is looking thoroughly despondent now.

It simply can't be. I cannot believe that anyone in this house could have stolen the manuscript. Suddenly, I remember something and walk back, "Grand-mère, you remember yesterday when Gerard's father arrived?" I ask excitedly.

"Yes, of course, Marie-Christine," she answers spiritedly. "What Helène ever saw in that man, I'll never understand. And the cheek of turning up at my house, uninvited!"

"But do you remember what he said?" I continue.

"What did he say, Marie-Christine?" she asks impatiently.

"Well, he said that when he rang the front door bell, no one answered. . . . "

"That's because the electricity was off," interrupts Grand-mère.

66

"True, but he also said that he then walked back to the kitchen door and it was unlocked, but Valérie commented that she could have sworn that she had locked that door."

Grand-mère looks up at me. She is silent for a moment as she considers the idea.

"You think that someone *outside* this house could have come in and stolen the manuscript while we were all having dinner?"

I know it sounds improbable, but it is a better explanation than one that points to a member of this household! I sit on the floor next to Grand-mère's feet and stare at the blazing fire in the hearth. Give the matter serious thought.

"Well, all the lights were out. Everyone knew Monseigneur d'Epinay was bringing those manuscripts to Grasse. Someone may have followed him up here last night and waited outside until we were all seated at dinner, and then entered the house and stole the manuscript."

Grand-mère seems to be recovering her spirits. The theft of the manuscripts, compounded by the thought that the perpetrator of the crime could be a member of her own family, was just too much for her. She is ready to cling to straws, and I have just given her one.

"You may have something there, Marie-Christine. Although this hypothesis of yours still does not explain how the person unlocked the kitchen door, or found my keys, or knew where I hid the manuscript."

"I know, I know." Am still staring at the flames for inspiration.

Grand-mère searches for her cane. It is lying on the floor next to me, and I hand it to her. She struggles out of her armchair, and begins slowly pacing up and down in *le petit salon*. Suddenly she stops. I gaze up at her from where I am sitting. Her despondency gone, she now has a very determined look in her eyes.

"Marie-Christine, this conversation must not leave the confines of this room."

I nod, not quite sure where Grand-mère is going with this.

"You will now telephone that police inspector who was so helpful this past summer."

"You mean, Inspector Pasteur, of Grasse's *gendarmerie*?"

"No, no," Grand-mère taps the floor impatiently with her cane. "That clever young man Claude . . . Claude . . . who saved your life?"

My heart skips a beat.

"Claude Bizzard, the Inspector from Paris?"

"*C'est ça*. I did mention to you, just two days ago, that we ought to invite him to spend Christmas with us, didn't I? That was because I feared that something like this would happen. I thought that if the bandits who were after the manuscripts found out that a police inspector from Paris was staying in this house, they would not dare try any tricks. But they were quicker than I thought."

"That's a great idea, Grand-mère! " What better way to bring Claude back to Grasse than to ask him to solve another crime!

"But, Grand-mère, what if he can't come? What if he has other cases to solve in Paris?"

"Marie-Christine, you don't understand. This is not just another crime. This is a case of national and international importance!"

I get up from my comfortable position next to the fire to call Claude to the rescue, but Grand-mère stops me.

"Marie-Christine, you must pretend that everything is normal. Go about your business as if nothing has happened. No one must know that the manuscript has disappeared. We do not want a great hue and cry over this affair. If word gets out, we will have all the French and European media on our doorstep. This has to be solved quickly and discreetly. Only the parties concerned and the police must know. Claude Bizzard will come as a friend and not as an inspector. Officially, we are inviting him to thank him for having saved your life, etc., and not in his professional capacity. Is that clear, Marie-Christine?"

◆

Have called Claude. He seemed happy to hear from me. I tried to explain the problem without revealing too much. He then asked to talk to Grand-mère.

"Marie-Christine, make sure she is alone and out of earshot. Use your cell-phone."

After the phone conversation in *le petit salon,* Grand-mère announced that Claude would be coming late this evening.

"Marie-Christine, go and help Valérie put up the crèche. Everything must seem completely normal."

Unlike in the United States where the Christmas tree is the traditional symbol of Christmas, in Provence it has always been the manger. Every home has its own little manger; every church displays large mangers with many characters which are essentially Provençal. It took me many years to realize that those *santons,* as they are called in Provence, could not possibly have been around when Christ was born.

Grand-mère has an old collection of those ceramic characters, which I loved as a child. Little men and women in traditional Provençal garb, all handmade and handpainted. Each with a story that Grand-mère used to tell me when she placed the *santons* in the manger. Samuel the blindman is led by his little boy Simon to visit the newborn Jesus. He will recover his sight because of his faith. *La Boumiano* is the gypsy who hides Jesus in her shawl so that the bad soldiers who are looking to kill all firstborns in Bethlehem cannot find Him. There is also the simpleton *Ravi* who is so poor he has nothing to offer to the baby Jesus, but then brings him sunshine. *Pescadou*, the fisherman with his sailor outfit, holds a big fish which he brings as an offering, and the hunter in Provençal, *Lou Casaire,* elegant in his high boots and brown hat, carries a duck that he has caught for the newborn child.

Valérie has set up the crèche in the formal sitting room and is busy situating the little figurines. I stand next to her and hand her each piece while trying to remember their story.

"Mademoiselle, where do you think I should place the *sage-femme*?" The midwife is carrying on her head a basket full of linen and diapers.

"She must be close to Mary. The baby will need to be changed."

Valérie laughs. "Just the way you used to say it when you were a little girl, Mademoiselle."

"But the *tambourinaire* must be put on the other side, far from the crib. If not, his drum beating will wake up the baby!"

The whole morning is taken up with the crèche. Grand-mère remains locked in *le petit salon*, no doubt calling Monseigneur d'Epinay. Everyone seems to have left the house after breakfast.

"Where have they all gone?" I ask Valérie, who is placing the baker, with his cotton hat and basketful of little loaves, on the road to the manger.

"Well," explains Valérie. "The roads were cleared this morning. Monsieur *le maire* sent a truck up here to clear the snow. Your aunt Geneviève and uncle Xavier took the dog out for a walk. Madame de la Rochereau also added that they needed to exercise and would be out for a while. The friend of Gerard, what's his name . . . ?"

"Alain LeMoine."

"Yes, he wanted to read *Le Figaro*, and we only get *Nice-Matin*, so the two of them drove off in Monsieur LeMoine's car."

Is that what they read in Strasbourg, *Le Figaro?*

Bending over to put the little donkey carrying sacks of wheat, next to the *santon* with his blue shirt and red scarf, on the hill behind the manger, Valérie complains, "My back is really stiff this morning!" She rubs her lower back. "Ah, yes, Madame Helène! She got up bright and early this morning and had a good breakfast. Seemed in very good spirits. She told me, 'Valérie, I have not finished my Christmas shopping yet. I am calling a cab and going to town. I won't be in for lunch.'"

I spread some straw on the cardboard surface where the manger stands, then place a little mirror for the pond. Unwrap the linen bags and pull out the two brown ducks and the little yellow ducklings and put them on the mirror.

"What about Gerard's father? Philippe Bousquet? Where is he?" I ask.

Valérie shakes her head, as she carefully places a cow behind the empty crib.

"I forgot all about him. After the shock he gave me last night! And Madame, your grandmother, was really upset at his coming to the house like this. But what could she do? This morning? I haven't seen him this morning. Perhaps he is still asleep, I don't know, Mademoiselle."

The crèche is near completion. Jean comes to set up the lights in the little houses on the hills around the manger. I decide to check in with Grand-mère.

Find her sitting in *le petit salon*, writing at her desk.

"Come in, come in, Marie-Christine," her voice is almost cheerful. I pull up a chair and sit beside her.

"So what is happening out there?" She points towards the door. Briefly tell her where everyone has gone.

"Just as I thought," she says grimly, continuing to write.

"What do you mean, Grand-mère?"

"Well, Marie-Christine," she answers, lifting her head from her papers and laying down her pen. "I talked at length to Inspector Bizzard on the phone this morning. His first reaction was, 'Don't let anyone out of the house. The manuscript may still be hidden there.'"

"You mean, that if it was someone in the house who stole the manuscript, he or she would not have had time to take it out of the house?"

"Yes, that was his thought. But of course, I knew it was too late. I heard doors banging, and cars driving off this morning. And now you have confirmed that everyone has left the house."

"Except, perhaps, Gerard's father. Valérie did not see him this morning."

Grand-mère shrugs her shoulder, "What do you expect of a man who has never done an honest day's work in his life? He'll probably sleep until lunch!"

Return to the theft of the manuscript.

"I guess you're right, Grand-mère. If the manuscript was stolen last night by someone in this house, it is gone by now."

Grand-mère's face is very serious. Pointing her finger at me, she adds, "And if your theory is correct and the *Trés Riches Heures* was stolen by someone outside the household, then it was removed last night and is therefore gone as well."

VII

"So what do we do now?" I ask, feeling quite dispirited. What was supposed to have been a Christmas family get together (boring, admittedly) has now turned into a family disaster.

"We are going to pay a visit to Monseigneur d'Epinay and Sister Felicity. Claude Bizzard has an idea, but we will need their cooperation. You, Marie-Christine, will play an important role in all this."

"Me? Are we going to play cops and robbers again like last summer, Grand-mère?"

Grand-mère looks at me over the rim of her eyeglasses.

"I'll tell you more on the way to the Cathedral, Marie-Christine. You can drive me there this afternoon. I have talked to Monseigneur d'Epinay, and he and Sister Felicity are expecting us at four for tea."

At a quarter to four we leave the house. All wrapped up in her black coat and hat, Grand-mère settles uncomfortably in my red Ferrari. Too low, too tight, too fast, and too red, according to her. This is a car for a race car driver and not for *une jeune fille de bonne famille*, or a nice young lady like myself.

Without too much difficulty I manage to drive up to the back of the Cathedral, on the *Place du Grand Puy*. Although it is officially called *Place du 24 Août*, the date when U.S. forces liberated Grasse from the Nazis in 1944, the people of Grasse still use its traditional name. Both names appear on the wall of the medieval buildings behind the Cathedral.

We climb the stairs up to the old door of this twelfth-century cathedral. It stands at the top of a rocky hill, while the old city of Grasse seems to cling precariously to the hillside. The bell tower though, is relatively new: Eighteenth-century lightning struck and destroyed it a number of times over the centuries, but it was rebuilt again and again by the Grassois. Every child of every family (including yours truly) was baptized at its font; every marriage celebrated at its altar; and every death mourned in its aisles. No building is more important to the citizens of Grasse than their beloved Cathedral. The bishop was going to help raise money for its renovation by bringing these old manuscripts and, instead, this disaster.

Grand-mère dips her finger in the holy water and crosses herself. I follow suit.

"A little prayer first, Marie-Christine. You know prayers help."

We sit on the dark oak pews. Grand-mère closes her eyes. Mine wander, looking at these twelfth-century pillars, aged yet still sturdy, a bit like Grand-mère. They have endured much, but have also witnessed Christmas celebrations, Easter processions, joyful family gatherings at weddings. . . . Thoughts linger on weddings. I look down the nave and imagine myself in a long white dress with a train. Definitely a veil of old lace (Grand-mère showed me hers . . . hmmm . . . maybe). If ever I do find the right man, I will get married here in this Cathedral.

We then return down the stairs and off to the right to the bishop's house. His old maid opens the door and ushers us into his library. Sister Felicity is already there, seated by an electric heater that has warmed the whole room. Electric heaters have made no headway in Grand-mère's house. Sister Felicity gets up and pulls a couple of chairs nearer to the heater.

"Come and sit here, it's so cold outside. Monseigneur d'Epinay will be back shortly. He is on the phone in the next room."

Just at this moment, Monseigneur "Pepy" comes in. He is dressed informally in a big blue sweater. A deep furrow crosses his forehead. He seems to have gotten older since last evening when he sat at the dinner table with the family. Rubbing his hands, he stands next to the heater while the maid brings in a tray with tea and coffee and a plate of biscuits. When she leaves the room, the bishop sits down and leaning over towards Grand-mère, shakes his head.

"This is terrible news, Madame de Medici. Terrible! How am I going to explain to the people of the Chantilly Museum, and the French Minister of Foreign Affairs, and the American ambassador, who will all be attending the Mass on New Year's Day, that the manuscript has been stolen?"

Sister Felicity, her hands folded on her lap, says quietly, "I have told the bishop that the police of Grasse will be able to catch the thief before he is able to leave the city. I am sure everything will be all right, and that he should not worry so much. It is not good for his health."

Grand-mère is looking surprisingly calm and composed.

"Dear friends, unfortunately, this may not be the case. If it was a member of my household who took the manuscript last night or early this morning, the manuscript has left the house because everyone went out this morning at one point or another. If, on the other hand, as my granddaughter, Marie-Christine, suggested, it was someone outside the house who managed to steal the manuscript last night through the back door of the kitchen, then the thief left with the *Trés Riches Heures* at that time. The manuscript may, therefore, be already in the hands of a third party, and on its way to Cannes, Nice, Antibes, Monaco, or Paris!"

Sister Felicity lowers her eyes and picks up her cup of tea. Monseigneur "Pepy" takes off his glasses and wipes them with a big white handkerchief. Neither speaks.

Grand-mère looking like the Rock of Gibraltar, continues, "I have, however, spent part of this morning on the telephone with the Paris Inspector, Claude Bizzard, who was so helpful last summer in the case of Monsieur Rondin. You remember him, don't you, Monseigneur?"

The bishop nods absently.

"He'll be coming tonight. But here is what he suggested we should do."

She stops and looks at the three of us with a mischievous twinkle in her eyes.

"Well?" asks the bishop impatiently. He shows no desire to play cat and mouse games with Grand-mère.

She re-arranges her collar, straightens her dress, and then looks up and smiles, "Nothing!"

"What do you mean, nothing, Grand-mère?" I jump out of my seat at the idea, hitting the table and almost spilling the tea from Sister Felicity's cup on the bishop. She catches the cup just in time. My Abercrombie genes just cannot accept the idea of doing nothing in a time of crisis.

"*Calme toi, chérie*," scolds Grand-mère, frowning. "Nothing, just as in pretending that nothing has happened. No one should know that the manuscript has disappeared because that would create an international brouhaha. On the contrary, Marie-Christine should go ahead and publish the story of the two manuscripts coming to Grasse for the eight-hundredth anniversary of the Cathedral. That will create an atmosphere of normality, while we employ the services of the French police to uncover the crime."

"But what is the point of this charade, if on January first we do not have the manuscript?" asks the bishop, whose furrow seems to have deepened, and whose jowls are sagging.

Grand-mère has obviously not finished what she had to say, "Well, I hope that we will have found the manuscript by then."

"But how, Grand-mère? How are we going to find the manuscript? You said yourself that the manuscript may already be in the hands of a third party, and far away from Grasse," I ask as I chew on a rather dry biscuit.

Taking a sip from her cup of tea, Grand-mère continues, "Let's put ourselves in the shoes of the thief, for a moment, to better understand the crime. Why has he (or she, but for the sake of convenience let us assume it is a man), why has he stolen the manuscript?"

"To sell it!" I jump in first.

"He is a collector and wants to add it to his collection," says Sister Felicity, stirring some sugar in her second cup of tea.

Monseigneur d'Epinay looks at Grand-mère thoughtfully, his eyes narrowing.

"What are you getting at, Madame de Medici? Are you thinking about the legend of the hidden treasure?"

Grand-mère clears her throat and says, "If the thief wanted to sell the manuscript, it would have to be to a collector. No one else would touch this manuscript, because it is too well-known— like stealing the *Mona Lisa*. What else can you do with it but keep it hidden and out of sight and out of the reach of the police?"

Monseigneur d'Epinay gets up and starts pacing up and down the room.

"There are people like this. Wealthy collectors who want to own unique works of art, and are willing to steal and bribe and commit all kinds of crimes to lay their hands on those works."

Grand-mère nods.

"And what would you say is their greatest motivating force, Monseigneur?"

"Greed, undoubtedly!" is the forceful response.

"Precisely!" answers Grand-mère triumphantly.

What is Grand-mère getting at? Is this a lesson of catechism? Are we talking about mortal and venial sins here? Or are we trying to catch a thief?

"Well, then," continues the venerable matriarch, turning towards Sister Felicity, "tell me, Sister, can greed be satiated?"

Sister Felicity looks thoughtfully at Grand-mère and then smiles. She seems to understand what eludes me totally, "Greed is insatiable. A person who is greedy for money never has enough. He constantly craves for more, even though he may be already very wealthy. A collector is the same. He will continue collecting and the search, purchase, or acquisition of yet another object will be only temporarily satisfying."

Monseigneur d'Epinay has stopped pacing and is listening to this dialogue with intense interest. I feel out of it. Thought that this was about stolen manuscripts and instead we are into the definition of greed, and sins big and small. Yawn discreetly. No one notices. They are all so engrossed in this theological discourse.

Crossing his arms and leaning backward, the bishop says, "I see, Madame de Medici. You are suggesting a trap. Using another item as bait, I presume?"

Grand-mère chuckles. What is Monseigneur talking about? Have this vision of a goat being set up to trap a tiger.

"Precisely, Monseigneur. Precisely!"

Sister Felicity has finished her tea and sets her cup down on the table. She turns to face Grand-mère and Monseigneur d'Epinay and says quietly, "And that's where I come in, isn't it?"

Sister Felicity, the goat for the trap?

"I'm afraid so," replies Grand-mère.

I've about had it with all this rigmarole.

"Will someone please tell me what's going on here? I have no idea what you are all talking about! Weren't we supposed to be discussing the theft of the *Trés Riches Heures?*" A frown appears on the old matriarch's brow. She disapproves of these sudden outbursts. But Monseigneur "Pepy" understands my predicament.

"Marie-Christine, we are talking about laying a trap for the thief of the *Trés Riches Heures,*" he says, smiling.

"I see," although I am not quite sure I do. "But how are we going to do this?" Am suggesting that an elaboration of the plan is in order at this point.

Sister Felicity gets up and says, "Madame de Medici, will you please explain the idea to Marie-Christine, while I go and get the 'bait'?" She winks at me and leaves the room.

Grand-mère clasps her hands together as in prayer and, addressing the heater, says, "The idea is that the thief may have stolen the manuscript for a collector somewhere. We do not know where. That collector in turn is ruthless and greedy and wants the manuscript so badly he is ready to steal and bribe, etc. We (that is, the people in this room) will tempt him with the second manuscript, the *Belles Heures,* which Sister Felicity has brought from the United States. We will let the thief know that the *Belles Heures* is at my house. No obsessed collector could let this once-in-a-lifetime opportunity to acquire *both* manuscripts pass him by. So he will try to steal the second manuscript as well. But this time we will be ready for him. With the help of Inspector Bizzard and his men we will catch the thief red-handed, and hopefully get the *Trés Riches Heures* back again."

Am beginning to grasp the relationship between the theological discussion and the goat as bait for the tiger. But a lot is still unclear. For instance, "Since we don't know who the thief is, how do we go about informing him about the goat?"

"What goat, Marie-Christine?" asks Grand-mère, looking at me as if I'm suddenly non compos mentis.

"Sorry, Grand-mère, I had been thinking of the goat that hunters tie to a tree as bait to catch tigers."

Monseigneur d'Epinay bursts out laughing.

"A very apt image, Marie-Christine! Yes, yes, very good. Ha, ha, ha!"

Grand-mère does not seem to think this is very funny. I suppose the loss of the *Trés Riches Heures* is affecting her sense of humor.

"To get back to your question, Marie-Christine. *You* will inform the thief about the presence in my house of the *Belles Heures* manuscript from the Cloisters Museum in New York."

Just when I thought I understood what the general plan was going to be to recover the *Trés Riches Heures!*

Crossing my legs and leaning against the arm of my chair, I examine Grand-mère and Monseigneur "Pepy" for signs that we are all three from the same planet earth.

"Grand-mère, am I hearing you correctly? You are saying that *I* should be cavorting with the thief of the *Trés Riches Heures* and, between two drinks, inform him that it is quite all right to drop by my grandmother's house and try his luck at stealing the *second* rare French manuscript. Furthermore, *I* should draw his attention to the fact that his collection could not possibly be complete unless he were in full possession of both manuscripts. And when that miscreant decides that I am right, and comes over to the house to have a look at the *Belles*

Heures, out from behind the living room curtain pops Inspector Claude Bizzard and nabs the thief, shouting 'Gotcha!' Is that the plan, Grand-mère?"

Monseigneur "Pepy" gets up and moves towards his desk. Turning his back to us, he picks up an old pipe and starts stuffing it with tobacco. He is chuckling and doesn't want Grand-mère to notice. She is still staring at the heater and ruminating about what? Ungrateful, ill-mannered grandchildren? Finally, she lifts her head and gives me the look that is meant to go straight to my inner soul.

"In your rather colorful jargon, Marie-Christine, you have managed to get the gist of the plan to catch the thief."

Having determined that we are definitely *not* on the same planet, star, or nebula, I now proceed to act as if 'the plan' were perfectly rational.

"Very well then, please give me the name and address of the felon, and I will do my very best to deliver him into the hands of Inspector Bizzard before the night is over."

Grand-mère smiles. The first smile since the manuscript disappeared.

"Marie-Christine, you forget the power of the media!"

The media? Have this sudden vision of a giant screen in the *Place aux Aires* in the middle of the old city of Grasse. A voice is announcing: *"Belles Heures du Duc de Berry"!* Authentic fifteenth-century manuscript located in the villa de Medici. Try stealing it without being caught!"

"Marie-Christine! Are you listening?" Grand-mère's voice brings me back to whatever planet everyone is on this afternoon.

"Yes, Grand-mère, I am listening. You were talking about the power of the media."

81

"*Le Loup-Garou!* That's what we were talking about, *chérie.* You can get this nice young man, Leon Baude, to write an interesting front-page article on the two manuscripts. He should mention, *en passant,* of course, that the two manuscripts are in the de Medici villa."

Have to admit I had not thought of this idea. Not bad. Could even work. And best of all this *would* be a "scoop" for *Le Loup-Garou.* The issue might sell well and we may even get some new subscribers.

Sister Felicity returns to the room. She is holding a large cardboard box that looks quite heavy.

"Is this the *Belles Heures?*" I ask, intrigued.

"Yes, it is. Let me put it on the desk there and we can all look at it."

Sister Felicity lays the box down slowly and carefully on the desk after the bishop clears some papers that were littered about. She opens the box that is tied with a little green ribbon.

"The original manuscript was burnt in the archives in Bourges in 1858, when a fire destroyed the place. However, this manuscript had been copied by an artist, the Comte de Bastard, who remained faithful to every detail. Of course it is not as valuable as the *Trés Riches Heures.*"

We all crowd around her to look at the manuscript.

I must admit: the art work is stupendous! The colors, the intricate vine designs of the borders. Full-length portraits of ladies and knights clad in brilliant reds and blues, on horses and in carriages. Saints tortured in every possible barbaric manner. St. Jerome tempted by a vision of two women (not too sure why—they are not particularly attractive).

"The most interesting part of the *Belles Heures* is the first special cycle," says Sister Felicity. "There are eleven scenes from the cycle of St. Catherine of the Wheel, or St. Catherine of Alexandria." Sister Felicity's eyes are shining as she explains. A real teacher with a passion for her work, her enthusiasm is communicative.

"What kind of a saint was she?" Never thought I'd be interested in saints.

"Well, she is supposed to have been the daughter of a King of Egypt, and was not only a very beautiful but also a very intelligent woman. Her reputation for learning made her the patron saint of libraries and librarians. She is on the seal of the University of Paris."

Suddenly the phone rings, loudly, insistently.

"Hallo, d'Epinay speaking. Yes, they're here. *What?!* Did you call the police? Yes, of course. I'll tell Madame de Medici. Yes, we'll be there in fifteen minutes."

Grand-mère, Sister Felicity, and I are staring at Monseigneur d'Epinay, mesmerized.

Grand-mère is the first to react, "Who was that? What happened?" she almost shouts.

Monseigneur seems to be in a state of shock and cannot answer immediately. He then turns to me and asks, "Marie-Christine, do you have your car?"

"Yes, I do," I answer as in a dream.

"Then you must take your grandmother and return to the house immediately. I'll join you shortly."

"Bernard, tell me right now, what has happened!" Have never heard Grand-mère call the bishop by his first name. Emotion must have overcome her sense of decorum.

He hesitates, then shakes his head, "I'm afraid, Eleanore, there has been an unfortunate . . . uh . . . occurrence." Astounding he uses her first name too. Well, after all they have known each other for over two-thirds of a century!

"Your son-in-law is dead. I think he has been killed."

"Xavier? Dead! Oh my God!" Grand-mère sits down in shock, her cane dropping on the floor with a clatter.

"No, Eleanore, it's the other one, Phillipe Bousquet."

VIII

Back at the house, pandemonium reigns. Valérie is running about clutching her head and repeating "*Mon Dieu! Mon Dieu!*" In the orchard Grasse's Inspector Dominique Pasteur (he of the red hair and red eyes) is in animated conversation with Jean. His side-kick, Deputy Inspector François Guerrier, is jumping about like a grasshopper, examining the orange grove and taking notes. Standing on the doorstep, Tante Geneviève is giving orders to the ambulance driver about where to park, while her husband, Xavier, is speaking on his cell-phone and gesticulating wildly. Meanwhile Pushkin, my aunt Geneviève's little white poodle, is yapping its head off and getting in everyone's way. Wants to be part of the game we all appear to be playing.

Grand-mère has recovered from the initial shock. Back in her own house, she takes control of the situation, takes Valérie by the arm and pushes her towards the sitting room. She asks me to call Claude Bizzard on his cell-phone and find out when he is coming.

"You'd better call your parents too, Marie-Christine. Tell them what happened before they hear it from the radio or the television and rush up here to see if you're still alive. Also take the manuscript from Sister Felicity and lock it up in the drawer of my desk in *le petit salon*."

Do as I'm told. Feel personally quite weak at the knees and somewhat nauseous. Not that I had particularly liked Phillipe Bousquet, but he was married to my aunt Helène, and was the father of Gerard!

I call the Carlton Hotel and am transferred to my parents' suite. Mother answers.

"Hi, Chrissy, how's everything? Haven't heard from you these last couple of days. Bet you had no electricity up there. Even in good weather that house of your grandmother's still functions like something out of the Middle Ages."

Not quite sure how I am going to approach this. Afraid Mother will freak out. I must mention the murder, but won't tell her about the manuscript since that story is not likely to hit the papers any time soon.

"I'm fine, Mother. Everything is OK. Aunt Geneviève and Aunt Helène have come up to Grasse for Christmas. Gerard is here as well. He has brought a friend."

"The place must be a zoo!" exclaims Mother.

"Yes . . . I suppose," I answer hesitantly.

"Chrissy! What's wrong? Now, don't say everything's fine. I know you," Mother has an uncanny way of sensing trouble. Perhaps that's the opening I need.

"Well, Mother, everything is fine, except that . . . that . . . Gerard's father, you know Phillipe Bousquet . . . "

"Of course, I know him. Your aunt's ex-husband. Well, what about him? Don't tell me he showed up too?"

"Yes, in fact he did. He arrived yesterday evening. He wasn't invited, of course." I hurry to add, as if that explains everything.

"I should think not. After the way he treated his wife! Disgraceful!"

"The thing is, Mother, he's . . . uh . . . sort of . . . dead." There I said it!

Silence on the other end.

"Mother . . . Are you still on the line?"

"Chrissy, I am not quite sure I heard you. Did you say Phillipe was *dead?*"

86

"Yes, Mother. He's dead."

"You mean his corpse arrived at the house?"

"Uh. Not exactly. I mean he was alive when he arrived . . . but now he is dead." This is getting really awkward.

"You mean he had a heart attack, or something? Speak up, child! You are mumbling and I can't hear you!"

"Not a heart attack . . . but I think he got killed."

For the next ten minutes Mother expresses herself forcefully on the subject of the French, eighteenth-century houses, and what happens when unruly daughters choose to live in France in old French houses with criminals lurking behind every tree. Finally, she announces that she and my father will be coming over this evening to check on me and on the rest of this mad household.

Relieved the ordeal is over, I then call Claude Bizzard to ask when he will be in Grasse. As he does not answer, I leave a voice message to the effect that there has been a death as well as a theft at the de Medicis, and that his assistance is urgently needed.

◆

Grand-mère is in the living room with Valérie, who is sitting on the sofa next to her, sobbing.

"Valérie, where are Tante Helène, Gerard, and Monsieur LeMoine? I have not seen them. Are they back?" I ask.

More sobbing. Hiccup.

"They haven't returned yet, Mademoiselle." Valérie blows her nose in a big, white handkerchief. Face all puffed up.

Grand-mère has her arm around her shoulders, and is making cooing sounds. Begin to understand why Valérie puts up with Grand-mère's tantrums and criticisms. She knows Grand-mère cares. That simple!

Finally, Valérie pulls herself together, and after a last sniffle, begins to tell the story.

"After you and Mademoiselle left for the Cathedral, I had some laundry to do. As it was still sunny, I decided to hang the laundry out in the garden, next to the orange grove. You know Madame, I don't like to give the fine damask tablecloth that was used at the dinner last night out for laundering." There is of course no washer or dryer in Grand-mère's house. All is given out to a laundering service, except what Valérie deems inappropriate.

"Yes, yes, Valérie. You are quite right. Please continue," Grand-mère urges.

"Well, you see, Madame, I thought everyone was out of the house, except for Jean and myself. So I put on my apron and prepared the tub with the water and the soap suds."

"Valérie, what happened after you washed the table-cloth?" There is a warning sign of a storm to come in Grand-mère's voice.

"No, Madame, not after, but before. I found I did not have enough soap powder and remembered that there was a brand new box in the bathroom of . . . Monsieur . . . sniff, sniff . . . Phillipe Bousquet." The handkerchief comes out of the pocket again and Valérie wipes her eyes.

"So you went into Phillipe's room," snaps Grand-mère.

"Yes, Madame. And as I knocked before entering, I remembered I had not made Monsieur's room this morning."

This time I interrupt. At this rate we will not get to the bottom of this story for another couple of hours.

"That's because he was not up this morning, like the others." Valérie turns to me with eyes red from crying.

"Yes, Mademoiselle, that's right. And when no one answered my knock, I entered the room." She stops, and heaves a deep sigh. Grand-mère is looking at her intently. No cooing anymore, I think she is now growling.

"Well." Grrr; "There was no one in the room, and, and, . . . "

Grand-mère's cane falls to the ground.

"Madame, the bed had not been slept in!"

Both Grand-mère and I stare at Valérie.

"But he did go to his room last night," I say, remembering Grand-mère telling Valérie to prepare the spare bed in the downstairs room.

Valérie nods.

"Yes he did. His suitcase was still there. He had set it on the bed and opened it, but had not unpacked. I thought perhaps that . . . that . . . "

"That what, Valérie?" Grand-mère is still irritated.

"Well, that he might have gone to Madame Helène's room. I believe I overheard Madame suggesting he come up to her room later for a drink, before they went to bed last night."

Grand-mère sighs, "Yes, that's my Helène. Never learns. She's still besotted with that man!"

"What happened after you found the soap, Valérie?" I try to get the conversation away from Grand-mère's reflections on her daughter.

"I put some order in Monsieur Bousquet's room. Closed his suitcase and put it on a stool next to the closet. I cleared some wrapping paper that was lying on the floor, and left the room."

It is getting cold and dark. I get up and switch on the table lamps. Pick up a couple of logs and add them to the dying fire.

Valérie with her hands crossed on her lap continues her story.

"It was only after I washed the table cloth and put it in the laundry basket, that I called Jean to help me. My back hurt me so I did not want to carry the basket outside. When Jean and I went to the garden, we passed by the orange grove. At first, we did not see what it was." Valérie begins sobbing again. Grand-mère waves to me.

"Marie-Christine, please get Valérie *un petit cognac.*"

On the sideboard next to the door there is always a tray with glasses and various drinks, in case someone drops in for a visit. Pour a cognac for Valérie. She drinks it in one gulp, then starts coughing.

"*Merci,* Mademoiselle. Yes, as I was saying . . . we could not tell. It looked like clothes on the grass. I thought the wind had caused some laundry to fly and scatter under the trees. So I went to pick them up. That's when, that's when . . . I found him." More sobbing. "Monsieur Bousquet was lying face down on the grass. There was blood at the back of his head. Jean and I tried lifting him, but he was so heavy, we could not. Then Jean said we should call you at Monseigneur d'Epinay's. I couldn't walk I was so shocked, so I just stood there next to the body. The ground was still covered with snow from yesterday. My feet were so cold. Jean went back to the house and called Monseigneur who told him to call the police. Monsieur *l'inspecteur* arrived just a few minutes before you did."

Valérie is looking pale and exhausted. Pour her another cognac.

◆

The rest of the evening went past in a big blur. Monseigneur d'Epinay and Sister Felicity arrived first and took Inspector Pasteur and his deputy, François Guerrier, in *le petit salon* to inform them about the theft of the manuscript. Then my aunt Helène, her son Gerard, and Alain LeMoine returned from wherever they had spent the day and were told of Phillipe's death by Grand-mère. Great display of shock and grief. Gerard started drinking and Alain sat next to him plying him with liquor. Tante Helène wailed hysterically and was joined by Pushkin, who howled in chorus. My parents arrived next, and tension mounted as Mother practically accused Grand-mère of staging murders and robberies in her house and endangering my life. My uncle Xavier quarreled with my aunt Geneviève saying that he should never have agreed to spend Christmas in this lunatic asylum. And Grand-mère, losing her patience, exploded and threatened to throw us all out of the house if we did not behave.

At this critical juncture Claude Bizzard showed up dressed all in black, unshaven with tufts of hair sticking out at the back of his head. His unexpected appearance caused the entire room to fall silent since most people did not know who he was. He could even have been, in the eyes of some, the criminal who killed Phillipe Bousquet!

"Claude!" I cried out. "I'm so glad you made it! We've all been waiting for you!"

Quizzical look on everyone's faces. Guess my statement applied only to Grand-mère and myself. Papa, who had said nothing while the crisis was unfolding and had retired to a corner of the room with a book, recognized Claude. He came forward with outstretched arms, "Monsieur l'inspecteur, welcome to the de Medici house." And after shaking hands, he turned to the silent group congregated in the *salon* and introduced him, "Inspector Bizzard from the *Police Judiciaire* of the *Quai des Orfèvres* in Paris."

◆

Twenty-second of December: Wake up with a headache, then remember last night. Claude has ordered us all to remain in Grasse (except for my parents). There is going to be an investigation in the death of Phillipe Bousquet. Despite the murder, the crackbrained plan to catch the thief of the *Trés Riches Heures* by luring him to the house, is still on.

At breakfast everyone looks glum and sullen. Decide that it is better to leave the house and drive to the headquarters of *Le Loup-Garou*. Must play my part in the scheme of things. It may even work. Who knows?

Drive off to the *Boulevard du Jeu de Ballon*. The elevator is not working so I climb the stairs to the office. Leon Baude, Vivianne, and Paul are hard at work planning the next issue of *Le Loup-Garou*. Leon pulls up a couple of chairs, Paul gets the coffee. We then settle around a table covered with papers, pens, photographs, and rubber bands.

Leon jumps in first, "I heard there had been a murder at your place last night. Is that true?"

News travels fast in Grasse.

"How did your hear that?" I ask, curious but not surprised.

"Claude Bizzard called me this morning. He also said that it was all right for me to stay on for another month with *Le Loup-Garou*. He said I would be needed here."

"Good, then that's settled. Now let me give you the scoop on what happened. You will also need to cover the manuscripts story. It is important that you write that."

For the next two hours I am deep into the articles for *Le Loup-Garou*. Give Leon all the information I have about the manuscripts, the legend of the rubies, the importance of having both manuscripts together, and the historical role of Grasse in providing a hiding place for the manuscripts. The team, however, is more interested in the murder.

"Marie-Christine, *Le Loup* is coming out tomorrow. We need all the gory details of the murder to beat *Nice-Matin* on this story."

"Frankly, Leon, that's all I know. I've told you what Valérie saw and did, but beyond that I don't know what happened."

"Very well, Marie-Christine. While we work on the manuscripts story, you get back to the house and find out all you can about the murder. You can call me on your cell this afternoon. This is big!"

Drive back feeling like the proverbial "Trojan Horse." To gather all the gory details of the murder for *Le Loup-Garou* also means to make public what is, after all, a family affair. That puts family loyalty up against my professional duty as a journalist. A catch 22 situation!

At the house, the family is gathered around the fireplace in the *grand salon.* Valérie has prepared a cold lunch which she is setting on the sideboard, and Jean is serving some aperitifs: Dubonnet, Amer Picon, Byrrh, St. Raphael, Pernod. Gloom and doom pervades the atmosphere.

Grand-mère is enthroned in her armchair looking like thunder. I go up to her and kiss her cheek. It feels cold.

"Everything all right, Grand-mère?" I ask hesitantly. Obvious to the naked eye that things are *not* all right.

"No, everything is all wrong!" explodes Grand-mère. Heads turn, Pushkin barks excitedly, Xavier drops the newspaper he has been reading.

"The inspectors have commandeered my private study to conduct police interrogations of members of my family and staff. This is unacceptable!"

At this point Claude Bizzard bounces out of *le petit salon,* followed by Inspectors Pasteur and Guerrier. Alain LeMoine dressed in a neat gray suit and blue silk tie comes out last. What a contrast to Claude, who is still unshaven and has not changed yesterday's black polo and leather jacket outfit!

Claude looks at the sideboard and smiles cheerfully, "Thank you, Madame de Medici, for inviting us to stay for lunch. I am starving!"

Grand-mère's stormy mood dissipates. It is extraordinary the effect Claude always has on her. She has already forgotten the commandeering of her private study!

"Come on, everyone, get up and serve yourselves," she orders.

Valérie has set out a plate of cold meats, a large bowl of green salad with endives, an earthenware terrine of lentils seasoned with ginger and nutmeg, a *tarte d'epinards* or spinach pie, a tray of cheeses including a Gruyère and a Brie. On the sideboard next to the door she has put a basket of oranges and tangerines, an apple tart with fresh cream, coffee, milk, and sugar.

The mood has lightened up. Everyone begins talking and serving themselves. Jean pours a chilled white wine, a *vin maison* from Grand-mère's cellar. I slide up to Claude and chat while he scoops a large serving of lentils. Have decided to get as much information out of him as possible. Must be professional. Family loyalty will have to wait.

I settle next to him on a settee by the French window. Need to be out of earshot of Grand-mère and my aunts. I then begin my interrogation.

"So, Claude, you think this case is interesting enough to come down from Paris for?"

With his mouth full, he looks up, "Which case?"

Taken aback, I hesitate, "I suppose you're right. There are two cases: a theft and a murder."

Stuffs his mouth with a large piece of spinach pie, and looks at me sideways. Forgot how long his eyelashes were.

"So which one were you referring to?"

I must get some information for *Le Loup.*

94

"I meant the murder, of course. That was a shock to the family. . . . " Claude chews on a piece of bread and ham.

"But you know, I was coming down here anyway before the murder."

Better have some wine and think about my answer, before I end up being interrogated by Claude. I wave to Jean to pour me a glass.

Claude smiles, a crooked smile that reveals his very white teeth.

"You know why I came down here? Your grandmother invited me to spend my Christmas vacations in Grasse!"

Cough and sputter in my wine.

"When did she do that?"

"Oh, about a month ago."

Grand-mère had planned this in advance. And then she asked me to call him about the theft of the manuscript! Must not appear to be surprised, "Yes, of course. She was worried about the manuscripts and wanted to make sure they were well-guarded." Only possible explanation, unless . . .

"I suppose so," he looks slightly disappointed.

Must change the subject.

"So what did you find out? About the murder, I mean."

Claude puts his very empty plate on the little side table and wipes his mouth with a large blue napkin.

"You want the police report? OK: Monsieur Phillipe Bousquet was found shot in the back of the head around five o'clock yesterday afternoon. He had been dead for at least twelve hours and perhaps as long as fifteen hours before he was found. The shot was fired at very close range, probably less than a meter, from a small semi-automatic handgun. The ballistics department is examining the bullet, as we speak."

"One shot?"

"A single shot to the head. Must have died almost immediately."

"And who? . . . " Am almost afraid to ask as the implications of the murder begin to dawn on me.

Claude looks very serious. He rubs his chin and discovers a stubble.

"Forgot to shave this morning. Hum . . . Are you asking who could have murdered your uncle? Well, frankly, anyone in this house. If a murder takes place in the middle of the night, no one needs an alibi. Everyone has the perfect right to say 'I was in bed and asleep.' Very difficult for the police to check if this is true for each person."

"Claude, someone who was *not* in this house could have come up here and shot Phillipe. Why do you think it was someone in the house?" Family loyalty demands that I stand up for members of de Medici household.

"Yes, it is possible, but unlikely," he answers eyeing the sideboard. Looks like a hungry wolf.

"Go and help yourself," I pat Claude on the shoulder. "Then come back and tell me why you think the 'external' suspect theory is so unlikely."

He returns with a plate full of lentils, a large slice of spinach pie and salad, and sits next to me.

"You see, two nights ago it snowed and the roads were closed."

IX

Time for coffee and dessert. Decide to circulate. Claude is not being helpful and I'm not inclined to believe his stories.

"I'm going to help myself with the apple tart," I say as I get up. Claude waves me away. Take a tiny slice of apple tart with just a wisp of cream, and some black coffee, and look around to decide where to sit. Alain LeMoine looks up from his plate and smiles at me. Definitely a charmer.

"May I get you a chair?" he asks, getting up and pulling one closer to the fire and to his chair. Well, perhaps I can find out what he was doing with the inspectors in Grand-mère's *petit salon.* Put my cup on the floor next to the chair, cross my legs, and slip my fingers through my hair. Alain follows every move. Feeling justifiably appreciated (even if I say so myself), I can now pursue my investigation. Pick up my fork and dip it into the cream.

"So, Alain, will you be spending Christmas with us?"

"Yes, I suppose so. That inspector from Paris does not want any of us to leave Grasse. It's quite incredible! Almost like being under house arrest!" His highly polished right shoe is shaking nervously, although the rest of him seems quite calm and composed. "Your grandmother has kindly invited me to stay here until the investigation is over, and as all hotels in Grasse are fully booked because of the Christmas season. I accepted—gratefully," he adds as an afterthought.

Savor a piece of Valérie's apple tart flavored with cinnamon. Without looking at Alain, I continue the subtle inquiry, "So, tell me Alain, *entre nous,* what are the police asking?"

"You mean what did they ask me in there?" he points to *le petit salon.*

I try to look indifferent, "In there, out here, I mean who cares? What do they want to know?"

"I am not sure what they are asking other people, but the Paris inspector, Claude whatever his name, asked me first where I was last night."

Nonchalantly picking up my coffee cup and placing my plate under the chair, I continue, "And what did you say?"

"That I was in my room, of course."

"Did he persist?"

"In fact he did. He asked me if I had left my room any time during the night."

"And had you?"

"Yes, I went down to the kitchen to get a glass of water."

"At what time was this?"

Alain looks at me curiously, "You sound like the inspector from Paris. Are you conducting an investigation as well?"

I must be careful not show my cards now.

"Me? No, of course not! Ha, ha, ha! What gave you this idea?" Laugh in a sort of carefree way. "Am just preparing myself for the police questioning when *my* turn comes."

After initial hesitation, Alain appears satisfied with my answer, lowers his voice, and adds in a confidential tone, "You know, I believe the police think it is someone in this house who killed Phillipe Bousquet."

As if I didn't know! Must appear to share confidences to build Alain's trust in me. Want him to be more forthcoming.

"I think you're quite right, Alain. I was just talking to Claude Bizzard, that's his name by the way, and he told me the same thing."

Alain frowns, "Did he tell you why he thinks it's one of us?"

I shrug, "He has this stupid notion that the road coming up to the house was closed that night because of the snow, and that consequently, it had to be someone who was physically here who killed Phillipe."

With his foot still shaking nervously, Alain looks thoughtfully into the fire, "But the bishop and the nun, as well as the mayor and his wife, left the house after dinner and returned to town."

Take a sip of coffee. It's lukewarm.

"Let me play the devil's advocate," I answer. "Claude will argue that it was only later that evening that the snow made the roads impassable. Remember, it doesn't snow much in Grasse but when it does, everything grinds to a standstill."

"But the next morning the road was clear, and we all went out!"

"I know, but the mayor sent a special truck with salt to clear the road to Grand-mère's house. After all he is an old friend of Grand-mère's and he had dinner at our house that night."

"Your grandmother gets special services, doesn't she?"

"She does; she's an institution in Grasse. Everyone knows her and seems to owe her a favor. So she gets pretty much what she wants around here."

Alain looks across the room to where Grand-mère is talking animatedly with Inspector Pasteur and his assistant, François Guerrier.

"Wonder what she's telling them, now?"

I laugh, "She could very well be telling them how to conduct the investigation."

Have not found out yet what happened between Alain and Claude in *le petit salon*. Ask Jean, who is pouring coffee, to fill my cup.

"So tell me, Alain, what happened after you went to get a glass of water in the kitchen the night of the murder?"

"Well, nothing much really. I went downstairs and saw a light in the kitchen."

Jean, who has been filling up my coffee cup, looks up in astonishment.

"Excuse me, Monsieur. May I say something, Mademoiselle?"

Am surprised. Jean and Valérie never interrupt a conversation with guests that takes place in the sitting room. They only answer questions when addressed directly.

"Well, what is it, Jean?" I asked a bit annoyed at the interruption. My investigation had been moving in the right direction until now.

"Well, it's just that Monsieur must be mistaken."

"What do you mean, mistaken?" This time it's Alain who is annoyed.

"He could not have seen a light, because the electricity only came back at eight o'clock the next morning."

For a second Alain's nostrils flair and anger appears in his eyes. Then he lowers his eyes and seems to make an effort to control himself. Turning to me and ignoring Jean completely, "I can only tell you what I saw. There was a light in the kitchen. It went off before I reached the pantry, and I did not find anyone in the kitchen when I got there."

"Thank you, Jean. I think my aunt Geneviève needs another cup of coffee." Point to where my aunt is sitting across the room—a clear indication that he should move away. Jean bows, "*Bien*, Mademoiselle."

Jean's remark has started me thinking, "Were you carrying a candle then, when you came downstairs?" I ask casually as I pick up my cup of coffee. Alain hesitates, just for a second, then shakes his head, "No, I had a flashlight."

"Oh, you brought a flashlight with you when you came to visit?"

100

"I got it later from the car, when the lights went out."

"You Alsatians are so much more used to cold weather than we are here in Grasse. So you went out at night, in the snow storm, to get your flashlight? How brave of you!"

Alain LeMoine looks furious. I think my question is the proverbial last straw that broke the camel's back.

"What is this? Do I have to answer your questions too? This is intolerable!" His raised voice attracts everyone's attention. He gets up and stomps out of the room.

"It's all right," I smile, tossing back my hair as if this was of no importance. Carrying my cup, I go and sit next to my aunt Geneviève. She has just put down today's issue of *Nice-Matin*.

"What's the matter with this young man?" she asks.

"Oh, nothing. The police have questioned him the whole morning, and then I asked him a couple of questions that annoyed him. That's all."

Tante Geneviève raises her delicately penciled eyebrows as if to say she really can't be bothered with people who behave like this. Then turns to face me and says, "Marie-Christine, perhaps *you* can help me."

A rare request from an aunt who always knows what she wants and how to get it.

"Sure, Tante Geneviève, if I can."

"Well, you see, I was so busy in Paris before we came down here that I just did not have time to shop for Christmas gifts. So, why don't you and I go to town this afternoon and shop? You can choose whatever you want for yourself, and give me ideas for gifts for everyone else."

I like this idea very much. It is getting a bit morbid and claustrophobic in the house, and I have not finished my shopping either. I had not expected so many people for Christmas!

At 3 PM, wrapped in a chinchilla fur jacket, Tante Geneviève climbs into my Ferrari and we drive up to town. We park in the modern *Parking de la Foux*, and set off on foot to the center of the old medieval town of Grasse. It is cold but sunny—perfect weather for shopping.

"Where shall we begin?" I ask.

"Depends for whom we buy a gift first," answers Tante Geneviève.

"What about Valérie? She may be easier to please than the others."

"Very well then, where do you suggest?"

"Let's go to *Cache-Cache*, it's close by. It's a large store, and I'm sure we'll find something."

The store is filled with customers, but Tante Geneviève moves decisively towards the hats.

A few minutes later Tante Geneviève, carrying a hatbox, and I are out and on the move again.

"I think I'll get my poor sister a bangle to cheer her up," my aunt announces.

Perhaps that's my chance to pursue the investigation, because I must find out if my aunt saw or heard anything the night of the murder.

"*Cassis Citron*, that's the place for handmade jewelry. And yes, she has taken it rather hard," I add as an afterthought.

"I can't think why, especially after the way Phillipe treated her." Tante Geneviève's tone makes it clear that she would never stand for this type of treatment from any man.

As we walk towards *Cassis Citron*, I pursue the subject.

"You know that Valérie overheard Aunt Helène invite Phillipe for a drink to her room that evening?"

"Ah! That explains why I heard voices and laughter in

Helène's room that night. At first, I thought it was the radio or television, and then I remembered that Maman does not have a television in the house."

"That's odd. Why didn't I hear anything? My room is closer to Tante Helène's than yours," I ask perplexed.

Tante Geneviève dismisses this with a quick gesture of the hand.

"I must have been going to the bathroom and passed by her room on the way."

We reach *Cassis Citron*. The owner is North African and creates her own jewels. She has lovely amber and pearl pins, long necklaces of silver and coral, rings set with semiprecious stones, earrings in the shape of flowers. There are beaded combs and shawls with beads.

I decide to buy my aunt Helène the beaded shawl. Tante Geneviève picks a striking bedouin silver necklace and matching bracelet. Carrying our carefully wrapped packages, we emerge on the street. A few minutes later on Avenue Thiers we find *Les Trésors d'Emilie*. I love this store! One can find anything from honey and liqueurs to furniture from around the world. We look at each other, "Xavier!" We exclaim in unison, and burst out laughing. Don't remember ever laughing with my aunt. She is more fun than I thought.

I find an exotic statuette of a goddess from Mali; my aunt, a ceremonial sash with printed motifs from the Sulawesi Island in Indonesia.

"He could wear it at auctions," giggles Tante Geneviève. I think she is secretly poking fun at her husband.

As we walk out loaded with gifts, I suggest we sit down and have a cup of coffee. *Café Olé* is the new place in town, so we go there. Find a table for two and order cappuccinos.

"That was fun," says Tante Geneviève, opening her Chanel handbag and taking out a gold powder case. "The atmosphere in the house is really getting on my nerves." Powders her nose and chin, and slips the case back in the bag.

"Did Claude Bizzard, the Paris inspector, question you too?" I ask, curious to know what happened between the two of them.

She sighs and sits back in her chair, looking bored, "Yes, he asked me where I was and what I saw and what I did that night, and if I went out of my room between 11 PM and 5 AM. A lot of hooey, if you ask me."

"And what did you tell him?"

"I told him, 'My dear Inspector Bizzard, what *do* you think I could possibly be doing in my mother's house, in Grasse, between 11 PM and 5 AM?'"

"Good for you, Tante Geneviève! He deserved that! And what was his reaction?"

"He blushed to the roots of his unkempt hair."

"But he didn't give up?"

"No, he did not. He apologized and said it was his duty as the investigating officer (I thought it was Pasteur), to ask these questions to everyone."

"So what happened next?"

"Well, I told him I was in bed fast asleep, and saw and heard nothing."

"But Tante Geneviève, you did. I mean you went to the bathroom and passed by the door of Tante Helène, and heard people laughing and talking!"

"You're right, *ma chérie*, I completely forgot to mention it. Anyway it's unimportant."

The waiter brings our cappuccinos with a little piece of chocolate on the side of the saucer, as is the custom in Grasse. I unwrap the chocolate and ask conversationally, "And Inspector Bizzard also questioned Uncle Xavier?"

Tante Geneviève wrinkles her nose and hesitates, "I don't think so. I'm sure Xavier would have complained if the police had questioned him. Perhaps they will this afternoon, while you and I are out here shopping," she adds, chuckling.

With my spoon I scoop the froth off the top of my cappuccino, "And Uncle Xavier slept through the night as well?"

"Xavier never sleeps. He is an insomniac, and frankly I don't know how he can live with just two or three hours of sleep a night."

Eat my chocolate slowly. Don't want to ask too many questions, before my aunt realizes that I'm conducting my own investigation. A young woman in high heels and tight black leather pants enters the café holding a miniature poodle in her arms that looks just like Pushkin.

"Oh! Look, there's another Pushkin!" I exclaim.

Tante Geneviève turns her head and looks at the dog with little interest.

"They're so small and need so much care. Shampoos, cuts, shots, vaccines, special diets. You can't imagine the trouble they are. Every time Xavier and I travel, we either have to take Pushkin with us or leave him in some dog hostel, which costs a fortune! And then he needs to be walked everyday, sunshine or rain."

"So Uncle Xavier had to take Pushkin out the other night even when it snowed?" I ask innocently.

She nods, then picks up her coffee and takes a sip.

"Yes, he could not sleep and Pushkin was scraping at the door, so Xavier got out of bed, dressed up, and took the dog out."

"But a little dog could freeze outside," I continue, as if I were interested only in Pushkin and not in my uncle Xavier.

"Don't worry, Pushkin has a little coat and booties. Xavier loves the animal although he curses him all the time. When it's cold, Xavier always dresses him up before going out."

"I suppose he let him run out in the snow for a few minutes then came up again," I know I'm pushing it, but that's the only way I'll find out what everyone was doing that night.

"Marie-Christine, you're beginning to sound like your Inspector Bizzard. I have no idea how long Xavier was outside with Pushkin. Unlike my husband I sleep soundly!"

Change the subject quickly, "We haven't finished shopping yet and it will get dark soon. Let's go to *La Place aux Aires*. There are quite a few shops there."

Tante Geneviève leaves some money on the table, and we walk out. *La Place aux Aires* is the market place of old Grasse. Every morning Valérie goes there to buy fresh vegetables and the fruits in season (at least those that are not grown in Grand-mère's orchard or vegetable garden). Even in the middle of winter one can find beautiful flowers arranged in pails around the fountain at the center of the *La Place*. As we approach, little donkeys carrying children are being walked around *La Place aux Aires*. This is part of the Christmas entertainment. There is also a small pet zoo under a great big white tent in the center of the square.

"Do let's go in and have a look," I urge.

"Very well, Marie-Christine, but afterwards we have to finish our shopping."

"We could come tomorrow, Tante Geneviève. The shops are opened until the twenty-fourth, you know."

We enter the tent, and find two small, furry donkeys rubbing noses. On the hay next to them is an old goat, sleeping. A gaggle of geese is making a rumpus in a corner cage. Brown rabbits are chewing on lettuce and carrots nearby. Their hands in another cage, three small boys are trying to catch the tail of a large rooster. A jolly-looking woman calls out to them from the doorway that it's late and they should be going home.

Outside there is music from the carousel. It is small and old and turns around slowly on a tune that I remember from when I was five or six. But the two horses on the carousel are still pulling the big white carriage, and the deer and the unicorn are still following to protect the carriage from the other more dangerous animals like the giraffe with its long neck, and the big black bear. The three little pigs still are still running away from the Big Bad Wolf, as they turn and turn and turn around.

Tante Geneviève puts her gloved hand on my shoulder.

"You were a very cute kid when Helène and I brought you here, all those years ago. Do you remember?"

"I do. And you told me that I would be safe in the carriage because the deer and the unicorn were there to protect me, and the horses were faster than the giraffe and the bear!"

She laughs and kisses me on the cheek. I remember her perfume.

"You still wear *Femme* of Rochas?" I ask.

"Always, *ma chérie*. It is a matter of personal taste and style."

Tante Geneviève lacks neither!

"One more errand, then home we go!" she calls out as she exits the tent.

At *Kali'graphie*, a small stationery across from the carousel, my aunt buys her nephew a beautiful set of pens in a dark navy leather case.

"Poor Gerard!" she sighs. "I don't think he'll get over the death of his father for a while."

I find a matching agenda and wallet and buy them.

It is getting dark and cold. I shiver as I set out towards the car. We walk quickly, in silence. My aunt's remark has brought back the fear at the pit of my stomach that shopping had temporarily dispelled.

X

Grand-mère has decreed that Christmas festivities will continue despite the loss of Phillipe Bousquet. His body has been transported to the morgue, where the forensic team will do an autopsy after Christmas. The family appears to have recovered from the initial shock of the murder, except for Gerard, who looks pale and haggard. After a bout of hysterical wailing, Tante Helène has now returned to normal: clicking with beads, and experimenting with various turbans and folkloric skirts. Pushkin and Uncle Xavier go out of the house several times a day—I wonder who is taking whom for a walk? Alain is avoiding me assiduously. After his outburst yesterday, I think he is a little embarrassed. Still dressed in black and unshaven, Claude Bizzard is asking people to step into Grand-mère's *petit salon*. Reminds me of that line from the nursery rhyme "Step into my parlor, said the spider to the fly." He has yet to question me.

Mother called this morning, "Chrissy, how are you faring in this hangout of mobsters and racketeers?"

"I'm OK, Mother. Really. Don't worry."

"Me? Worry? Why should I? I mean people get murdered everyday, even in the best of families. One's daughter gets thrown off yachts, discovers corpses in her backyard, and is in cahoots with bandits. Why in the world would a mother a worry?"

"Mother, everything is under control. We have that nice inspector from Paris, Claude Bizzard, you remember? The one who saved my life last summer. Well, Grand-mère has invited him to stay with us and investigate Phillipe's murder."

"How comforting! A policeman spending Christmas under the same roof as my daughter to investigate a murder!"

Must change the subject. Mother will go on and on if one doesn't stop her.

"You and Papa are coming up for Christmas supper and midnight Mass tonight, aren't you? I mean this *is* Christmas!"

"Well, of course we are, darling. That's what we came to France for, didn't we? Although I can think of many more enjoyable and safe ways of spending Christmas."

"Yes, Mother, yes. Also, do remember to bring the gifts with you. At Grand-mère's gifts are opened on Christmas Eve after dinner, not on Christmas day."

"I know, dear. I've been married to your father long enough to remember all those quaint customs that he is so attached to. By the way," Mother's voice sounds more cheerful, "I've had to do some shopping in Cannes this week, after I found out that the whole de Medici clan was going to be in Grasse. Hope your aunts will like what I got them."

Must finish my shopping too. Perhaps I'll take Tante Helène for a drive and find out what happened the night of the murder. Knock on her door.

"Come in," she calls out. "Just watch your step."

Open the door and find complete chaos. Wrapping paper everywhere on the floor. Suitcases half unpacked. The cupboard is open with a few garments on hangers, others lying pell-mell at the bottom. Every chair and table is covered with articles of clothing, shoes, belts, books, and assorted bottles and toiletries.

Am not quite sure whether to enter or stay at the door.

Tante Helène, flustered but happy, is standing in the middle of the chaos holding a long loofah in one hand and a flowery umbrella that has seen better days in the other.

"I wonder where I should put these? What do you think, Marie-Christine?"

My first thought is: throw them in the garbage! But restrain myself.

"Tante Helène, are you done with your Christmas shopping?"

At the mention of shopping, Tante Helène drops loofah and umbrella. Wrapping up the edge of her long trailing skirt around her waist, she climbs over the mountain of scattered clothing and comes over to me.

"Are you planning to go shopping?" she asks with a big grin of anticipation.

"Yes. Want to come?"

She looks around the room and makes up her mind.

"I'll clear all this up when I get back."

A few minutes later, wrapped in multi-colored shawls, she squeezes into the Ferrari and we drive off to Cannes. It is only twenty minutes away, but long enough to have a good conversation.

"Tante Helène, I want to tell you how sorry I am about Phillipe. I didn't have a chance to before, but now that we are here. . . . "

"That's all right, Marie-Christine. And thank you. You're the first person to say anything to me about that. Everyone else seems to assume that because Phillipe and I were divorced, we no longer cared about each other. But that is not true. Not true at all." Her voice cracks, as she tries to find a tissue in one of the pockets of her sprawling skirt. After blowing her nose stertorously, she continues, "In fact, do you know why he came up that night, despite the storm and the snow?"

"Why?" I ask.

"Because he wanted to see me. He said he wanted bygones to be bygones."

111

More blowing of the nose and some wiping of the stray tear. I must press on, "When did he tell you that?" I ask as I swerve to avoid a truck. The sky is gray and it looks as if it will rain.

"That night. When he sat in the living room answering all these horrible questions that Maman was putting to him, about why he had come, and where he planned to spend the night, and so on. I felt so sorry for him then, all alone and cold, and no one caring a hoot about him. You know, if I hadn't put my foot down that night, Maman would have thrown him out of the house. So before he went to his room, I told him to come upstairs and have a drink in my room so that we could talk. I really wanted to know how he was doing, and I wanted to talk about Gerard. After all he was his father, although he hadn't done much fathering, and had not paid alimony once, and was never there when . . . "

I must stop her before we end up talking about her divorce instead of about what happened that night.

"And did he come?" Drops of rain are beginning to fall on the windshield.

"Of course, he came. I took a bottle of champagne from the tray on the sideboard, and Phillipe brought two glasses. And we talked, and drank—it was wonderful."

Her face has cleared. No more tears, no more sniffles. There is something else though. Something she does not want to say. "Phillipe was doing well? I mean was he working and all that?"

She hesitates, "He told me that he had found a great opportunity to make money. He would not say what it was, but he seemed very pleased with himself."

"What was he planning to do with this money? Did he at least tell you that?"

More hesitation. Tante Helène is playing with her rings, twisting them back and forth.

"Not at first. He said that it was great to see me and Gerard, and that I looked beautiful. He admitted that he was a lucky man to have two people who cared for him the way we did. Then he added that he knew we would be happy for him when he told us his news."

"The money-making scheme?" Phillipe always had projects like that. They invariably ended up with him borrowing money from his wife, and later from Grand-mère, his mother-in-law. I suppose borrowing can be considered a money-making scheme too.

"I thought so," remarked Tante Helène. Falls silent and looks out at the rain. We're approaching the circle with the big green road sign, which shines phosphorescently through the rain: Mougins, Frejus, Antibes, Nice.

"It was not money then?" I egg her on, afraid we'll reach Cannes without getting the whole story.

"No, it was not money: . . . it was . . . love." Almost bump into the car in front of me.

"What?" I exclaim.

Her voice is dead. Can't see her face because I need to keep my eyes on the road. It is raining very hard now.

"He told me that he had met this young woman and that they were getting married. He just needed to make that money, and then everything would be fine."

Finally a traffic light. I stop and turn towards Tante Helène. She looks grief-stricken. I wonder if it is because of Phillipe's death, or because he was getting remarried.

La Croisette, the "boardwalk" of Cannes, is a great place to shop, that is, except when it rains. There is really no place to hide then, except in restaurants, cafes, or hotel lounges. Call my parents at the Carlton on my cell-phone, after I've parked under a tree.

Mother answers.

"You're in Cannes, Chrissy? In *this* weather? And with your aunt Helène? What in the world for?"

Tante Helène understands English, so my answers must be monosyllabic.

"Yes, yes, and yes, Mother. We had to finish our Christmas shopping, but it's raining too hard. Will you be in, let's say in five minutes? We'll drop by for a snack at the Carlton. Perhaps it will stop raining afterwards, and we can get to the stores."

A few minutes later we climb the marble steps of the Carlton and enter the lounge. In the summer, the *Bar des Célébrités* is full of people who want to see and be seen. But in winter it is the habitués who fill the plush wine-red armchairs. Like migrating birds they gather everyday with friends for coffee or drinks. Waiters in mustard-yellow jackets stand behind the art deco bar surveying the scene and chatting with each other. Snacks and desserts from the restaurant kitchen are available upon request.

Tante Helène's long cotton skirt is wet, her hair is damp, and her mood matches her general appearance. Flopping in one of the red velvet armchairs, she begins to unwrap the shawls. Mother shows up, in an impeccable navy pantsuit and a Chanel scarf.

"Good morning, Helène; good morning, Chrissy." Peck on the cheek of her sister-in-law. More effusive hug for me. Waves to the waiter and orders a Perrier with lemon. Tante Helène wants to see the menu card. She hesitates between a curry concoction and a tongue sandwich.

She calls back the waiter to discuss the ingredients, wants to know who the chef in the kitchen is, if he prepares the curry from scratch or if it is brought in from another restaurant, if the tongue is canned or smoked. Mother's perfectly manicured red nails are clicking impatiently on the table. Finally, orders are taken, and a very much relieved waiter rushes off to the kitchen.

"I meant to ask you earlier, Chrissy, at what time are we expected at your grandmother's for dinner this evening?"

Mother likes to have a clear-cut program with exact times for everything.

"The aperitifs are served around seven, and dinner around seven-thirty. We'll probably be done with dinner by nine or nine-thirty depending on whether we have coffee and dessert at the dinner table or in the sitting room. The opening of the gifts takes place before we leave the house for midnight Mass at the Cathedral."

As we settle to consume the smoked-tongue sandwich, the Perrier, and my small *salade niçoise,* which the waiter brings to the table, Mother spots someone she knows entering the Carlton and waves to him.

"Hi, Peter! Didn't know you were in Cannes!"

A tall, gray-haired American approaches.

"Hallo, Priscilla! This *is* a surprise!"

"How have you been, Peter? Why don't you join us?"

"Well, just for a minute. I am expecting to meet someone here."

"Have you met my daughter, Chrissy? And this is my sister-in-law, Helène Bousquet. Peter Thompson is an old friend from New York."

Thompson shakes hands, and looks at Tante Helène with much interest.

Pulling a chair from another table, he sits between my mother and my aunt.

"Helène Bousquet? Any relation to Phillipe Bousquet, by any chance?" he asks.

A sudden pall descends upon the table. Tante Helène answers somewhat melodramatically, "I *was* his wife."

Thompson nods, "Yes, I know. Phillipe told me."

Drawing her partly wet shawls around her, Tante Helène turns towards him, "Phillipe told you what exactly?"

Thompson shrugs as if it were of no importance.

"That you two were divorced."

Before Tante Helène makes a scene, I interrupt.

"Mr. Thompson, you must know that Phillip Bousquet died . . . uh . . . recently."

Thompson looks shocked, then apologizes profusely. Tante Helène begins sniffling and searching in the pockets of her damp skirt for a tissue. Mother, holding her glass of Perrier as if it were a prickly rose, asks, "Did you know Phillipe Bousquet, Peter?"

"Yes, I do. I mean, I did."

"In what capacity?" I ask. Am curious because Thompson does not look like any of Phillipe's friends or shady business associates.

"Well." Thompson hesitates, then makes up his mind. "I'm sorry. This is confidential."

"For goodness sake, Peter! The man is dead!" exclaims Mother.

That is just too much for Tante Helène, who starts bawling. Embarrassed, Thompson stands up and waves to an elderly gentleman who has just entered the lounge.

"Excuse me, ladies, but the person I was waiting for is here." Hurriedly, and without looking at Tante Helène, he leaves our table.

A waiter rushes to see if everything is all right with my aunt. Mother, who detests public scenes, orders a Scotch on the rocks.

"Nothing that a little Scotch won't cure," she says. "Drink up, Helène, and for Pete's sake stop making such a ruckus!"

After gulping her Scotch, Tante Helène hiccups twice and then falls silent, looking dazed.

"Mother, who in the world is Peter Thompson?"

"Peter? Oh, he's the vice-president of Tiffany in New York."

XI

Christmas Eve! The house is buzzing. Valérie has brought in help from a nearby village to organize this very special dinner known in Provence as *Le Gros Souper* or the big supper. It has its unchangeable customs that Mother calls quaint, but I suspect enjoys all the same.

It is seven, and I hear Mother's voice. Time to go downstairs. Dressed in a black velvet sheath with a gold pendant and small diamond earrings, I join my parents. Papa is wearing a crimson silk tie. A matching handkerchief is elegantly pointing out of his breast pocket. Holding a glass of glowing red wine, he is talking with Gerard, who looks pale and gaunt. In a long tartan skirt, Mother wants to assert her Scottish roots and asks Jean for *un whisky s'il vous plait*. Surveying the goings on like a general on the battle field, Grand-mère in black silk with a diamond brooch is seated next to the fireplace. She taps impatiently with her cane, "Where is everybody? We have to begin the burning of the log."

Some noises on the stairs, then a crash. Rush out of the living room to see what happened. Tante Helène, carrying all her gifts, missed the last step of the stairs. Boxes, papers, ribbons are strewn about. She scrambles to get up and starts collecting the packets nearest her. Alain, who was coming down behind her, is helping to pick up the packages. The commotion has attracted Pushkin, who runs down the stairs, barking joyfully. He gets hold of a big golden bow and shakes it as if it were a rabbit.

Carrying the gifts wrapped in brown recycled paper with trailing ribbons, Tante Helène, Alain, and I deposit them next to the manger. The other gifts, more colorfully wrapped in silver and gold or in bags with bows and cards, are also piled there on a Persian carpet.

As if to emphasize the contrast, Tante Geneviève, on the arm of her husband, Uncle Xavier, makes a grand entrance into the sitting room. She is wearing a long, slim cashmere skirt and a delicately beaded cardigan in a warm fuschia color. He is in a royal blue, satin dinner jacket. They could be stepping right out of the latest fashion issue of *Vogue*.

The bell rings. More excited barkings from Pushkin. Jean brings in the guests: Monseigneur d'Epinay and Sister Felicity. Monseigneur moves directly to Grand-mère.

"Thank you for inviting us to share the Christmas celebrations with you. I will have to leave immediately after dinner, however, because I must be at the Cathedral for the preparations of the midnight Mass. But Sister Felicity can stay and come with you all to the Cathedral later."

Grand-mère looks pleased.

"Thank you for joining us. I know how difficult it must be, on such a busy night as this, to leave the Cathedral and come."

Suddenly Claude Bizzard appears, seemingly from nowhere. Tonight, he does not look like a Paris inspector at all. He is actually wearing a well-cut navy suit and a conservative silk tie! Has even shaved and put some shiny mousse on his hair to keep it under control. With his hands in his pockets he tries to slip into the room unnoticed. Despite his arrogance and know-it-all attitude, Claude is shy sometimes—one of his more endearing qualities. He has others, which I discovered last summer. Neither of us has brought up in conversation the events of last summer. But then we have not had a serious conversation lately. In fact, he has not even questioned me in Grand-mère's *petit salon* about the murder of Phillipe.

119

Decide it's never too late to have a little heart-to-heart chat.

"Good evening, Claude. I must say I did not recognize you when you came in. Looking good!" He smiles, a crooked smile that reveals his incredibly white teeth.

"Good evening, Marie-Christine. I am in disguise. An undercover agent!"

"You're sure that's the reason? It isn't that Valérie burnt your old clothes by any chance?"

"Not at all. I was going to sit next to you at dinner and ask you all kind of probing questions about your whereabouts on the night of the murder. But you found me out!"

"I'm so sorry. To make up for my unforgivable behavior you may sit next to me at dinner tonight, and I will tell you all I have discovered."

He picks up a glass of wine from the tray that Jean is passing around and looks at me sideways, from under his long eyelashes.

"So you have been carrying out your own investigation, have you now?"

"Well, I *am* the editor of *Le Loup-Garou* after all. And this is news, although a bit too close to home. Still, my guess is I found out more about the whereabouts of everyone in this household than you have."

Flip my hair, turn on my heels, and move towards Grand-mère. Hope that this is enough of a hook to get him interested in asking *me* questions about the night of the murder.

Grand-mère taps on her wine glass and asks for silence.

"Tonight is Christmas Eve, and we will celebrate it the way families in Provence have celebrated it for centuries. We will begin with the ceremony of the burning of the log, the *cacho fio* in Provençal. As you all know, this log must come from a fruit tree. To mark the special occasion of the gathering of the de

Medici clan at Christmas this year, I have chosen an olive tree. This particular tree was over a thousand years old and grew on our land. Last spring, it was struck by lightning and died. So we chopped it and prepared the log for tonight's celebration."

Pointing to Papa and to Gerard, she calls them to stand by her.

"Jean-Pierre is my eldest child, and Gerard my youngest grandchild. Together they shall carry the log and place it in the fireplace. But first, they must turn around the dining table three times. Jean-Pierre, Gerard, please pick up the log, and all of you move to the dining room."

Both men pick up the heavy log which is on the tiled floor in front of the chimney and lead the way to the dining room. The table is set and some of the cold dishes are already there. As we stand by the door, Papa and Gerard begin to walk slowly around the table while Monseigneur d'Epinay intones the age-old prayer in the Provençal dialect, and we all follow suit,

"Allègre! Allègre!

Mi Bèus enfant, Diéu nous alegre!

Emé Calèndo tout bèn vèn . . .

Diéu nous fague la gràci de vèire l'an que vèn

E se noun sian pas mai, que noun fuguen pas mens!"[3]

I translate it in a low voice to Mother, as we stand behind the rest of the family.

"It means 'Joy, Joy, my beautiful children! God rejoices with us. With Christmas, (Calèndo is Christmas in Provençal) all is well. May God's grace allow us to see the year to come, and if we are not more, then may we not be less.'"

Just then Papa and Gerard complete the three circles around the table and move back to the sitting room. They stand before

3 See Marion Nazet, *Noël Provençal: Saveurs & Traditions* 2nd Edition (Aix-en-Provence: Edisud, 1998), p. 36.

the fireplace waiting for Grand-mère to sit in her armchair. Jean brings a small jug with cooked wine and Grand-mère pours a little wine along the log. Then slowly and in unison my father and my cousin place the log in the fireplace, and Jean lights the newspapers under it. The flames crackle and the whole room fills with the smell of the olive tree and the fruity wine. Monseigneur d'Epinay settles on the sofa next to Mother.

"Tell me, Monseigneur, what is the origin of the burning of the log?" she asks.

Everyone falls silent and listens.

"Symbolically, in our traditions the log represents Christ sacrificed for our sins. The fire is a sign of joy and light, symbolizing the resurrection of Christ. The roots of this tradition, however, are to be found in pagan rituals. The burning of the log was a tribute to the sun which remains undefeated by the winter solstice—a pre-Christian tradition known in Roman times as *Natalis Invictus*. The sixth-century pope, St. Gregory the Great, recommended that the early Christians adopt pagan rituals and turn them into Christian celebrations of the one and true God. He believed that this was the most efficacious way of converting pagans to Christianity."

Mother mulls this over for a few seconds, "But Monseigneur, once everyone was converted why keep up those pagan traditions?"

Monseigneur smiles, "Well, they became Christian traditions. And are they not a wonderful way to celebrate Christmas and to bring together all the members of a family, from the youngest to the oldest?"

Grand-mère, who feels very defensive of things Provençal, especially when Mother is around, breaks into the conversation, "My dear Priscilla, your Christmas tree is a pagan tradition too. Probably a Germanic celebration of the winter solstice as well."

Just as a transatlantic debate about the merits of Christmas traditions is about to erupt, Valérie enters the sitting room and announces that dinner is ready.

And so we move into the dining room: Grand-mère sits at the head of the table and Father, the eldest son, at the foot. To Grand-mère's right as usual is Monseigneur d'Epinay and Uncle Xavier is seated to her left. The rest of us are seated in order of seniority and paired off man and woman. Claude gets to sit next to me.

After Monseigneur d'Epinay says grace, Mother, who is seated beside him, pursues her anthropological research.

"So do tell me, Monseigneur, what is the significance of going around a dining table three times carrying a heavy log? You have to admit this is not very Christian."

"Madame, you are quite right. Turning around a table cannot be found in any of the holy scripts. Neither Jesus nor any of His apostles ever mentioned turning around a table. But like all rituals, this one holds many symbols: it is intended to remind family members that they are tied together by faith as well as by blood. It symbolizes Christ's death and His resurrection three days later. It is an affirmation of the Holy Trinity: turning three times for the Father, the Son, and the Holy Spirit. It is also a ritual found in many early traditions of Christianity. Even today in the Eastern Christian rites, for example, when certain sacraments such as marriage and confirmation are performed, those being married or confirmed in their faith turn three times around the altar."

I think Mother's curiosity has been satisfied. She graciously bows her head and says, "Thank you, Monseigneur, for explaining what was not immediately understandable to someone from another culture."

Monseigneur smiles and points to the table.

"I don't know if you have noticed, but Madame de Medici's table is covered with three tablecloths in true Provençal Christmas tradition."

I had forgotten this Christmas custom of the three tablecloths. Sure enough, Valérie has put the largest, the damascene tablecloth that she hand washed the day she found the body of poor Phillipe, at the bottom, then a second smaller tablecloth in linen on top of it, and finally we are having dinner on the smallest, the third which is cotton.

"Aha!" says Mother triumphantly. "The Holy Trinity!"

"Yes," agrees the bishop somewhat hesitantly. "There are many other references to this custom such as the symbolism of the holy family, Jesus, Mary and Joseph, and . . ."

Grand-mère interrupts, "There are also very mundane reasons for these three tablecloths: each stands for a different meal. The simplest and lightest meal is eaten on the cotton tablecloth. That's the dinner on Christmas Eve. Lunch on the twenty-fifth is served on the second tablecloth. And the last meal before the family disperses again, is eaten on the twenty-sixth, known in Grasse as the second Christmas day. Speaking of which," Grand-mère adds, looking at the door of the pantry from whence Valérie emerges with a big tureen of soup, "here comes the first course."

Valérie places the tureen on the table and lifts the lid. Smell of sage and garlic wafts across the room.

"*L'aigo boulido!*" trumpets father from the other side of the table. "My favorite soup! I always identify it with Christmas and with Christmas gifts!"

"Jean-Pierre always ate faster than we did. When he'd finish, he would urge us to gobble up our food so that he could run to the sitting room and open his gifts!" says Tante Geneviève, laughing.

"Well, you and Hélène were always so slow! I wanted to go and play, and all you two did was complain that the soup was too hot, or that it needed more salt, or had too much garlic!"

Papa and my two aunts look suddenly like the kids they must have been eons of years ago. Even Grand-mère appears surprisingly young as she beams happily at her family. Meanwhile, Claude has already finished his soup, while I have barely tasted mine. Turning to me, he says in a low voice, "You don't know how lucky you are, Marie-Christine, to have such a warm and loving family."

"Yes, I know. And yet some at this table think that one of its members is a murderer!"

That's it. I have thrown the glove and declared war! Claude stiffens, and passes his fingers through his hair with the most unfortunate result. Tufts begin sticking out on top of his head, and hair cream sticks to his fingers. After some wiping of his hands, he asks:

"So, do tell me. What nefarious goings on have you discovered that I have overlooked?"

Supercilious air does not become him. I tell him so, and add:

"What did *you* find out about everyone's movements that night?" Lower my voice so that those gathered around the table don't overhear what I'm saying.

He shrugs his shoulders, "As I suspected. Everyone was in bed and asleep and heard and saw nothing."

"Ha! And you call yourself a detective? I found out that everyone, except yours truly, was up and about that night."

"You don't say?" Claude's tone makes me want to kick him.

"I *do* say. For example, did you know that my uncle Xavier sleeps only a couple of hours a night, and took Pushkin out for a walk that night, after we all went up to bed?"

"Did he now?" This time Claude shows definite interest and glances across the table at Xavier, who is looking morosely at his soup which he has left untouched.

"Yes, he did. And that Alain went downstairs to fetch a glass of water and saw a light in the kitchen?"

"He saw a light? What kind of a light?" asks Claude looking doubtful.

"I asked him the same question, especially after Jean reminded me that electricity had not returned until next morning. That made him angry and he just got up and left the room. He has been avoiding me ever since."

"Well, playing the devil's advocate, he could have seen the light of a candle, or even of a flashlight," he adds.

"You're missing the point here, Monsieur *l'inspecteur*," I say in a sarcastic tone.

"And what is the point, may I ask, Mademoiselle?" adopting the same tone.

"The point is: Alain is either not telling the truth, and if so why? Or he is telling the truth and if so, who was walking about at this late hour of the night, in the kitchen, on the night of the murder?"

Claude smiles, that crooked smile with the flashing white teeth. Despite his sarcasms and superior attitude, he can be quite attractive.

"You *are* good, Marie-Christine. I could even find you a job on the police force in Paris. Mind you, you would have to start at the very bottom, fining people for littering, that sort of thing. But within ten years or so you could become a junior detective."

It was too good to last!

"No, I leave these menial tasks to you. I solve crimes only when the police are too incompetent to do their job."

Valérie has cleared the soup and Jean is bringing in the next course: a large plate of stuffed snails or *escargots* (not my favorite dish). Grand-mère addresses one and all, "And as most of you know the dinner on Christmas Eve is light. We never serve meat, but Valérie has prepared some traditional dishes."

Father is delighted with the food, and explains to Mother across the table:

"There are always seven courses served on Christmas Eve, Priscilla."

Mother has begun to figure out the rhythm of these traditions, "Let me guess, another pagan custom?"

Monseigneur d'Epinay interrupts, "Please remember, Madame de Medici, that those pagan customs were adopted almost two thousand years ago to explain to the people living in this region some of the basic Christian tenets of faith. The seven courses represent the seven sorrows of the Blessed Virgin Mary."

Valérie carries in a lovely ceramic dish of *cardons* or wild artichokes covered with a creamy *bechamel* sauce. Jean goes around the room serving slices of baked cod with capers and golden leeks. Two pie dishes with baked cauliflower in one and an onion pie in the other complete the meal. A large bowl of endives and chicory had been placed on the table earlier.

Picking up where the bishop left off, Sister Felicity who has not said much all evening, continues:

"Today's young people in the United States have all but forgotten the seven sorrows of Mary. If they are not instructed in school or at college, they have no idea what those are. Here, in Provence, every kid learns this lesson while eating a garlic and sage soup, the escargots, or the baked cod fish we are now consuming."

Uncle Xavier savoring an escargot, smiles for the first time this week.

"Delicious way to learn!"

"And you don't need books," adds Alain the librarian.

Gerard, pale and unkempt, looks up from his cod and asks in a lugubrious tone, "What are the seven sorrows of Mary? I've forgotten them. It would be appropriate, I think, to mention them tonight."

A pall falls on all gathered. Gerard has just reminded us all that his father is dead. Sister Felicity, who is sitting next to him, puts her hand on his.

"You're right, Gerard. It is appropriate to mention the sorrows of Mary tonight. They are in historical order: the Prophecy of Simeon, the Flight into Egypt, the loss of the Child Jesus in the Temple, the meeting of Jesus and Mary on the Way of the Cross, the Crucifixion, the Taking down of the Body of Jesus from the Cross, and the Burial of Jesus."

Gerard has lowered his head and is looking blankly at his plate. Sister Felicity turns to the rest of us around the table and says, "Although we are in the middle of our meal, Gerard has reminded us that it is not too late to pray for those who are no longer with us, and more especially for Phillipe Bousquet."

Gerard's pain is obvious, as is our embarrassment. In our excitement to prepare for Christmas we had shown little respect or affection for someone who, after all, was still part of the family through his son.

"Let us hold hands around the table," says Sister Felicity, "and let us pray together for Phillipe's soul."

And so it is that we end our Christmas Eve meal in prayer.

◆

Chastened but cheerful, we move to the sitting room. Gerard apologizes and says he is going to lie down before midnight Mass. Totally satiated, we settle on various chairs, armchairs, cushions, and settees. The scent of burning wood, olives, and fruit fills the room. There is an undercurrent of excitement and expectation as eyes glance discreetly at the gifts piled next to the manger. Valérie has arranged on the table the desserts and the coffee, while Papa, standing next to the sideboard, is examining the liqueurs.

Addressing the bishop, Mother boasts:

"Monseigneur, I know all about the thirteen desserts of Christmas."

Monseigneur, picking up a tangerine and beginning to peel it, smiles politely but not enthusiastically. He knows that Mother is going to tell him what they are whether he wants to hear it or not.

Pointing to a plate of candied fruits and black and white nougats, Mother explains:

"The thirteen desserts represent Christ and His twelve apostles." She stops and frowns, "But isn't that sort of a Last Supper, Monseigneur, and a bit premature for Christmas? It would have made much more sense to have had thirteen desserts at Easter instead, don't you think so?"

Papa calls out:

"Who is for a Benedictine? A Cointreau? A Provençal quince liqueur? Or a cognac?"

As he takes orders, Sister Felicity points out to the plate of dried fruits and nuts.

"A teacher of mine once told me that the dried fruits served on Christmas Eve in Provence represented four religious orders. Is that true Monseigneur?"

Monseigneur d'Epinay has finished his tangerine and is wiping his hands and mouth on a white napkin. He nods, "Yes, they are called the four beggars: the dried figs, raisins, hazelnuts, and almonds are supposed to represent the orders of the Dominicans, Franciscans, Augustines, and Carmelites."

"Why beggars? Were these beggar orders in medieval times?" Mother has not given up her investigation of Provençal folklore this evening. As long as it keeps her from arguing with Grand-mère, I don't care what her hobby horse is. But Monseigneur is looking at his watch. After agreeing that those were indeed beggar orders and the reason why these desserts were called the four beggars, he gets up and says he will see everyone at the Cathedral tonight, and departs. That is the signal for opening the gifts.

Grand-mère waves to Papa to come and stand by her side:

"Jean-Pierre has always loved most this part of our Christmas traditions," she says with a twinkle. "So tonight he will orchestrate the opening of the gifts."

Caressing the tip of his mustache, Papa looks at me, then at Claude.

"You two," pointing to us, "pick up gifts from the pile there, and begin distributing them. Make sure that each person in this room gets at least one gift before we all start opening ours. They should all be marked to indicate who the recipient is."

Claude stands at attention and salutes, "*Oui, mon capitaine.*"

I get off the sofa reluctantly.

"Papa, you're soooo old-fashioned. Why can't everyone pick up their own gift?"

"Where's your Christmas spirit, Marie-Christine?"

"Very well."

A few minutes later amidst "oohs" and "aahs" everyone is opening gifts. Ribbons are flying around much to delight of

Pushkin, who has come out of the kitchen, wagging his little tail. Valérie has given him his Christmas dinner and now he's ready to play. Alain crumples his wrapping paper into a ball and tosses it to Pushkin. Gerard had bought him a gift and put it under the crèche. Tante Helène seems delighted with my gift of the beaded shawl and immediately puts it on. She now looks like a fully decorated Christmas tree. Uncle Xavier puts on his glasses and inspects with great interest the ceremonial sash from the Sulawesi Island of Indonesia. Turning to his wife, he says, "You know, my dear, this is a complete fake. I believe it is made in Hong Kong."

I open my gift from Mother, "Hey, that's cool!" I exclaim, holding up a diamond lizard pin from Tiffany. "Thanks, Mother!"

Suddenly Grand-mère utters a cry:

"What's the meaning of this?"

All eyes turn towards Grand-mère, who is sitting in her usual armchair next to the fire. She was having some trouble with the ribbons of Tante Helène's brown paper wrapping, but she has now opened the package.

Tante Helène gets up and walks toward Grand-mère.

"Don't you like your gift, Maman?" She asks, looking concerned.

Grand-mère seems really angry, "If that is supposed to be a joke, Helène, it is *not* funny!"

"But what is it, Maman? I thought you liked . . ."

"I never liked jokes. And this is one I appreciate even less than your other scatter-brained ideas."

Clinking all over with the beaded shawl and her many long necklaces, Tante Helène leans over to look at what Grand-mère is holding on her lap.

She then raises her head, looking quite bewildered, and says, "But this is not my gift!"

Grand-mère, still angry, stares at her daughter.

"But my name is on the label. And all your gifts are wrapped up in this atrocious grocery store paper, are they not?"

Tante Helène is shaking her head, "But this is not . . . I mean this is, this is . . ."

"What are you babbling about, Helène?" asks Papa, marching up to his mother and sister.

"What on earth!" he exclaims as he sees what Grand-mère has unwrapped.

"For goodness sake, Jean-Pierre, what is it?" asks Mother impatiently.

"It's the manuscript! *Les Trés Riches Heures de Jean, Duc de Berry!*"

XII

Claude Bizzard jumps up from his seat and rushes to Grand-mère. Apart from her and Monseigneur d'Epinay, only Claude and I and Sister Felicity know that the manuscript disappeared three days ago. And of course whoever took the manuscript.

"Is that the manuscript?" Claude asks without specifying which or why he is asking.

Grand-mère nods. She has regained her composure. Realizes that Tante Helène had nothing to do with this.

Unaccountably, Tante Helène begins to sob and rushes out of the room. Pushkin thinks she wants to play and runs after her, barking joyfully and wagging his little tail.

Sister Felicity has followed Claude to look at the manuscript. She puts her hand out to touch it, but Claude stops her.

"Don't touch it, Sister!"

Sister Felicity draws back her hand and says, "Fingerprints, I suppose?"

"Yes, and there may be a number of other clues as to who took it."

Father is observing Grand-mère, Claude, and Sister Felicity, trying to understand what is going on.

"Can someone explain what this is all about?"

Claude looks at Grand-mère, seeking her permission. She nods in silent assent.

"Well, you see, Monsieur de Medici, this manuscript was stolen from your mother three days ago, on the twenty-first of December."

"What? Where was the manuscript?"

Grand-mère holds up her hand and asks everyone to sit down.

"I am delighted to find between my hands this very precious manuscript. It had been left with me for safekeeping by Monseigneur d'Epinay. On the night of your arrival at my house, the manuscript disappeared from *le petit salon*, where I had kept it under lock and key. I do not know how or why it was taken, and if it was supposed to be a joke, it was in poor taste and we will say no more about it. I am sure Monseigneur will be delighted to learn that the *Trés Riches Heures du Duc de Berry* has been recovered. This time, however, I am putting it in the custody of Monsieur l'inspecteur." Grand-mère hands over the manuscript to Claude, who seems slightly taken aback by the offer. However, he graciously accepts the *Trés Riches Heures* and asks for the brown wrapping paper as well.

"The manuscript was obviously not wrapped up in this paper originally. I wonder how it got to be that way? Perhaps the paper holds some clues to the perpetrator of this disappearance. In any case the police will need to examine it."

"But Maman, why didn't you say anything?" asks Tante Geneviève irritably. "I mean we *are* your family. And Xavier worked so hard to get that insurance company to insure the manuscript while it was in Grasse. So how could you have kept the disappearance of the *Trés Riches Heures* from us like this?"

"I would have told you sooner or later," says Grand-mère placatingly. "I just did not want to spoil your Christmas. The murder of poor Phillipe was bad enough. I just hoped against hope that Claude here would be able to find the manuscript in time for New Year's Day and the eight-hundredth anniversary of the Cathedral. God must have listened to my prayers, because the manuscript is back again and hopefully in safe hands."

Mother has been on her best behavior all night, but the discovery of yet another crime under Grand-mère's roof is just too much for her.

"Outrageous! This is just outrageous! First a murder, then a robbery! Chrissy, I think you should come down to Cannes with us *this* evening. I just can't let you stay in this house any longer! Your life is in constant danger here."

"I am all right, Mother. Don't worry. All that has nothing to do with me. It's just about the manuscript. And now the police have it," I add, pointing to Claude, who is standing holding the brown wrapping paper and gazing at the manuscript. But Mother is not finished with her tirade.

"How do you know you are not in danger? What did Phillipe have to do with manuscripts? He wouldn't have known the difference between a medieval manuscript and a musical score. And yet *he* was murdered!"

Claude looks at Mother thoughtfully.

"This is a very important point you are making there, Madame de Medici."

"You mean about a possible relationship between the murder and the theft?" I ask, hoping that the conversation will move away from the question of my future residence.

"Yes. You see the night the manuscript disappeared, Phillipe Bousquet was murdered. It cannot be a coincidence."

This opens up a great big can of worms.

"Then, are you saying that whoever killed Phillipe Bousquet also stole the manuscript?" asks Papa.

"Possibly."

"But why kill Phillipe?" persists my father.

"I can think of a number of reasons."

"Such as?" I jump in. Bet Claude has not thought of any.

"Well . . . " He scratches his head and immediately hair begins sprouting in all directions like weeds. "He might have unexpectedly witnessed the theft of the manuscript."

"And the thief shoots him and then returns the manuscript a couple of days later? That does not sound very likely, does it, Monsieur l'inspecteur?" I say sarcastically.

Claude looks annoyed.

"I know, I know. Well, he might have stolen the manuscript, and someone shot him to get it from him."

"Does not hold water either," I argue. "In the first place, he knew nothing about manuscripts, as Mother just pointed out, so why steal one?"

"To sell it. He might have needed money."

"Phillipe always needed money. But why go for the *Trés Riches Heures*? He could just as well have stolen the family silver or Grand-mère's antique jewelry."

Grand-mère is waving everyone away.

"Go and prepare yourself for midnight Mass. We should leave here in the next half hour. Jean will have the cars ready to drive up to the Cathedral. It is very cold tonight, so dress warmly. Remember the Cathedral is not heated." She gets up slowly from her armchair and walks with her cane out of the room. Everyone follows, except Sister Felicity.

Claude and I remain standing by the fireplace discussing the likelihood that Phillipe stole the manuscript and was killed for it.

Claude stares at the manuscript as if for inspiration.

"It could be that he was sent here to steal the manuscript by someone else who knew the value of the manuscript, and who promised to reward him handsomely for it."

"I agree, this sounds more like Phillipe. But then why in the world would that person (presumably the one who wanted the manuscript) kill him for it and then return the manuscript?"

Claude looks at me and smiles—somehow feel weak in the knees. I felt better when we argued.

"You know what, Marie-Christine? You're absolutely right! It makes no sense, and I have no explanation either. It is also 11:15 PM," he adds, consulting his watch. "And you should be preparing yourself to go to midnight Mass."

"Aren't you coming too?"

"No, I am staying here. I have to keep guard on the manuscript before it disappears once again." Then leaning over, he kisses me lightly on the cheek, "Merry Christmas, Marie-Christine. I'm really glad I'm spending my holidays with you in Grasse!"

And with that he turns around, and marches out with manuscript, brown wrapping paper, and ribbons hanging loosely and trailing behind. Am left standing, unsure of what I should have said or done. Sister Felicity, who has been silent throughout, follows Claude, and I hear her say, "Inspector Bizzard, after you've finished examining the manuscript for finger prints and other clues, would you mind showing it to me? I think I may have the beginning of an explanation as to why the manuscript was stolen, and then returned."

"But of course, *ma soeur.*"

◆

By 11:30 PM the family has gathered in the hallway: women wrapped up in furs, men with hats, berets, scarfs, and mufflers. Pushkin is howling plaintively in the kitchen. He knows we're all going out and he is not. Jean and Valérie are also dressed up. Jean is driving the old Citroën with Valérie sitting next to him. Grand-mère has asked Tante Helène to sit with her at the back of the Citroën (probably wants to get to the bottom of this whole manuscript affair). Alain has invited Gerard and me to join him in his old BMW sedan. I agree eagerly. Don't want to have to ride with my parents and get another lecture from Mother about my living in a "hangout of mobsters and racketeers." Father understands. He winks at me, and before Mother can say anything he suggests that Tante Geneviève and Uncle Xavier ride with them in the Jaguar. Sister Felicity is left alone on the doorstep, so I wave to her, "Jump in, Sister Felicity, we have a place for you in here."

It's a cold and clear night. The sky is luminous with a full moon and zillions of stars. The Citroën is leading the way. It climbs slowly up the hill that leads to the Cathedral. Bells are ringing joyfully, and getting louder and louder as we move closer to the center of town. We park across the *Palais des Congrés*, as we must go the rest of the way on foot. Grand-mère, leaning on the arm of Jean on one side and Valérie on the other, trails behind. The rest of us hurry down the narrow, cobbled street of *Rue Jean Ossola*.

Hands in pockets, Alain and Gerard walk together silently. Tante Helène slips her arm in mine and sniffles.

"I feel a cold coming," she complains. "You know, I am a daughter of the sun. I wake up with the twittering of the birds. Midnight Masses are really not my thing anymore. But Maman insisted that we all go to Mass."

Behind me, I hear Mother saying to Papa, "I mean this place is *ancient*. How can people live on these narrow streets?"

"Medieval, Priscilla, medieval. Some of the houses go back to the fourteenth and fifteenth centuries, but most date to the seventeenth and eighteenth centuries. That's not too old."

"Not old? Three hundred years is not old?"

138

Papa decides to change the subject. He calls out to me, "Marie-Christine, can you still remember the names of the bells of the Cathedral?"

When I was six years old, my father taught me the names of the eight bells of Notre Dames des Fleurs. So I laugh and sing out, "Of course, Papa: Sauveterre is Do, Martin is Ré, Veran is Mi, Bernard is Fa, Thècle is Sol, Agathe is La, Joseph is Si and Honorat is Do!"

"Great, Marie-Christine! And you, Helène, do you remember the story of how the notes got their names?"

Tante Helène turns around and chuckles, "How can I forget Mademoiselle Huguette, our music teacher? She was tone deaf and would repeat at least once a week the story of *Guido d'Arezzo*."

"Who was he?" I ask as we go down the narrow steps towards the Cathedral.

"He was a Benedictine monk who, in the eleventh century, composed a hymn in Latin to St. John the Baptist, the patron saint of musicians, giving the first syllable of each verse the name of a note," replies Tante Geneviève, who has caught up with us. For the second time this evening I can see what my two aunts and my father were like when they were kids. Fleeting thought that as an only child I may have missed something.

Hunched and wrapped against the cold, dark forms are hurrying in the same direction. Children bundled up in coats and mittens are running in front of their parents, laughing. The pealing of the bells is almost deafening now as the Christmas carol *Les Anges dans nos campagnes* . . . sounds just above our heads. Alain and Gerard reach the steps of the Cathedral first and wait for the rest of us to gather there, before entering.

Inside the lights are dim. Feels as if I have stepped back in time. These huge, carved stone pillars that support the great arches in the nave give a sense of reality to the past. The air is thick with the smell of incense mixed not with myrrh but with eucalyptus of Provence. We move to the front of the Cathedral where a member of the de Medici clan gave, a generation ago, a pew that bears the family name. Grand-mère is last to arrive. The first seat is reserved for her on the pew.

Monseigneur d'Epinay enters and kneels before the altar, and the traditional midnight Mass begins as it has in this Cathedral for eight hundred years. Readings from the Book of Isaiah read by the mayor, Psalm 95 sang by the choir as the music from the organ echoes against the aged walls, a letter of St. Paul delivered by Papa, the Gospel according to St. Luke—the past and present woven in the same burnished Christmas tapestry.

Grand-mère has pulled out a pen. She tears a sheet out of her diary and begins writing furiously. Meanwhile, Monseigneur d'Epinay, head bowed, moves slowly, almost reluctantly, towards the pulpit. It is time for him to address the congregation and give his Christmas sermon. Grand-mère turns to Gerard, seated just behind her, and whispers something. He hesitates, then takes the paper from Grand-mère's hand and walks quickly towards the pulpit. As Monseigneur d'Epinay begins ascending the steps, Gerard hands him the paper and whispers something in his ear. They then both turn and look at Grand-mère. Monseigneur reads the paper and raises his head. His brow has cleared and his face is alight with joy. In the space of thirty seconds he has shed ten years. Gerard returns to his seat, and the bishop climbs the steps to the pulpit with alacrity.

"Tonight I come bearing glad tidings of great joy! It is Christmas and Jesus is born! God has given His only begotten Son that we may be saved! Alleluia!"

The bishop is inspired and for the next fifteen minutes he

preaches love and hope and redemption with such enthusiasm that he has the congregation riveted. Then he concludes, "And tonight I want to announce that with the assistance of some members of this community," he looks towards our pew, "the Cathedral of Notre Dame Des Fleurs will celebrate its eight-hundredth birthday, on January first, in a manner that befits the occasion. Two rarely seen Books of Hours originally owned by Jean Duc de Berry will be brought together for the first time in over five hundred years and exhibited in this Cathedral. The French Minister of Foreign Affairs and the Minister of Culture, as well as the American Ambassador to France and other high dignitaries of the Republic, will be present for the occasion. On that day, the eyes of the world will be turned to Grasse, and many will want to discover for themselves the beauty and warmth of our town. I therefore urge you to give a warm welcome to all the visitors who will come here, and to show them the hospitality and generosity for which the Grassois are renowned."

The choir and organ then burst into the triumphal hymn,

"Alleluia! Sing to Jesus! His the scepter, His the throne.

Alleluia! His the triumph, His the victory alone!"

XIII

I wake up slowly. Open one eye, then the other, and peer over my goose down comforter. It is Christmas morning! Valérie has already come in and prepared the wood fire burning in the grate, but the room is still chilly. My nose above the blanket is cold. Light is filtering through the shutters, and my gifts, still wrapped, are piled next to the armchair. Did not have time to open my gifts last night with all the hullabaloo over the recovered manuscript. Need a cup of hot coffee. A couple of croissants with Valérie's mouth-watering strawberry jam won't hurt either. Guess I'll just have to go downstairs and get them myself. The family and guests are keeping Valérie busy. Something to be said for the only child; she gets all the attention. Now I am just one of the brood. Must fend for myself.

A peremptory knock interrupts my dark thoughts. I know who it is before she enters.

"Still in bed on Christmas morning? With the sun shining outside?" The old matriarch is in my room before I have time to say "enter."

"Grand-mère, I am a night person, not a morning person like you. I am fully awake at midnight, but it takes me time to get up in the morning," I answer, irritated at this invasion of my privacy at the crack of dawn.

"Nonsense! No such thing as morning and night persons. All new-fangled ideas that you got in America! Anyway this is neither here nor there, you and I must talk."

"Grand-mère," I plead, "I am still in bed, and have not had breakfast or a shower."

"I thought you'd give me some lame excuses. So I asked Valérie's niece, Huguette, to bring you some breakfast. And, if

142

you open my gift right here," she picks one of the wrapped-up packages and hands it to me, "you'll find something that will keep you warm."

Cheering news about the breakfast, but not sure about the gift. Grand-mère has her own ideas about what people should get as gifts versus what they really want to receive. Eye the package on my bed with apprehension. Too early in the morning for me to put on a happy face for something I don't like. But Huguette arrives just in time with breakfast on a bed tray! A steaming pot of coffee, a little basket of fresh croissants, a few curled balls of butter on a butter dish, and two tiny bowls of Valérie's apricot and strawberry jams.

"Thank you, Huguette! That's a lovely Christmas gift! Merry Christmas!"

"Thank you, Mademoiselle. Merry Christmas to you too," answers Huguette and leaves.

"Grand-mère, I'll open your gift after I've had my breakfast. Why don't you sit next to the fire and tell me what's on your mind."

Grand-mère decides that this is the best thing to do under the circumstances, and settles in the armchair from which she can best keep an eye on me.

"Very well, Marie-Christine. Have your breakfast while I tell you what has been bothering me. Of course, there is first the very serious matter of the murder of Phillipe. Thank goodness Claude is here with us and can pursue the investigation *sub rosa*, because of course this is a matter for the police of Grasse and not of Paris. But our dear inspector Pasteur and his deputy Guerrier are not doing much because of the Christmas holidays. I can't say I blame them. They have families too, and need a break sometime. But we do need to clear this matter up as soon as possible, for the sake of your cousin Gerard, if for no other reason. He's looking terribly depressed, and I don't like it. We need to find out what Phillipe came up here for the other night, and who was after him."

My mind has cleared after sipping coffee and biting into a crunchy croissant with Valérie's heavenly strawberry jam.

"Grand-mère, I talked to Tante Helène, yesterday. She told me that Phillipe had come up that night to tell her that he was getting remarried. He went to Tante Helène's room and they drank champagne, and then he said that he had met a young woman and had fallen in love with her and was going to marry her."

Grand-mère frowns and then shakes her head, "It does not make sense . . . " she leaves the sentence unfinished.

"Why not, Grand-mère? I mean he wished to tell his ex-wife, and I guess his son too, that he was getting married. He didn't want it to come as a shock, and he wanted their blessing too."

I pick up another croissant and try the apricot jam. Close my eyes to better savor the sweet and tangy taste of last spring's fruits from Grand-mère's orchard.

Grand-mère taps her cane on the floor impatiently.

"You know why not? Because that man never, in his entire life, asked for anyone's permission or blessing, least of all his poor wife's, before embarking on some idiotic scheme."

"Perhaps you're right, Grand-mère. And getting remarried at his age and without a penny to his name was idiotic."

"How do you know he didn't have a penny to his name?" Grand-mère is suddenly alert.

"Well, because he told Tante Helène something to the effect that he was coming into a lot of money soon, and that afterwards everything would be fine and he would be able to marry that woman."

"So he was up to his old tricks again, was he?" Grand-mère's eyes are shining.

Drink my coffee slowly, and remember something.

"You know, he must have been pretty sure he was going to get that money," I say thoughtfully.

"He was always sure that he was going to make money with his wild schemes, and they never came to anything. Phillipe had no money sense whatsoever. Making money for him was a matter of luck, like winning the lottery." Grand-mère still gets angry when she remembers Phillipe's stories.

"Yes, Grand-mère, but in this case I think he knew he was getting the money."

"What makes you think so?" asks Grand-mère; she seems definitely interested.

"Well, let me tell you what happened yesterday, when Tante Helène and I went to the Carlton to have a snack and wait for the rain to stop."

Recount the meeting with Mother and Peter Thompson, and how Thompson had mentioned he knew Phillipe. I added that Phillipe had told him that he was divorced from Tante Helène.

"So, what's the point of your story?" asks Grand-mère in a surly tone.

"Peter Thompson turned out to be the vice-president of Tiffany! And when pressed by Mother and me to tell us more about his relationship with Phillipe, he refused."

Grand-mère looks at me thoughtfully, "And what do you deduce from this conversation?"

"First, in order to meet a man like Peter Thompson, Phillipe must have been moving in wealthy circles. I mean, a poor man does not usually have the opportunity to mix with the likes of a vice-president of Tiffany."

Grand-mère nods, "Good point. Please continue."

I know I'm on shaky ground on this one, but I think my hunch is right.

"Phillipe must have developed a relationship with some rich people who perhaps offered him a job of some kind. I don't know. Anyway, I think he was planning to buy an engagement ring from Tiffany for his fiancée, and might have mentioned to Thompson in conversation that he had been married previously. This would explain why Thompson knew of the divorce, and also why he refused to tell us more about his relationship with Phillipe. I mean, how could he inform someone he had just met that her ex-husband was planning to buy an engagement ring for another woman?"

Grand-mère smiles.

"Marie-Christine, you have a lot of imagination, *ma chérie.* But the first part of your argument does not hold water. Who in his right mind would offer your Uncle Phillipe a job that was worth as much money as he was suggesting? As to your second point, you may very well be right. At the moment, I cannot think of a better explanation for Phillipe's strange behavior nor for that of the American jeweler. But then why in the world would anyone want to kill Phillipe?"

Put this way, a terrible idea occurs to me. A piece of croissant gets stuck in my throat and I start coughing. Grand-mère looks at me and the same idea seems to cross her mind. A look of horror appears on her face and she drops her cane with a clatter on the floor. We stare at each other, and then Grand-mère shakes her head.

"No, no. It cannot be. She is a fool but not a murderess. Yes, I know she was still in love with the man. But kill him? Never! Helène would not hurt a fly."

I say nothing. Remember Tante Helène's grief-stricken face when she told me about Phillipe being in love with that young woman. However, I just can't imagine, Tante Helène holding a gun to the head of her beloved Phillipe and shooting him in cold blood. But what's the saying about a woman scorned?

Grand-mère has not finished yet. Coughs, clears her throat, and changes her position in the armchair. She definitely looks uncomfortable.

"Grand-mère, what is it? There is something you're not telling me."

She heaves a big sigh, and then makes up her mind.

"Yes, Marie-Christine, you're right. There *is* another matter we have to talk about. I had a long talk with your aunt Geneviève this morning. She told me certain things. I had no idea. No idea at all. I thought they were doing so well." She shakes her head sadly.

Wipe my mouth. I have eaten the last crumb of croissant and swept clean the two little bowls of jam. Lift the tray and set it aside on the bed. I need to sit up to better focus on what Grand-mère is saying.

"Grand-mère, what did Tante Geneviève tell you?"

She bends down to pick up her stick.

"Ouch! My lumbago is back. It must be this cold weather."

She rubs her back and looks in pain. Bite my tongue. Was going to suggest that installing central heating in the house would help with the lumbago. But I must not go down that road; if I do I'll never find out what Tante Geneviève told Grand-mère.

"Is Tante Geneviève in some kind of trouble?"

"*Ma chérie,* you can't imagine! Apparently Xavier's auction house has not been making money for the past three years. What am I saying? The auction house has been steadily losing money in the past three years. So Xavier asked his wife, Geneviève, who has her own business consultancy, to help put some order in the finances of his auction house. That is, after all, what she does everyday as part of her work. When she examined the financial situation of Xavier's auction house, however, she discovered that the problems were so severe that there was no other solution than for her husband to declare bankruptcy. But Xavier refused to do so. He said his reputation would be ruined, he would never be able to go back into that business again, that his clients would leave him, etc."

Am stunned. Always thought that Uncle Xavier was making tons of money with all the art work and antiques he was selling to the rich and famous.

"But, Grand-mère, how can auction houses go bankrupt? I mean even if they don't sell their antiques and works of art immediately, they can still store them and sell them later. The value of those collectibles, paintings, furnishings, and so on, might even increase if sold later."

Grand-mère is rubbing her hands. The arthritic pain in her joints gets worse when she is upset. She nods.

"Yes, my argument exactly. But Geneviève said that Xavier had borrowed heavily to buy works of art which he was unable to sell. And when repayment on the debt came due, he just did not have the money to repay his loans."

"So what did he do?"

"He borrowed more and at higher interest."

"And Tante Geneviève did not know? Couldn't she have advised him?"

"No, that's the problem. He never told her how bad things were with his business until it was too late."

"But why, it doesn't make sense?"

Grand-mère continues rubbing her hands.

"Pride, I suppose. Geneviève was doing very well in her business and making money. He did not want to seem less capable than his wife. Men are funny that way. They'd rather get deeper into debt than admit they'd made a mistake."

Am beginning to feel too warm in bed and want to get up. But Grand-mère has not told me the whole story yet.

"So what did Tante Geneviève do when Xavier refused to declare bankruptcy?"

"What do you think? She put family first, and against her better judgment loaned him the money from her own business to repay his debts."

I shrug my shoulders, "Well, that must have taken care of his auction house, I suppose? Even if they are not as wealthy as they once were, they must still be well off?"

Grand-mère leans back in her chair and looks at me across the room.

"You see, child, when my daughters got married I gave each her share of the de Medici inheritance as part of her dowry. You, of course, got your father's share. Helène and Phillipe squandered their money, and Helène subsequently divorced. I put up a little trust for her and Gerard, so that she could live decently and bring up her son. Geneviève, on the other hand, kept her money under her own name and invested it into her consultancy. The man she had married was wealthy and had his own thriving auction house. They kept separate accounts and separate businesses. Now, however, Geneviève has drained her own account by loaning money to Xavier. She has no reserves left, and she has just found out that Xavier did not pay back all he owed. Instead he . . . he has . . . a new interest."

"What new interest?" Am not sure I want to know.

Grand-mère shakes her head in disbelief.

"After Geneviève almost bankrupted her own business trying to help him out, she discovered that her husband had an ongoing liaison with his secretary." Grand-mère pulls out a large cotton handkerchief and blows her nose.

"Uncle Xavier was cheating on his wife?" Uncle Xavier, who looks sooo ascetic? An affair? I can't believe it.

"Don't be vulgar, *ma chérie*. A *liaison* is what we used to call it when I was young."

Refrain from pointing out that cheating is cheating, whatever the term used.

"So what's going to happen now?" Am a bit shaken by all these revelations.

Grand-mère is unhappy and in pain. She rubs her back and scowls.

"Geneviève wants a divorce. But I have counseled her against it. We are good Catholics, and one divorce in the family is already too many. I told her that once she straightens out their financial affairs, the rest will take care of itself."

Grand-mère is quite enigmatic sometimes. I fluff up my pillow and turn towards her.

"How in the world can a liaison come to an end by simply straightening out financial matters, Grand-mère?"

Grand-mère nods wisely and wags her tongue at me.

"You are very young still, Marie-Christine. You do not understand men. When a man gets older, sometimes he needs to be reassured that he is still powerful and, hum . . . hum, virile, and so he embarks on a liaison to prove himself. The urge is stronger when the man is not doing well in his work, or his business is failing."

Am beginning to get the drift.

"So you mean, that if Uncle Xavier is back in the saddle, so to speak, he will no longer need a mistress to—er—prove himself?"

"*Exactement,*" answers Grand-mère, looking relieved that she does not need to explain further. Her generation finds it very difficult to discuss sex and extramarital affairs. She'd be *really* shocked if she knew what my friends talk about!

"Is there anything we can do to help?" I ask after a brief silence.

"We must try to save this marriage. Geneviève needs a quick loan of one hundred thousand euros to get her through the next three months. She believes that before the end of March she'll be able to pay it back. Frankly, I cannot lend her this money. Everything I have which is not tied up in real estate and agricultural land is in stocks and bonds. I do not want to sell anything now, because the market is very weak. Grasse, as I had mentioned to you earlier, is in a recession."

Begins to dawn on me that Grand-mère is in my room to ask my help for Tante Geneviève. I understand now why my aunt and uncle came to Grasse for Christmas! Tante Geneviève desperately needed the money and did not want, or could not take, a bank loan. She managed to convince her recalcitrant husband to join her by suggesting the possibility of taking a loan from Grand-mère. It was obvious from the start that Xavier was unhappy about coming to Grasse, and that he had done so only under pressure from his wife.

"So Grand-mère, are you saying that you think I should lend Tante Geneviève the money?"

She looks at me gratefully and smiles, "Yes, Marie-Christine. That's exactly what I am asking. Thank you for making it easier on me. I feel quite embarrassed to ask my granddaughter to help my daughter, but this is a family matter and we should settle it within the family. I am sure that you will get your money back very soon, and that you won't really miss it during those three months."

Am not so sure that this family business is all it's cracked up to be.

"Grand-mère, if I lend this money to Tante Geneviève, what guarantees do I have that she won't give it to her husband who will then use it for—er—other purposes?"

"She promised me, Marie-Christine, that she will pay back every centime within three months." Grand-mère looks a bit less confident now.

"But Grand-mère, why is she so sure that she will have the money within three months?"

"I don't know. She didn't explain. But she did say something about expecting to be paid a large sum of money in the next few weeks, money that was owed to her."

"Sounds like Phillipe."

Grand-mère looks up sharply, but says nothing. I decide to open Grand-mère's gift. Am preparing to smile and to thank her for whatever it is, whether I like it or not.

After struggling with the bow (half chewed by Pushkin) and the Scotch tape, I manage to open the packet without tearing the paper. I hate tearing gift-wrappings. It's almost like eating chicken with one's hands and throwing the bones on the floor.

A glorious crocheted shawl in gold, cashmere wool tumbles out of the box.

"Grand-mère, that's magnificent!" I exclaim, genuinely enthusiastic.

"I crocheted it for you, *ma chérie*, when you were away in America this autumn. I missed you and crocheting this shawl brought you closer to me, everyday."

I jump out of bed and rush to give Grand-mère a big hug.

XIV

Christmas lunch is served at 1 PM. Family members are expected to attend either of the two morning Masses, at 9 AM or at 11 AM. But the only person who has gone to church this morning is Valérie. Everyone else has either slept late (like yours truly), or has been outside enjoying the bright sunlight. Have put on a little red dress with a black jacket and high-heeled boots. As I come downstairs, I hear Pushkin yapping joyfully in the garden. Assume that he is accompanied by Xavier. The front door is opened and family members are wandering about. Alain enters, holding Pushkin on a leash.

"So you are taking care of Pushkin today?" I call out in a friendly way. Have not had much chance for conversation with Alain since our brief discussion the other night. He looks great in a dark green wool sweater and brown loafers.

"He was standing by the door with his leash in his mouth, waiting for Monsieur or Madame de la Rochereau. Felt sorry for him, and took him out for a walk."

Alain bends down and unleashes Pushkin, who rushes to the kitchen wagging his little tail.

"I think he smells the stuffed goose that Valérie is preparing for lunch," he says, grinning.

"What are you doing until lunch?" I ask.

"Nothing in particular. Want to go for a walk? The sun is warm."

"Great idea. Let's go!"

We walk out into the garden and open the big iron gates. Once in the street we turn right and start climbing uphill. The road is lined with pines and olive trees. The bright yellow house

153

next door was sold to an English tycoon who drops in one day a year. The rest of the time it remains shut.

"So tell me about yourself, Alain. How did you become a librarian?"

With his hands in his pockets, Alain looks anything but a librarian. A movie actor, a model for Ralph Lauren, a ski instructor perhaps.

"I grew up in an old house in Alsace. My father had this large wood-paneled library with literally thousands of old leather bound books. He had inherited many from his father and grandfather and added more to the collection. There was a bookbinder nearby and father always sent his books there to be bound, 'So that they last for you, your children, and grandchildren,' he would say. The library was my favorite room in the whole house. Father and I would sit there by the fireplace, and he would read me stories when I was very young. Later, I would do my homework after school in the library. During the weekends and holidays I would pick up books from the shelves and sit in one of the big leather armchairs and read. That's where I discovered Charles Dickens, Alexandre Dumas, Robert Louis Stevenson, Mark Twain, and many, many other great writers. . . . "

Alain's voice trails off. He seems to be back in that library and far away from here.

"I see. So of course you love books and, therefore, it was natural for you to become a librarian," I say trying to bring him back to Grasse.

He looks at me, surprised, as if he had not realized I was walking beside him.

"No, you don't see at all," he answers roughly. He strides forward leaving me behind.

"Hey, Alain, don't walk so fast! I can't keep up with you," I call out.

He stops and slowly turns around, "I'm sorry. You're right, I became a librarian because I'm a bibliophile. So why don't you tell me about yourself. Where did you study?"

The conversation proceeds in a desultory manner. I try to return to the wood-paneled library. But Alain has had a Jesuit upbringing, so he answers a question with another question. Cannot beat him at this game. We pass Madame Dutreuil's house. The red wooden gate is chained. She must have gone to Paris to be with her son and his family for Christmas. But further up on the road there is a trail of cars. The Galloudecs are receiving a crowd of old and young in their salmon-colored villa. Monsieur Galloudec waves cheerfully to us from the doorstep. "Merry Christmas!" he calls out. We wave back.

"Let's go back to the house. Lunch will be served soon," I suggest. Realize that Alain is on his guard for some reason. Holding something back? But what? And especially why? What has his father's library got to do with anything?

◆

Christmas lunch in all its glory! The table is set on the second tablecloth. Beautifully starched, the linen glows. Grand-mère's best Limoges dishes, polished family silver, and crystal glasses are a feast for the eyes. Table is decorated with holly and winter roses. Sitting atop the napkin on each plate is a little gift for each of us wrapped in gold foil. Even Mother who has come up from Cannes with Papa is enthused, "What a beautiful table! Reminds me of the Christmas we spent with the Thompsons in New York a few years ago."

Wonder if it is the same Peter Thompson whom we met in Cannes yesterday? Must follow up on that trail.

Monseigneur d'Epinay is not here today to say grace, so Papa bows his head and prays, ending with, "And we pray for the departed that they may at last find peace."

Father's acknowledgment of Phillipe's death. No one looks at Gerard.

Jean begins to serve the Strasbourg truffled *foie gras* or goose paté out of a crusty golden pastry. Papa at one end of the table pours wine out of a crystal decanter. I turn to Gerard, who as usual is seated to my left.

"How's everything?" Remaining vague as to my exact meaning.

"Fine," he answers quietly.

"Gerard, I meant to ask you, how long have you known Alain?" Have noted that Alain is seated far down the table talking to Mother and cannot overhear our little conversation.

"Around six months. He was very helpful to me when I was preparing a major paper for my History of Law class. He gave me some really great sources." Looks at me curiously, "Why do you ask?"

Squirm a little on my chair.

"Well, he and I went for a walk earlier today and he began talking about his home in Alsace."

Gerard's eyes widen in alarm, "You talked to him about his *house?*"

"Yes, I mean, why not? Why shouldn't I?"

"He didn't tell you?"

"Tell me what? He spoke of his father's library, and how he used to go there and do his homework when he was a little boy."

"What else did he say?"

156

"Well, nothing much. That's the point. He suddenly stopped talking about himself, and just wouldn't get back to his father's library, nor why he became a librarian. Every time I tried to get him to tell me more, he'd change the subject of conversation."

Gerard nods, and looks across the table to Alain.

"I understand. It must have been hard for him to speak about it."

At this point Jean wheels in a serving cart. Valérie's stuffed goose surrounded with chestnuts is on a silver tray on the top shelf. I can hear yapping in the pantry. Pushkin is protesting that his lunch has flown the coop.

Jean first places the silver tray with a serving knife and fork before Papa, who begins to slice the goose ceremoniously. Then he picks up the two other dishes from the bottom shelf of the serving cart and sets them in the middle of the table. Tante Helène claps her hands in delight.

"Thank you, Maman. You remembered the *Gibelotte de lapin!*"

Mother looks across the table to my aunt Geneviève.

"What is this—gibo, gibili?"

Geneviève laughs mischievously.

"It is a traditional rabbit stew in white wine. But Valérie uses a secret family recipe which, she once assured us, she will divulge to no one, even under torture. Between you and me, I believe she adds some Marc de Provence to the wine. Helène has also discovered that the secret recipe includes an eel sauteed with the rabbit."

The part about the eel does not appeal to Mother. Her expression remains unchanged. She has had too good an upbringing to display any emotion about eels. However, when asked if she wants some rabbit stew, she answers politely but firmly, *"Non merci."* She does, however, help herself to the salad of beets and endives.

Plates are passed around the table to Papa, who serves each person a slice of the goose with the stuffing and the chestnuts. Uncle Xavier takes a Byronic pose. Closing his eyes, he inhales the aroma of the goose. Then, raising his glass, he says:

"Members of my beloved family, dear friends. We must recognize that this is truly the best prepared Christmas goose that any of us has eaten in a long time. Let us drink to Valérie's *chef d'oeuvre!* A culinary masterpiece worthy of the greatest French chefs."

Grand-mère calls Valérie from the kitchen. She pops in and curtsies shyly. We all raise our glasses and drink to her health. She turns bright red. Mutters *"Merci Messieurs, Dames,"* and rushes back to the kitchen. In the meantime, Gerard and I have not finished our little conversation about Alain.

"So, Gerard, what is your friend's story?"

Gerard hesitates. Picks up a chestnut and chews it.

"Well, if he didn't tell you, perhaps I shouldn't either."

That's it. I've about had it with these shenanigans.

"If you don't tell me, I won't speak to you until next year. Is that understood?"

Gerard chuckles.

"Oooh I tremble before such threats! Anyway I better tell you before you put your foot in it and ask him embarrassing questions."

"Well?" I ask, piqued at my cousin's total lack of appreciation for my diplomatic skills.

Gerard takes his time before answering. Looks furtively at Alain, who is conversing with Mother about Benedictine music manuscripts.

"Well, a few years ago, when Alain was away at school, there was a fire that destroyed his house. His father was alone, because his mother had died when he was young. The tragedy is that, while trying to save some of his favorite books, his father was killed. Apparently a bookshelf collapsed on him. Alain never forgave himself for not having been with his father then. He has vowed to rebuild the house and fill the library with all the books that were once there."

What a devastating experience! No wonder he said I did not understand. How could I've guessed? I glance at him but can't find a trace of that tragedy anywhere on his handsome face.

"Thanks for telling me, Gerard. Helps me better understand his character and his odd behavior at times. But tell me, does he have the money to repair or rebuild his house?"

Gerard shakes his head.

"No, he has no money. There is just the land on which the charred ruins still stand. But he won't sell the land because he wants to build a new house on the very same spot on which the old house once stood."

"But he won't be able to afford the cost of rebuilding the house on his salary as a librarian," I argue.

"Yes, I did mention this to him. He just smiled and said that he had figured things out and that he knew exactly how he was going to raise the money to rebuild his house."

"Nothing else?" I am curious.

"No, he never explained, and I didn't press him. He gets really upset at the mention of the house."

Remember how he strode away earlier this morning, leaving me behind. Guess he was trying to hide his pain.

After Valérie has cleared the dishes, Jean brings in a large tray of cheeses: Roquefort, Gorgonzola, Gruyère, *tommes de chèvre* (my favorite: little disks of goat cheese wrapped in chestnut leaves). He goes around the table with the tray, followed by Valérie, who places two baskets of small oval breads at either end of the table.

Grand-mère, directing her remarks to Mother as if it were a challenge, "These breads are called *fougassettes de Grasse*."

"Ah," responds Mother, quite in the fog.

Papa, from the other side of the table sensing a storm brewing between wife and mother, jumps in to calm the waters.

"The sweet Christmas breads of Grasse, Priscilla. They are flavored with grated orange zest, orange blossom water, and made with olive oil instead of butter or margarine."

"Interesting," responds Mother. She, however, makes no effort to taste the *fougassettes*.

Need a diversion before something unpleasant is said. Mother and Grand-mère have been intensely polite to each other for the past two days. It may not last much longer. Must think of something to say quickly to avert a clash.

"I wonder who put the manuscript of the *Trés Riches Heures* in Tante Helène's room?"

I blurt out the first thing that comes to mind.

Am a bit too successful. A frigid silence follows my question. I have reminded everyone of the tragedy, the theft, the suspicions.

"Why did you say that the manuscript was put in Madame Bousquet's room?" asks Claude, always the inspector even on Christmas day.

"I don't know. I just thought that that's the way it came to be part of the gifts around the manger. After all Tante Helène," I turn towards my aunt who is gobbling up a little *fougassette*, "didn't you bring your gifts downstairs after dinner?"

Tante Helène stops chewing for a moment to consider my question.

"I did. However, earlier that afternoon, I had brought the gifts down and placed them next to the manger. Each packet was wrapped up and had a really nice bow on it. But an hour later I found Pushkin standing in the middle of the gifts and tugging at one of my bows. I think it was the one on your gift, Marie-Christine. Anyway, I then had to take the packets back upstairs."

More silence follows. Valérie bustles in and begins closing the shutters of the dining room. Mother pushes her chair away from the table and prepares to get up. Explanations are in order, "Mother, dinner is not over yet." I call out across the table. "Valérie is closing the shutters before she brings in the dessert."

Mother looks at me as if I am not all there.

"And why does the dessert require that we stay in the dark?" she asks quite rationally.

Just then Jean comes in from the kitchen carrying a round plate with the Christmas pudding. Valérie follows, holding a small translucent bowl and a long match that she has lit in the fireplace. Both come and stand next to Grand-mère. She takes the lit match from Valérie and touches the liquid in the bowl which immediately catches fire, filling the room with a wonderful aroma of brandy and burnt sugar. In slow motion Valérie then pours the flaming liquid over the pudding and sets it on fire. The scent of sweet oranges and cranberries mixes with that of the brandy. The room is aglow. Like a Caravaggio painting the center is lit by the flames. Around the table eyes look enormous; faces partly disappear in the shadows. Feelings are highlighted. Surprise, delight, joy, and also fear.

"Ooohs and aaahs," and finally clapping as the fire dies down. Grand-mère smiles happily and begins slicing the pudding.

Places the slices on plates that are then passed from hand to hand around the table. From an antique silver bowl, Valérie pours a warm, rum-flavored custard on each slice.

"This, my dear Priscilla, is for you. *Le plum pouding Anglais.* When I planned the menu for the Christmas festivities, I made sure that the favorite dish of each of you would be served."

Mother smiles. The storm has bypassed us for the time being.

"Thank you, Maman." Can't believe my ears. Mother is actually addressing Grand-mère in that familiar French way! She must really be moved.

"This is not a Provençal tradition, strictly speaking," says Grand-mère with a twinkle. "But it became one among some families in Grasse and Nice, after members of the British royalty made the Riviera their winter resort over a century ago. They introduced us to tea, tennis and *le pouding*. Everything else, of course, they learned from us!!"

XV

After lunch, decide to soak up some sun in the garden, and walk through the French windows to the terrace overlooking the valley. It is so peaceful out here. Far away, little sailboats bob up and down on the horizon. It feels almost like spring. Suddenly, I hear footsteps behind me, and Claude's voice, "Marie-Christine!"

"*Oui,* Monsieur l'inspecteur?" I reply, a bit annoyed. Wanted to be alone to think things over. But perhaps Claude can help.

"I thought we could have our little chat now."

"You mean, you're actually going to question me about the murder of my uncle Phillipe?"

"Yes, of course. You're high on my list of suspects. And though it's Christmas, I must ask you some questions—just as I had to with the others. Don't have much time left here, you know. I must be getting back to Paris soon."

Shrug my shoulders and comment, "As long as we stay outside here, and I don't have to go and sit in Grand-mère's *petit salon,* you can ask me any question you want."

Claude Bizzard smiles. Crooked smile that weakens my knees for some reason.

"I promise, upon my honor as an *inspecteur de police,* to conduct my questioning entirely on sunny terraces overlooking beautiful valleys." He places his right hand on his heart.

"In that case, I am entirely at your disposal." Lean over the balustrade to watch Pushkin chasing joyfully a large leaf blown by the wind.

"Very well then: Mademoiselle de Medici, did you hear or see anything unusual on the night of the murder?"

Straighten myself and look at him directly.

"Monsieur l'inspecteur, everything about that evening was unusual. First, my uncle Phillipe turning up uninvited in a snowstorm. His excuse? That he had this urgent desire to spend Christmas with his son and ex-wife whom he had not visited in six months. Then, what does he do? He tells them he is getting remarried. I mean, how insensitive can that be? And my aunt's behavior? Wasn't it unusual? She invites her ex-husband for a drink in her room. Why? Does she think he'll fall to his knees and beg her forgiveness?" Am thinking out loud. Claude is a good listener.

"Very good, very good. Please continue," he says encouragingly.

"Then, there is the behavior of everyone else. Why do they tell you they were all in bed, fast asleep and heard or saw nothing, when that is manifestly untrue? Take my uncle Xavier, for example; he took Pushkin out for a walk that night. Why didn't he come out and say so?"

"Perhaps he forgot?" Claude sounds unconvinced.

I shake my head.

"Does not sound like my uncle Xavier. He doesn't forget a thing. On another tangent, did you know that he has gone bankrupt?"

"How do you know that?" he snaps.

"It's a long story," I reply. Repeat what Grand-mère told me about my uncle and aunt's financial situation.

"So what does your uncle and aunt's financial problems prove?" Claude asks, looking from under his dark bushy eyebrows.

"It proves nothing," I say somewhat irritated. "You asked me if I had seen or heard anything unusual, and I am relating all the unusual things I have noted in the past two days. Nothing makes any sense at all, least of all the return of that manuscript gift-wrapped in Grand-mère's name."

Claude bows his head and looks thoughtfully at one of his shoes.

"Everyone had a motive and opportunity," he mutters to himself.

"Claude, why are you looking at suspects in the house? Yes, you told me there was snow and the roads were closed. But you know, in the States, this snowstorm would be considered just a minor storm, nothing really serious. Anyone could have walked up to the house in that snow and entered from the backdoor. Remember Phillipe said it was unlocked."

Claude nods, and puts both hands in his pockets as if he is looking for something there.

"Yes, I remember. But, Marie-Christine, you have just described the problem. How was the manuscript returned? Wrapped up in your aunt's brown paper gift wrap, and placed with the rest of the gifts next to the manger. Tell me then, how could that be the work of an outsider?"

I am silent. Lean on the balustrade and look at the garden. Pushkin is staring disconsolately at a prickly holly bush on top of which sits the dry leaf. He barks at it, but it won't come down and play with him. Feeling sorry for him, I call out, "Pushkin! Come! Come, Pushkin!"

He looks up, wags his little tail in acknowledgment, then turns his attention back to the leaf. I have to turn mine to Claude.

"If what you say is true, then the thief *and* the murderer are both in this house. Don't you think one criminal in a family is more than enough?"

Claude scratches his head, with unfortunate results. His hair starts sticking out at odd angles. He too is now observing Pushkin. Neither of us wants to look at the other. Feel rather defensive about my family.

"Marie-Christine, I did not say that. While the theft of the manuscript appears to be an entirely domestic affair, the murder could, in theory, have been committed by someone outside the family circle."

I hear the hesitation in his tone. I know there is going to be a "but" in the next sentence. "But . . . , " Claude pauses and then decides to change his approach, "why was Phillipe murdered in the first place?"

"I can think of many reasons why he would be killed: He might have owed money to some mafia guy, he could have embezzled money and ruined someone. Perhaps he had an affair with a married woman whose husband found out. . . . My uncle Phillipe was not exactly a model citizen, you know. I'm sure he must have made a lot of enemies in his life."

"That's not the point, Marie-Christine," replies Claude, still looking at Pushkin.

"Then what *is* the point?" I ask. Am irritated, and don't know quite why. Claude has a way of getting under my skin.

Staring ahead, he answers calmly, "Why was Monsieur Bousquet killed *here*? What was he doing out in your grand-mother's garden in the middle of the night?"

Have to admit that he has a point. I glance at him surreptitiously. He looks worried and is frowning. Knitted eyebrows look like one long furry tail across his forehead.

"Are you afraid that our troubles may not be over yet?"

He doesn't answer—just stares ahead. Suddenly he asks, "What do you know about Alain LeMoine?"

"Alain? Why? You don't think he has anything to do with all this, do you?"

"You haven't answered my question," Claude insists.

Pushkin has found another leaf, and is now chasing it and

barking happily. Decide to tell him my cousin Gerard's story. After listening to me in silence, he says, "After the murder of Monsieur Bousquet, I contacted the *Police Judiciaire* at the *Quai des Orfèvres* in Paris. I had them check out Alain LeMoine. He is a bona fide librarian in Strasbourg and a specialist on medieval manuscripts. This is why I was suspicious of his turning up here at such a convenient time, when two of the most important European manuscripts are going to be exhibited together for the first time."

The idea had crossed my mind. Must share my thoughts with Claude, "Although the timing was 'convenient,' as you put it, Alain did not ask to stay. In fact he most emphatically wanted to leave. It was my cousin Gerard who insisted that he have dinner with us, and later that he spend the night in Grasse rather than drive back in the snowstorm." Claude has found a rubber band deep in his pockets. He rolls a piece of paper into a ball (found in same pocket) and places it on the rubber band turning it into a sling. He sends the ball flying in Pushkin's direction. Very excited at this new toy, Pushkin abandons the leaf and runs after the paper ball.

"The *Quai d'Orfèvres* also checked the story of the fire. It happened five years ago. And Alain's father was killed. But do you know the circumstances of that tragedy?"

Shake my head. Gerard just gave me the bare facts.

"LeMoine senior was in debt. He did not tell his son. Probably wanted him to complete his studies and not worry about his old father. Anyway, one day five years ago, LeMoine senior called an auction house in Paris and offered to sell one of his own rare manuscripts."

Have a sinking feeling at the pit of my stomach.

"You don't mean—you don't mean?"

Claude nods, not looking at me.

"Yes, he called Xavier de la Rochereau's auction house."

"Oh my God!"

"According to the police report, Xavier de la Rochereau offered to come to Strasbourg to view the manuscript, because LeMoine did not want to send it by mail to Paris. So, Alain's father invited your uncle for dinner. He was an excellent cook, apparently. It is not clear what happened that night. LeMoine accidentally spilled something in the kitchen and the fire spread rapidly throughout the house. Xavier de la Rochereau ran out to the neighbors and alerted the firemen. LeMoine stayed behind and tried to rescue his books, and was killed in the fire."

Stare silently at the valley below. The breeze is getting colder and the sun is setting over the sea. I shiver as I look up at the sky. Dark clouds are gathering "like a herd of angry elephants" as Papa used to say when I was small. Even Pushkin has decided to call it a day. Carrying the little paper ball between his teeth, he trots back to the kitchen to see what Valérie is cooking.

"Does Alain know that my uncle Xavier was there that day?" I finally ask.

Still leaning on the balustrade, Claude looks at me from under his long eyelashes.

"What do *you* think?"

"Then why didn't he say anything? Why did he pretend he never met him before?"

"The same can be said of your uncle, Marie-Christine. He never acknowledged Alain, at least not in public, not at dinner, nor in the sitting room when we were all gathered together. In fact, I never saw them speak to each other at all. They have been studiously avoiding each other."

168

As I look back at the last three days I can't remember seeing them talk to each other either. But then, "What would they say? I mean, it would make the situation even more tense if they brought up Alain's tragedy."

"I would be curious to know if Alain LeMoine decided to stay in Grasse after he realized that your uncle Xavier was spending Christmas in this house."

Claude begins striding up and down the terrace. He is nervous and unhappy. Something else occurs to me, "Alain could have found out, weeks ago, that my uncle Xavier was coming to Grasse. When Gerard told him he was spending Christmas in Grasse with members of his family, he must have mentioned their names and perhaps even said something about what they did for a living."

At that moment, Gerard appears on the terrace.

"Hey, you two, what are you doing out here? It's getting cold and Valérie has prepared coffee and her *vert-vert*, your father's favorite pistachio cake."

After the *vert-vert*, Papa and Mother leave for the Carlton. Am deeply grateful that parents and grandparents have behaved themselves and that there has been no family feud. In the meantime we, the younger generation, i.e. Alain, Gerard, and I feel that we have been cooped up long enough at home. I decide to let off steam at a disco in Cannes. Claude says he has work to do and cannot join us. This man does not have an iota of fun in him!

Around 11 PM, when the family retires for the evening, we take Alain's old BMW sedan and race down to Cannes. (No self-respecting discotheque opens before 11 PM). I sit in the front seat next to Alain. My cousin Gerard is behind, smoking.

I decide to do some investigating before we reach Cannes. The disco will be too loud to hear anything.

"So, I finally found out why you became a librarian," I begin in a chatty sort of way.

Alain swerves sharply at a corner. Gerard starts coughing in the back seat. Afraid I'll mention his role in elucidating that mystery? "Did you?" His voice is icy.

"Yes, I was chatting with Inspector Bizzard, and I happened to mention your name."

More coughing in the back seat.

"Gerard, throw that cigarette away. I can't breathe up here." Don't like cigarettes. They're bad for the skin, and the smell sticks to you like bad company.

Gerard rolls down the window and throws his cigarette out. Cold air fills the car.

Alain has accelerated and is driving nervously.

"So what did the good inspector tell you about me?" he asks.

"Well, he told me about the fire that burnt your house." Feel I am entering the proverbial minefield. Gerard has heard enough and leans over the back of my seat.

"Marie-Christine, why don't we talk about something more cheerful? I mean it's Christmas for God's sake!"

Alain interrupts him.

"That's all right, Gerard. I do want to know what the inspector told Marie-Christine. After all, there has been a murder at your grandmother's, and many of us are suspects, I guess. The *Police Judiciaire* has to carry out its investigation, Christmas or no Christmas."

Good! I am glad Alain is a reasonable man. Hope he'll stay that way until I finish what I have started.

"The inspector said that he had checked you out. He said that you were a librarian and a specialist in medieval manuscripts, and that it was rather a coincidence that you came to Grasse when two of the most important fifteenth-century French manuscripts were going to be displayed . . . "

Alain brakes suddenly—just as we were going through a red light.

"So the inspector suspects me of stealing the *Trés Riches Heures*, does he now? And how does he explain the return of the manuscript, then? A change of heart? Or was it his presence that so scared me that I gave up what I had come up to steal?" Do I detect a note of sarcasm here?

"No, Alain, he never said that. He was just doing his job and investigating all possibilities, that's all." Try to reassure him. He starts the car jerkily and races down the road to Cannes.

"But you haven't finished, Marie-Christine. What else did Inspector Bizzard tell you about me?"

"He told me about your father's accident, Alain."

Alain is silent. His profile is set in stone. Not a muscle moves. Gerard lights another cigarette, and opens the car window slightly. I think he's decided to stay out of this.

"Well, now you know," Alain says finally.

"I'm sorry about your father, Alain. I really am. It must have been very difficult for you."

Alain does not answer. We are speeding at 150 kilometers an hour. But I'm not done yet. Must bring up the subject of my uncle Xavier before we reach Cannes.

"Alain, why didn't you say something when you met my uncle Xavier?"

More silence. Then Gerard asks, "What are you talking about, Marie-Christine?"

"Uncle Xavier was with Alain's father the night of the fire." There I've said it.

171

"What?" Gerard almost screams. The smoke from his cigarette is going to asphyxiate me.

"Is that true, Alain?"

"Gerard, get rid of that cigarette!" I order.

Gerard throws his cigarette out the window. Then leans over the back of my seat, "Alain, is it true that Uncle Xavier was with your father that night?"

We have entered Cannes. The shops are closed because it's late and it's Christmas night. Some decorative lights shine over store windows and across the streets. A car of rowdy teenagers rushes pass us.

"Yes, it's true," answers Alain quietly.

"Did you know he was coming to Grasse when you drove up with Gerard the other day?"

I've got to get to the bottom of this.

Gerard hits the back of my seat.

"Why didn't you tell me, Alain? Why? I thought we were friends!"

Decide to ask Gerard. Turn to face him as he leans over the back of my seat and tries to get some response from Alain.

"Gerard, did you tell Alain who was coming for Christmas at Grand-mère's?"

"No! I just said the family, that's all." Then he turns to Alain again, "So you found out about Uncle Xavier when you arrived?"

Alain finds parking on the street and stops. He unbuckles his seat belt and turns to face me and Gerard. Appears in complete control of his feelings.

"Look, you two. My father died five years ago. It's over. I don't want to talk about it anymore. Yes, I recognized your uncle Xavier, but he didn't seem to know me. Why do you want me to bring up the matter again? There is nothing more to be said. My father's dead and the house is gone. Xavier de la Rochereau cannot bring either of them back. OK? So let's go to Le Jimmy'z and have some fun."

Know when I'm beaten. Alain will not speak. I guess I should enjoy Le Jimmy'z and forget this story. After all it's none of my business. Claude is the inspector on this case. Let him find out who killed Phillipe and why. At least we have the manuscript now, and it can be exhibited with *Les Belles Heures* on New Year's Day at the Cathedral.

Suddenly I remember something. Isn't it tomorrow that the article on *Les Belles Heures* being located in Grand-mère's house will appear in *Le Loup-Garou*? The idea of that article was to lay a trap for the thief of the *Trés Riches Heures*. But now that we have both manuscripts we don't need a trap. Won't the article attract the attention of some other crooks?

XVI

December 26 in Provence is known as the second Christmas Day. For many it's a holiday. One gets to relax and enjoy one's gifts. The hustle and bustle of Christmas is over. Plans for next year are hatched. Photo albums are examined to see who got married or divorced; whose children did well, or not as the case may be; who put on weight; and whose hair needs a trim or a dye! Old friends get to call each other and catch up on a whole year of news. Lots of leftovers are consumed. And I get to stay in bed a couple of hours longer, play with my gifts in my room, call a girlfriend in New York on my new cell-phone, and send an e-mail to another friend from my new laptop (both much appreciated gifts from Papa).

Must find out what Leon has been doing at *Le Loup-Garou*. He is at work and must have got the new issue of the paper out this morning.

"Leon, it's Marie-Christine. Merry Christmas!"

"Merry Christmas, Marie Christine! Everyone here sends you their best wishes!" Leon sounds excited. "By the way, did you see the new issue of *Le Loup-Garou?* No? It's great! The local stores are running out of the paper. I'll order a second printing. OK with you?"

"By all means, go ahead! By the way what does the front page look like?"

"Just fabulous! Headline reads '*Les Trés Riches Heures de Jean, Duc de Berry* back in Grasse after 500 years.' We've got some great photographs and interviews with Monseigneur d'Epinay and the American, Sister Felicity. She is quite the expert, isn't she? People just loved the story! I mean no one is reading *Nice-Matin* this morning!"

"Have people been calling you? Asking questions about the manuscripts?" I now am worried that *Le Loup-Garou* may have become too successful for our own safety.

"Yes, there have been at least a dozen queries," answers Leon. "Things like: Are the manuscripts the genuine thing? Why is one of the manuscripts in a museum in New York? Isn't it against the law to sell manuscripts to foreigners?"

"Leon, do you remember if anyone called to ask about the location of the manuscripts?"

"Well, Marie-Christine, you did say that we should mention that the two manuscripts were in the de Medici villa, remember? Is there a problem?" Leon seems puzzled.

"No, no problem," I say vaguely. "Just curious."

"Let me ask Vivianne. She picked up the phone a couple of times." I hear him calling Vivianne. "Vivianne says that she remembers someone asking if both manuscripts were at the villa, or if it was only the *Trés Riches Heures* that was there. But she doesn't remember if it was a man or a woman, and the person didn't leave a name."

"Thank you, Leon. One last question: Will the sale of this issue of *Le Loup-Garou* make a significant difference to our finances?" Must know the bottom line.

Some hesitation, then, "Well, Marie-Christine, a few more sales like today's and we'll be in the black. This is a great start."

After we hang up, I decide to dress. Need to go to town and get a few copies of *Le Loup-Garou* for the family. I also want to get a feel for what people are saying about the manuscripts being in Grand-mère's house.

Wrapped in my new pink cashmere sweater and matching cap and gloves (gift of Tante Geneviève), I go downstairs and bump into Claude at the front door.

"Going to town?" he asks casually.

"Yes, need a lift?"

"No, but I'd enjoy the ride and the company."

We get into my red Ferrari. He does not even look at it as he slips in. I start the engine, and we are off on the road to town.

"So what are you up to this morning, Marie-Christine?"

Recount my conversation with the managing editor of *Le Loup-Garou*.

"What I should have told you earlier," I add, "is that when the *Très Riches Heures* disappeared, Grand-mère and Monseigneur d'Epinay planned to lay a trap for whoever stole the manuscript. So they asked me to tell Leon to mention in the new issue of *Le Loup-Garou* that both manuscripts were located in Grand-mère's house. I forgot all about it until late last night, and of course by then it was too late. Leon did what he was told, and now everyone knows where the manuscripts are. I'm afraid that someone may break into the house and try to steal them."

Claude is silent, looking straight ahead at the road. Then he says thoughtfully, "Marie-Christine, if someone outside the house really is trying to steal the manuscripts, then certainly that break-in could occur in the coming few days. To pre-empt a burglary I'll ask Pasteur and his deputy Guerrier to send someone to guard the house. After all they are valuable manuscripts and the local police should be able to provide protection until New Year's Day. But . . ."

He hesitates and begins ruffling his hair, a sure sign that he is unhappy with this scenario.

"I know what you're going to say," I say sarcastically. "It was not an outsider who stole the manuscript; it was someone in the house."

"Hey, careful! You don't want to get us killed here!" he admonishes, as I swerve dangerously around a bend on the road.

"Marie-Christine, if I'm right and it is someone in the house, then you have nothing to fear."

Am not sure I understand his logic, and say so.

"Well, it's very simple. Whoever took the manuscript in the house has no further use for it and has returned it. So why would that person try to steal the manuscript again?"

Thinking it over in a nanosecond, I decide he's right.

"Very well then. I'll drop you off at the police station and you can discuss security matters regarding the manuscripts with Pasteur and Guerrier. Meanwhile I'll go and see how my paper is doing."

◆

Tonight, in my room, catch up with my diary writing. The temperature has dropped again, and the wind is howling outside. An icy rain is beating against the shutters. Valérie has built a crackling fire in the room, and put a pile of logs next to the fireplace in case I need them. Have settled into my big armchair, upholstered in a primrose paisley, cotton print. Wrap myself up in Valérie's knitted throw blanket, her gift to me this Christmas. Gerard has bought me a big box of chocolates that I have set on the table before me with my mug of hot cocoa and the last issue of *Le Loup-Garou*. It is a really good article on the manuscripts. No mention, however, of the disappearance and reappearance of the *Très Riches Heures*. I have not told that story to Leon.

So where was I? Begin writing. The house is quiet. Everyone's gone to their room. Writing is relaxing. I feel myself unwinding. . . .

Suddenly I wake up. It's dark and cold. I shiver. The fire has died down, only glowing red ambers are left that give no heat. Must have fallen asleep while I was writing. But why is it so cold? The curtains of the French window are moving? It must be the wind. The wind? I jump up from my chair, dropping my diary, pen, and throw blanket on the floor. Rushing to the window, I pull the curtains and step on something that cracks like, like glass? The window is opened. The glass pane has been broken. The wooden floor is wet. Little pieces of glass are everywhere. My balcony is littered with broken twigs. Must be from the branches of the tree that overlooks it.

Fear, horror begin to sink in. Someone broke into my room—again, like a recurring nightmare. It's easy to get in. One can climb up the tree to the balcony. Someone climbed into—into my room! Oh my God! Is he still in my room? I turn around quickly to look inside the room. It's dark, just the glowing ambers. The person who broke in must have unplugged the floor lamp. I can hear my heart beating against my ribs. Try not to breathe too loudly, lest someone hears me. Stupid of me, the person can see me outlined in the window. But the room is silent. I can't hear anything.

Barking! Pushkin has woken up too. He is barking furiously.

"Shut up, you mutt!" The voice of Uncle Xavier.

More barking. Then a bang and a yelp. Sounds as if Uncle Xavier has thrown something at Pushkin.

I must alert the household. Cross my room and find the door open. Whoever broke into the room left through the door and must be roaming about the house. Rush out of my room, and stop. How do I alert everyone? Knock on each door and try to explain, behind the door, what's happening? There are too many doors, too many people in the house. The burglar, or whoever broke in, might run out, and we won't be able to catch him. Worse, he might be lurking around the corner and might attack me. Stand paralyzed at my door. Suddenly Pushkin barks again. That energizes me. I start screaming:

"Help! Help! *Au Secours! Voleur!* Thief!" in French and English. Pushkin understands from the sound of my voice that there is danger. He starts howling: Woooooo! Wooooo! The more he howls, the louder I scream. Feel better. Rush to every door and bang loudly. Doors open. Sleepy faces stare out. Pushkin comes running out of my uncle and aunt's room, barking.

"What's the matter? What's happening?"

Gerard, Alain, and Claude are the first to rush to action when I explain. They switch on the lights all over the house. Preceded by Pushkin, they run downstairs, check windows, the front door, the kitchen door. Grand-mère comes out in her powder-blue woolen dressing gown, looks at me, and asks sharply, "Someone broke into your room?" I nod. My throat feels terribly sore. I screamed too much.

"Quick, *le petit salon!*" she urges.

Uncle Xavier, followed by my two aunts, Grand-mère, and me go downstairs. Sure enough the door of Grand-mère's private study is open. The light from the corridor shows the room in chaos. It is littered with papers and the desk drawers are open.

"*Mon Dieu! Mon Dieu!*" Valérie, holding her face in both hands, is weeping at the mess in *le petit salon.*

Grand-mère, looking at the drawers, says very quietly:

"The manuscripts are gone."

XVII

Silently we troop into the sitting room. Wearing his old, brown woolen coat, Jean is putting some logs in the fireplace. Grand-mère, looking weary and dispirited, hobbles painfully towards her armchair. Valérie goes upstairs to fetch her cane and brings it down to her. Alain and Gerard gravitate towards the table with the drinks and start taking orders. In a loose, emerald silk kimono, with red hair flowing on her shoulders, my aunt Helène looks like a Titian painting of Flora or Maria Magdalene as she reclines on the sofa. Quite a contrast to Tante Geneviève, who is deadly pale and appears thin and desiccated in a tailored navy housecoat. She sits straight and stiff on a chair and orders *un whisky sec*, with not even one ice cube. Looking and sounding like thunder, Claude is railing at Pasteur on the phone outside the sitting room.

"Why wasn't someone watching the house?" he shouts. Then after an interval, "Then how come the house was burglared?" The other side is trying to explain. "And where is the d . . . guard?"

The front bell rings. No one looks particularly surprised despite the fact that my watch says it is 3 AM. Jean pulls his old coat to his chest and goes to see who is at the door.

"*Bonsoir*," says a familiar voice.

"*Bonjour*, Inspecteur Guerrier," answers Jean sarcastically.

Claude pounces on the inspector and the gendarme who is with him.

"You call yourselves policemen! The house was burglared tonight! And I came expressly to warn you this morning at the gendarmerie to keep an eye on this place! What is the meaning of this? Were you both asleep or what?"

Feel sorry for Guerrier and his companion. They are soaked, half-frozen, and appear quite terrified of Claude. Guerrier tries to explain, but Claude won't let him talk. Decide to intervene, "Inspector Guerrier, you and your friend are dripping wet. Do take off your coats and boots and come into the sitting room. It will be easier to talk inside. Jean, will you please see what these gentlemen want to drink."

Looks of deep gratitude from the inspector and his assistant. Claude raises his eyebrows but stops bawling them out. Valérie collects their wet coats and asks them to carry their boots and leave them in the kitchen. I hear barking and decide to follow the two men into the kitchen. Don't feel like staying behind in the hallway with Claude, who is still fuming. Wearing his raincoat and boots, Uncle Xavier is talking to Guerrier. Pushkin, all wet, is energetically shaking off the water and sprinkling everyone and everything around him. He looks even smaller than he is because his hair is stuck to his body, but he still barks ferociously at the gendarme.

"I went out in the garden and walked around the house to see if I could find traces of the burglar," Uncle Xavier explains to Guerrier as he takes off his coat. "I didn't find anything. Guess it was too dark." He looks down at Pushkin, who is now licking his front paw, and adds, "The dog also needed to go out for a walk."

"Why don't we all move to the sitting room?" I suggest. "We will be more comfortable there to discuss the break-in."

Finally, everyone is gathered in the sitting room. The fire that Jean has been stoking is blazing, and the two policemen are ensconced on two armchairs with a glass of wine that Valérie has warmed up when she saw how cold they were.

"Well," says Claude, eyeing them with a cold, cruel stare, "What have you got to say for yourselves?"

Guerrier drains his glass and looks at Valérie. She understands and pours him another glass. Color returns to the inspector's face.

"Inspector Bizzard, my assistant here, Dupont, from the gendarmerie and I have been in Madame de Medici's garden since eight o'clock tonight." He looks at his watch and blinks. "I mean it has been five and a half hours in the d . . . rain! Sorry, Mesdames. We did not stay in the police car, which was parked outside the gate. We walked around, checked the front and back doors to see if they were shut. They were. And they were locked too. We tried them to see if there was any way someone could get in."

Dupont sneezes and apologizes. He looks unhappily at his socks. There is a big hole in one of them. Probably wishes he could have kept his boots on. Valérie returns with more warm wine.

"Let me explain things here, Guerrier. This time the burglar came in from the window and not from the door." Claude's icy tone does not conceal his anger. It seems to make it even more threatening.

"This time?" asks Dupont, puzzled. Obviously no one has told him about the first disappearance of the manuscript.

Guerrier waves his hand at Dupont.

"I'll explain later." He then turns to Grand-mère, who has been sitting gloomily in her chair, watching the policemen, "Madame de Medici, I apologize for this. But truly we did not see or hear anyone in your garden in the past five hours. It was dark and raining of course, and we could have been in your vegetable garden when the burglar broke into the house."

Everyone is silent. Tante Helène stretches out an arm above her head and yawns loudly, then covers her mouth.

"I don't know about you all, but I am going back to bed. I am tired and I am cold. Furthermore, I heard and saw nothing until my niece screamed. So I don't think I can be of any help to the police." As she stands up to go to her room, Claude stops her.

"One moment, Madame Bousquet. Is this your official statement about what you were doing at the time of the burglary?"

"Yes, Inspector Bizzard, that is my official statement," she answers impatiently, throwing back her red hair that is tumbling over her face. "I have nothing else to add," and with that she sweeps out of the room, green kimono somewhat askew.

My aunt Geneviève stands up and hands her drained whisky glass to Valérie, who is hovering around.

"*Messieurs les inspecteurs,*" she addresses the police officers in the plural, "may I congratulate you on your inefficient and blundering conduct tonight? It gives a deplorable picture of our Grassois police system."

Stiff as the proverbial poker she walks out of the room. The three men look distinctly embarrassed. They have been reprimanded like a group of lazy schoolboys who have not done their homework.

Leaning on her cane, Grand-mère struggles out of her armchair. Valérie rushes to help her and she waves her off.

"I can get up on my own, Valérie. Thank you. And now, inspectors, I also have to say goodnight. I must get some rest. Perhaps sleep will bring good counsel, but at the moment there is nothing more I can say or do. Let us all make our official statements tomorrow morning when we are more awake."

Claude calls Pasteur at the gendarmerie and asks him to send two other men to guard the house. Guerrier and Dupont are sent home and ordered to return in the morning at 9 AM. Bundled in a towel, Pushkin is brought in by Jean. His little black snout sticking out from the towel, Pushkin manages to bark at Dupont as Xavier carries him off to Tante Geneviève's bedroom. Finally, I am left alone with Claude.

I can't help it. Have to rub it in:

"Sooo, it was someone in the house who robbed the manuscripts. It was someone in the house who killed my uncle Phillipe! How do you explain, then, the break-in tonight, Inspector Bizzard?"

Claude ruffles his hair which has begun to stick out again in its odd way.

"I have to admit, Marie-Christine, that you were right, and I was wrong. You also warned me about your grandmother's plan to trap the crook and how it might backfire, and it just did. My profound apologies for not heeding your warning."

Am definitely mollified by this abject recognition of my superior deductive powers. I must be equally magnanimous, "But you did heed my advice, Claude. You asked Pasteur to send two men to watch the house and, judging by the state of their coats and boots, they must have been out there for quite a while tonight."

"They might as well have been in their beds and asleep for all they saw and heard!"

Claude is still angry at Guerrier and Dupont.

"Claude, what happens next?" Realize that this is a new situation.

He does not answer. Instead he walks over to the table where the drinks are still standing, "Do you want a little cognac? I need one."

"Yes, thank you." I then move closer to the dying fire for warmth. With only my red woolen robe and slippers on, I am feeling cold. Claude, on the other hand, is fully dressed.

Carrying two cognac snifters, he hands me one and sits across from me in Grand-mère's armchair. He inhales the aroma and then drinks slowly, looks up, and smiles, "We seem to be destined to meet only to discuss crimes and criminals, aren't we?"

Feel warm suddenly. Not sure if it is the cognac or that crooked smile, but I must not let either go to my head.

"Well, that *is* your profession, isn't it?" I answer rather brusquely.

Holding his glass in both hands, he observes me under his long eyelashes.

"Why are you always on the defensive with me, Marie-Christine?"

Not quite sure what to answer, I'd better drink and think quickly. The cognac burns my throat and I begin coughing.

"Are you all right?" Claude asks, looking concerned.

"Yes," cough . . . cough . . . "yes I'm fine, thank you." There I go, snapping at him again.

"Well then, why?" He has not given up.

Could I do the Jesuit thing and answer with a question? Or just deny flatly that I am on the defensive? What if I tried to have a real conversation with him? He obviously is not sleepy, nor am I, so perhaps we can talk seriously.

"I'm sorry, Claude. You're right. I do have a tendency to snap at you for no reason. Or at least—I mean—there is a reason." Not sure how to proceed.

He leans forward, eyes shining.

"I was afraid you were going to say there was nothing the matter."

My heart is behaving somewhat oddly. Feel it thumping on my ribs.

"What would you have done if I had said so?" I ask, trying to postpone explanations.

"I would have said 'good night' and gone to bed," he answers calmly.

I squirm on my armchair. Have pulled my feet up and tucked them under me for warmth. Suddenly feel self-conscious about how I must look to him. Drink the last drop of my cognac. Warms me and gives me courage to continue.

"Well, Claude, it's like this," I pull my robe closer around my neck and look at the fire. "Ever since I met you, last summer that is, I have felt that you—that you . . . " Am floundering.

"Yes, Marie-Christine?"

"That you never took me seriously!" There I've said it.

Claude looks completely taken aback. He had not expected this at all.

"What do you mean, Marie-Christine? I have always taken you seriously!"

It is going to be more difficult than I thought.

"No, you don't understand. You, and you are not alone, think that I am just another pretty face, a spoiled, rich kid enjoying the pleasures of the French Riviera. . . ."

"That's not true, I never . . .," he protests.

"Oh, yes you did. Remember last summer, when I was trying to run *Le Loup-Garou?*"

"Well, then, I didn't know you. But when I got to know you, I changed my mind."

"But you still don't take my ideas seriously. For instance, earlier this evening or morning, I asked you a question. You never answered me, as if I were not intelligent enough to understand the repercussions of this latest theft of the manuscripts."

"I am sorry, I did not mean it that way," Claude answers apologetically. "I was trying to figure things out for myself. I really cannot understand how someone broke into the house, stole the manuscripts, and disappeared without anyone apparently seeing or hearing anything."

"Claude, you're doing it again," I shake my head impatiently. "You are not answering my question. I did not ask how the burglar broke into the house. I asked what was going to happen next. Meaning: Will the information about the loss of the two manuscripts be made public? Are we going to have the press covering the theft? Are we going to alert the *Quai d'Orsay?*" I am referring to France's Department of State. Am afraid this is going to create tensions in U.S.-French relations. "You see when you don't answer my questions, or answer them in a way that implies that I cannot understand the broader picture, it irritates me. And when I'm irritated I snap. It's really very simple, you know."

Claude has put his snifter on the table between us and sits back in his armchair. Holding his chin in his left hand, he looks at me thoughtfully.

"I confess I have underestimated you at times, and have not been as candid as I should have. In my defense, it is because I wanted to protect you," he clears his throat and looks embarrassed. I am not quite sure I understand.

"Why did you want to protect me?"

"It's not that you can't stand up for yourself, but that—but that . . ."

"Yes?" It's my turn now to get him to speak frankly.

"Well, since you bought *Le Loup-Garou* you seem to be getting into trouble."

"The stealing of the two manuscripts had nothing to do with me or my newspaper," I snap (again!) at him.

"Perhaps not. But, in the hope of catching the thief of the *Trés Riches Heures,* your grandmother used your newspaper to spread the rumor that the manuscripts were in her house. The result is that someone broke into your room to steal the manuscripts."

"It's just because I have a tree growing under my balcony, that's all."

"Be it as it may. You did get into trouble. I came to spend my Christmas vacation to see you again. And what happens? I find you in the very midst of another crime. Some people are like that: they attract crime, like others attract money, or fame, or . . . "

I laugh. Claude is really very old-fashioned.

"Mother would say this is all balderdash, you know. And a girl can take care of herself. But I appreciate your desire to protect me. I would much prefer however, if you took me into your confidence and if we worked together, instead of arguing with each other."

Claude smiles his crooked smile that shows his very white teeth, and stretches out his hand across the table.

"Let's shake hands on this. You tell me everything you've seen and observed, and what you think happened, and I'll do the same, to the extent that it is permissible for a police officer to share information with others beside the officers in charge of the case."

I suppose I must be content with his promise. We shake hands.

"Now, Marie-Christine, can you tell me exactly what happened tonight? I'm taking notes. So you see how important your statements are to me? I'll report them to Pasteur and the police of Grasse because this is not my case, and I cannot carry on an official investigation in Grasse unless I am given the express order to do so from the *Quai des Orfèvres*."

"Let's have some more cognac first, and let's put some wood in the fireplace. The room is getting colder by the minute." I shiver.

Claude gets up and places a dry log on the dying embers. He revives the fire with a poker.

"What a beautiful fire!" he exclaims. "I don't think we need the lights on."

He switches off the lights, takes our snifters, refills them, and returns. I drink some cognac and watch the flames dancing in the fireplace. Feel warm again and drowsy.

"There's nothing much to tell," I begin. Then recount what happened in the wee hours of this morning. After I finish, he asks, "Marie-Christine, would you like to come upstairs with me and show me what you saw in your room?"

Have no desire whatsoever to go upstairs. Don't want to see the broken glass or feel the cold wind rushing into my room. I am just fine in my armchair next to the fire.

"Claude, why don't you go upstairs. I don't feel up to it. It was quite a shock, you know, and I don't think I've quite absorbed it all yet."

"That's all right, Marie-Christine, you don't need to come. I'll go upstairs alone. Will you be all right down here on your own?"

The cognac has made me really sleepy. My eyelids are closing. I mutter something and fall asleep. I dream that Claude is carrying me and laying me down on the sofa. That he brings me my eiderdown comforter and covers me with it. I feel warm and comfortable. Dream that he caresses my hair and bends down to kiss me.

XVIII

December twenty-seventh and the household is humming. Valérie has prepared a light lunch for Grand-mère and me in *le petit salon*, to keep us out of the way of the comings and goings of the police. Since nine o'clock this morning, Claude has been leading a thorough search of the house and the grounds with a whole battalion of Grasse's police force. Wonder if there are any gendarmes left in Grasse today to catch criminals or even give tickets to wayward drivers. Grand-mère's study, the scene of the crime, was cordoned off, then thoroughly examined, photographed, and dusted for fingerprints. Finally we're allowed back in.

Pushkin got into everyone's way this morning. He rushed up and down the stairs in mad pursuit of various gendarmes. Must have been difficult for him to decide who was or was not an intruder. Better suspect everyone. This strategy backfired, however, when, in an excess of zeal, he grabbed the left ankle of Dupont, who promptly nose-dived into Tante Helène's open suitcase. Claude then had to ask Tante Geneviève to take Pushkin out for a long walk.

Over chicken bouillon, goose paté, a Roquefort and a Brie, accompanied by a glass of Grand-mère's *vin maison*, we take stock of the situation.

"Marie Christine, the situation is very serious," begins the venerable matriarch.

Spreading some Roquefort on a toasted bread, I agree.

"I need you to be my eyes and ears and carry out an investigation at a more discreet level."

I nod, as I sip Grand-mère's wine that has a faint taste of nuts and berries.

190

"I want you to go and talk to Sister Felicity. Despite being American, she is a particularly well-educated and knowledgeable woman. I feel that she may have the answer."

Grand-mère's views of Americans have never been flattering. But at least she recognizes talent when she sees it. Prejudice does not completely cloud her mind (except when it comes to Mother and her side of the family).

"Answer to what Grand-mère?" I ask somewhat in the dark.

She wipes her lips with her napkin and lays it down near her plate.

"I cannot believe that the manuscripts were stolen for their monetary value, whatever some people may think. They are unique and cannot be sold on the market."

Remember the discussion I had with the staff of *Le Loup-Garou*. Was it only last week? Feels like years ago.

"Grand-mère, there are people who will pay a fortune just to possess some rare and beautiful item. They are obsessive types. Want things that no one else has, I guess."

Grand-mère shakes her head.

"You may be right, but there is something else, something that eludes us. Do go to the Cathedral and speak to Sister Felicity. She must have heard the news by now, and must be terribly worried. Tell her we are doing our best to find the manuscripts."

I agree. However, I need to know what Grand-mère hopes my conversation with Sister Felicity can accomplish.

"Grand-mère," I begin after biting into a juicy red apple that Valérie has brought in a straw basket. "Sister Felicity is a scholar. She is not a detective. I don't think she has the vaguest idea who the crooks are who are after the manuscripts. She lives in Scholastica Abbey, away from all that is wicked and evil."

Grand-mère shakes her finger at me.

"Never underestimate the Holy Orders, Marie-Christine. Priests and nuns rub elbows with evil everyday. In fact, they may have much more experience than you or me, or even the police, in dealing with evil. You see, they deal with people's hearts and souls. That's where evil first takes root and grows surreptitiously. The police deal with criminal behavior, which is the final stage: the outer expression of that evil that has been festering inside perhaps for years."

◆

Call Sister Felicity at the bishop's house to see if she is in. She is, and will be happy to see me at four o'clock this afternoon. The sky is gray and a cold drizzle has begun to fall; put on my long, white cashmere coat and white beret, and slip into my Ferrari. Fifteen minutes later I am knocking at the bishop's door. Sister Felicity opens the door herself. Her face is calm and serene. Thought she would be distraught, knowing that the manuscript she had brought from the United States had been stolen.

We settle in Monseigneur d'Epinay's library, where the old electric heater is warming the room.

"Monseigneur is not in?" I ask after removing my coat and beret and settling on one of the rather uncomfortable chairs next to the heater.

"No, he has work to do at the Cathedral. He'll be back this evening," answers Sister Felicity, pulling up another chair. She has set up a little table with a teapot and a plate of dry cookies which she offers me. Chewing on a cookie, I begin my investigation, not sure where it will lead me.

"Sister Felicity, you have heard what happened last night, haven't you?"

She nods, still supremely serene.

"Grand-mère has sent me to talk to you. She thinks you may have a better explanation for why those manuscripts were stolen than anyone else."

Sister Felicity looks at me and smiles, "And you, Chrissy, are not very sure that I can help?"

Am taken aback by her bluntness, but I suppose she is right. I do have reservations.

"Well, Sister, it's not that I doubt your expertise in manuscripts . . .," I begin somewhat hesitantly.

"No, you wonder what my expertise has to do with crime and criminals."

Speaking of dealing with people's hearts and souls, Sister Felicity can read people's minds as well.

"That is more in the realm of the police. . . ." Feel embarrassed and leave the sentence unfinished. She leans over and pats my hand.

"That's all right, Chrissy, I am not sure myself that I understand why those manuscripts were stolen. But I have been praying this morning after I heard of the theft. I have asked God to guide me and help me understand what the thief was after when he, or she, took those manuscripts."

"And have you figured out why they were stolen?" I ask eagerly.

She stands up and puts her cup of tea on the table.

"Come with me, Chrissy, and let me show you something."

I follow her to the far end of the library. That side of the room is paneled from floor to ceiling with bookshelves. In front of those shelves is a very large oak desk on which papers and what seems to be photocopies of pages of a medieval manuscript with colored illustrations are spread out.

193

Sister Felicity points to those pages.

"This is a photocopy that I made of the *Belles Heures du Duc de Berry* before I left the States. I kept it in my suitcase and forgot all about it until the manuscripts were stolen. . . ."

Curious, I bend over the copy to look more closely. Lots of rather gory pictures.

"This is St. Catherine of the Wheel or St. Catherine of Alexandria, which we were looking at when you were here with your grandmother last week," Sister Felicity points out. She shows me a number of other illustrations and explains some of the stories depicted in that manuscript.

"What about the *Trés Riches Heures?*" I ask. "Did you make copies of that manuscript as well?"

Instead of answering, Sister Felicity walks to the bookshelf behind the desk and picks up a rather large book. She brings it back, and after pushing aside some of the papers, places the book on the desk. From the title I realize that this is a printed copy of the *Trés Riches Heures du Duc de Berry.*

"Yes," she nods, "This is the published edition of the *Trés Riches Heures*. It was first published by George Braziller in 1969. This is the 1989 edition, which reproduces each of the illustrations, the miniatures painted by the brothers Limbourgs between 1413 and 1416, in full color and to exact scale."

Am beginning to get an inkling of what Sister Felicity is trying to do here.

"So you are putting the two manuscripts, or rather the copies of the manuscripts, next to each other to get a better understanding of what the thief was after?"

"I've put myself in the shoes of the person who stole the manuscripts, and imagined what he or she would want with them."

Am quite shocked—a woman dedicated to the service of God imagining herself to be a crook!

"*You*, Sister Felicity? You put yourself in the shoes of a crook?"

Sister Felicity smiles mischievously.

"But of course, Chrissy. How do you want me to help people if I don't understand them?"

Have no clue. Guess it's the same argument Grand-mère was making earlier this afternoon. I shrug, "Very well then, Sister Felicity, what was it that the crook saw in those manuscripts?"

She begins turning the pages of the published book of the *Trés Riches Heures*.

"What do you see, Chrissy, when you look at this book?"

I look at Sister Felicity, and wonder if the shock of the loss of the manuscripts has not been too much for her. If she wishes to step in the shoes of crooks and thieves, that's her business. I have no intention of playing this game.

"Sister Felicity, I hope I am not one of your suspects. I assure you I have no understanding of medieval manuscripts, have never been a collector of anything except Italian shoes, and frankly have inherited enough money to keep me afloat for the next few years."

Sister Felicity bursts out laughing. It's contagious, and I begin laughing too although I am not quite sure why.

"No, Chrissy, you are not on my list of suspects. I just need someone besides myself to look at the manuscripts (the copies of course), and tell me what they see. That's all. You've already told me something."

I think I understand.

"You mean if the thief was not an expert on medieval manuscripts, was not a collector, and had no one to sell the manuscripts to, what would he want with the two manuscripts?"

Sister Felicity looks impressed.

"Very good, Chrissy. Yes, that's exactly what I'm trying to get at."

I begin flipping through the printed book.

"But why, Sister Felicity, are you discarding the monetary and the collector's motives for the crime?" I ask quite reasonably.

Sister Felicity pulls a chair up to the desk and sits down. She gazes at the book and the photocopies on the desk, "I'm not discarding anything, Chrissy. I only want to widen the search to see if there are other reasons, in addition to those you've mentioned, to steal the manuscripts. I think I've found one, but I'm not sure. I want you to look at those miniatures, Chrissy, and tell me what you see. Because you are not an expert, nor have any interest in those manuscripts, you may have a fresh perspective on things. Study the images carefully."

As I hesitate, she places her hand on my shoulder and says very sweetly, "Chrissy, humor me please."

What can I say? I mean she has come all the way from Cape Cod, trusted us with the safekeeping of the manuscript by placing it in Grand-mère's house, and we've lost it. I really should do everything I can, even play this silly game, if it can be helpful.

"Very well, Sister Felicity. I'll do it."

Start with the photocopy of the *Belles Heures*. The illustrations are highly stylized and painted in bright blues, rich reds, and gold. There is a series, a bit like today's comic books, on that poor St. Catherine who refuses to worship idols. She is thrown into prison, a very small prison because the guards have to stuff her in it. Then there is another illustration of some kind of wooden contraption that is going to crush her bones, as she refuses to give up her Christian beliefs. How did people come up with those things? Did someone just sit down one day and

sketch a big wheel and think "this is the best way to break someone's bones"? Really sick! In another illustration angels come
down from heaven and shatter the wheel. Too late. St. Catherine
is already dead. The angels fly her body off to Mount Sinai in
the desert of Egypt. They could have come a bit earlier and
swooped her away, like super heroes, dropping something really
heavy on her tormentors.

Time passes and the room is growing dark. Sister Felicity has
been sitting next to me very quietly. Her eyes are closed. I think
she's praying. I look carefully at each illustration, although I don't
share my thoughts with Sister Felicity. She might find them rather
iconoclastic. There's a very interesting picture entitled St. Jerome
tempted by a vision of two women. It's a full-length page illustration of a monk kneeling on the floor in front of the gate of a
cathedral. He has dropped a red purse with what looks like a
rosary with rather large red beads. He looks behind him at the two
temptresses (rather plain women with long necks and protruding
bellies). A little black-winged and horned monster is floating
over his head. Guess it must symbolize temptation.

"Look, Sister Felicity," I say finally, to break the silence.
"That's an interesting illustration."

She opens her eyes, and looks at the illustration.

"God bless you, child!" she exclaims when she sees it. Her eyes
are shining; her hand is trembling as she holds the photocopied
image of St. Jerome.

Am surprised at her enthusiastic response. The painting is
not *that* spectacular.

"Why do you think it is interesting?" she asks.

I look at St. Jerome kneeling in front of the cathedral. . . .

"The entrance of the cathedral reminds me a bit of the
entrance to Notre Dame des Fleurs." Sister Felicity is glowing.

197

"Yes, Chrissy. What else do you see in this picture?"

There is a tremor in her voice. Her eyes are fixed on the image. Am beginning to feel excited as I examine the picture more closely. There is something else, "The winged monster looks very much like the gargoyle over the stained glass window on the west side of Notre Dame des Fleurs."

Sister Felicity is beside herself. She gives me a big hug.

"You're wonderful, Chrissy!"

"But what does this mean?" I ask, a bit overwhelmed. "What has that manuscript got to do with Notre Dames des Fleurs? I mean the illustrations were painted by the de Limbourg brothers for the Duke of Berry in Bourges, weren't they?"

"We are not sure," replies Sister Felicity, sounding like the scholar that she is. "The paintings in the *Belles Heures* and the *Très Riches Heures* show different castles that belonged to the Duke of Berry. This means that the de Limbourg brothers may have accompanied the Duke on different trips around the realm. They traveled on their own as well. We know that from archival materials and letters that were discovered years later."

"You mean to say, Sister Felicity, that the de Limbourg brothers may have come to Grasse as well?"

She gets up and switches on the lights in the library. A warm glow fills the room. She then walks to the bookshelves and pulls out an old book, and brings it back to the desk.

"Remember, Chrissy, that first evening when I came to dinner at your grandmother's house with Monseigneur d'Epinay?"

"Yes, of course. It was just a few days ago."

"Feels more like years. At that dinner there were other guests, among whom the mayor of Grasse . . . "

"Monsieur Martel and his wife, Mathilde. She actually writes a column in my newspaper *Le Loup-Garou.* . . . "

"Yes, yes," Sister Felicity waves her hand impatiently. "But do you remember what we were talking about?"

I try to think back, "I remember we talked a lot about manuscripts."

"Yes, we did. And at one point in the conversation Monsieur Martel brought up the legend of the de Limbourg brothers, who were asked by the Duke of Berry to encode in the two Books of Hours, the *Belles Heures* and the *Trés Riches Heures*, information about the location of twenty rare rubies."

"Ah yes, I remember! He also said something about the manuscripts being brought to Grasse for safekeeping."

"That's right, Chrissy. The mayor said that upon the death of the Duke of Berry an inventory of his belongings was made. Although very detailed, there was no mention of the *Trés Riches Heures*. Listed however was the other Book of Hours, the *Belles Heures*."

"And the *Belles Heures* was bought by someone at half its actual value." I remember Gerard kicking me under the table because I was asking too many questions and he was bored by the conversation.

"The *Belles Heures* was bought by Yolande d'Aragon."

"And who was Yolande d'Aragon?" Am trying to figure out who all those historical figures were.

"She was the mother of Louis d'Anjou, who was then Count of Provence. According to legend, the count had been entrusted by the Duke of Berry with the *Trés Riches Heures,* when de Berry's chateaux were burnt and pillaged by the Burgundians all over France."

"I see." Am beginning to get the picture, so to speak. "And so after the death of the Duke of Berry, Louis d'Anjou got his mother to buy the second manuscript, the *Belles Heures*, because he was already in possession of the *Trés Riches Heures.*"

Sister Felicity nods approvingly. But the history lesson is not over.

"The reason why Louis d'Anjou wanted to have both manuscripts, Chrissy?"

"To find the rubies?" I ask. Remember Monsieur Martel trying to tell his story and being continuously interrupted.

"Exactly! The twenty rubies, one of which weighed two hundred forty carats, which disappeared at the time of the death of the Duke of Berry."

"Are you saying, Sister Felicity, that the legend of the rubies is true?"

Sister Felicity sits down and buries her face in her hands.

"Chrissy, I have to admit that at first I did not believe this story. I thought it was just a legend. After that dinner at your grandmother's, I discussed it with Monseigneur d'Epinay. The bishop did not pooh-pooh the story. He expressed the opinion that stories can be transmitted quite accurately from generation to generation among people who are illiterate, which was the case of most Grasseois in the fifteenth century. He argued that this is the only way they have of remembering their history. We, today, rely on books. We make no effort to remember names and dates. Everything is stored for us in books. We can always go back and check facts. People who cannot read or write have to rely on their memory."

"In other words, you are saying that this legend was not a legend after all?" I ask, holding my breath.

"Well, I decided to look at the books that the mayor was referring to. I found an early printed history of Grasse. It was here in this library." She points to the old book she had brought from the bookshelf. "A whole set of old books were recently moved from the mayor's office to the house of the bishop, because of space constraints. The office needed the library for some of its newer records and books."

"So, what did you find, Sister Felicity?" I ask eagerly.

Sister Felicity opens the book and points to a page in Latin, "This passage here mentions that two men, who were in the service of the Duke of Berry, spent a couple of months in this very house in 1410. Although their particular profession is not clearly described, there is some reference to their ability to draw or sketch. They seem to have spent time sketching the Cathedral!"

"Oh my God! You mean that the miniature painting of St. Jerome in front of the cathedral is actually our Cathedral, Notre Dames des Fleurs?"

"Yes, Chrissy. After reading this medieval history of Grasse, and coming across the reference to the two men from the Duke of Berry's entourage showing up here the same year that the de Limbourg brothers are thought to have begun illustrating the *Belles Heures*, I became convinced that the mayor's story was not a legend after all."

Am silent as I reflect upon this stunning revelation. There is something else though, "Sister Felicity, the so-called legend stated that both manuscripts were needed to find the rubies. If that is so, then the *Belles Heures*, which was illustrated first, must contain the first piece of the puzzle. This would be the painting of St. Jerome indicating that the rubies are located in the Cathedral of Notre Dames Des Fleurs. I guess then that the second manuscript, the *Trés Riches Heures*, would have to show where in the Cathedral the rubies are hidden. Is that a plausible assumption?"

Sister Felicity stretches her arm across the desk and picks up the photocopy of the miniature painting of St. Jerome.

"Chrissy, I came to the very same conclusion. So I looked again at this painting of St. Jerome to find a link to the second manuscript, the *Trés Riches Heures.* I noticed the little red purse that had fallen from St. Jerome's pocket and out of which a rosary with big red beads had spilled out. Do you see it there?" She points to the painting. "Now, examine the rosary closely and tell me what is odd about it."

Am really enjoying this. Solving a five-hundred-year-old mystery! As I look at the rosary I see immediately what Sister Felicity means, "There is no crucifix at the end of the rosary!" I exclaim.

She claps her hands.

"Excellent, Chrissy! You'd make a great detective! And yes, you are absolutely right. There is no crucifix, meaning that. . . . " I interrupt her excitedly, "It cannot be a rosary! Those red beads must be the rubies!"

"Undoubtedly," agrees Sister Felicity.

Both of us peer at the picture, "You see, Chrissy, there are at least three clues in this painting: the entrance of the Cathedral, the gargoyle, and the red beads. There is another, but you'll see it when you look at the second manuscript."

Sister Felicity stretches her arm across the desk and retrieves the 1989 edition of the *Trés Riches Heures du Duc de Berry.*

"This morning I went through the second Book of Hours, this printed edition of the *Trés Riches Heures,* to find the other half of the puzzle. I had come to the same conclusion you had, namely, that the second manuscript would tell us where in the Cathedral the rubies were hidden. I wasn't sure, however, what to look for. Finally, I went back to the red beads next to St. Jerome and counted them. And sure enough there were twenty beads pointing clearly to the twenty missing rubies. So I re-examined the second manuscript, the *Trés Riches Heures,* to see if I could find red beads in any of the illustrations. I couldn't find beads, but I did find something else."

She opens a page of the printed edition of the *Trés Riches Heures* and points to a full-page illustration of a nativity scene! A golden-haired Mary in a long blue robe is looking down at a little naked Jesus on a bed of straw surrounded by four gargoyle-like creatures!

"This is quite extraordinary," I comment. "I know nothing about medieval manuscripts, but I have never seen a painting of a nativity scene, where the infant Jesus is surrounded by what looks to me like gargoyles!"

Sister Felicity's eyes are shining and she is almost breathless with excitement.

"I know, I know. It's incredible! The text says that they are cherubims. However, in no other de Limbourg illustration are cherubims painted entirely black. I would not have noticed it either had I not been searching for clues that would link the illustrations in the second Book of Hours with those in the first. And there are other clues. Chrissy, look closely at this Christmas manger and tell me what else you see that is similar to the painting of St. Jerome."

I pick up the photocopy of the illustration of St. Jerome and place it next to the painting of the manger. After studying the two paintings closely, I notice another similarity.

"The de Limbourg brothers must have used the same live model for the Virgin Mary in the *Trés Riches Heures*, and for the woman in blue that St. Jerome is looking at in the first manuscript. Not only are the women in the two paintings identical, they are also dressed in the same way. The only difference is that the Virgin Mary is wearing a white scarf, which does not hide her long blond hair, whilst the other woman is not."

Sister Felicity pats my back, "Bravo, Chrissy! I am very impressed. Why do you think the de Limbourg brothers chose to do that? I mean, use Mary as a clue?"

That's a no-brainer!

"Because the Cathedral is dedicated to the Virgin Mary! *Notre Dame* is Mary."

"Precisely! It is a way of reinforcing the message in the first manuscript, the *Belles Heures,* that the rubies are in the Cathedral."

She turns the pages of the printed edition thoughtfully and adds, "And of course, it also points to the matching illustration in the *Trés Riches Heures.* Since there are over three hundred illustrations in the two manuscripts, it was important for the de Limbourg brothers to indicate which illustration in the *Belles Heures* matched that in the *Trés Riches Heures.* They chose to do so by using the same model in both pictures, the same gargoyles, a similar hill in the background, and. . . . "

I look down at the two paintings again and frown.

"But there is something odd with that picture of St. Jerome. I mean, why did the de Limbourg brothers paint the temptation of St. Jerome in the first place—a picture of sin just outside a cathedral?"

Sister Felicity nods.

"It occurred to me that the de Limbourg brothers were trying to depict the temptation to steal the rubies, and not sexual temptation as the text mentions. It was their way of explaining why the rubies were being hidden in the Cathedral."

I suppose she is right. But there is also the choice of gargoyles, "How do you explain the gargoyles, Sister Felicity? Isn't that an odd choice as well?"

She shakes her head, "That I have not figured out yet. There must be a reason, of course, but I can't tell you what it is at the moment."

Sister Felicity then gets up and picks a side lamp from a small table next to the desk. She carries it and puts it on the desk so that the light shines directly on the book and the photocopied image of St. Jerome that I am holding in my hands.

"There is still more to be gleaned from this nativity scene, Chrissy. Look more closely," she bids me.

I'm beginning to get tired. My initial excitement has died down as I realize that we still don't have a clue where the manuscripts are, or who took them. The reason they were stolen may very well be the rubies, but frankly so what? The important thing is to find them, not to speculate about why they were stolen. But I have promised to help out Sister Felicity. Must humor her a little while longer. So I go back to looking at the nativity scene. There are a great many sheep on a hill, and angels appear to be singing from a book over the stable. Joseph, wearing a strange pointed hat, is kneeling next to Jesus. There is no star shining over the manger. Instead, there is an image of God, depicted as an old man with a long white beard, wearing a crown and holding a globe in his left hand. He is surrounded by . . .

"Oh, my God!" I shout almost dropping the book. "Those those red angels!"

"Yes, Chrissy," says Sister Felicity with a tremor of excitement in her voice. "These are the twenty 'flaming seraphims.' And in case one does not understand what they stand for, there are two shepherds searching the skies and pointing to the seraphims. These angels have the identical color to the twenty beads in the illustration of St. Jerome. The nativity miniature is also the only illustration in the whole *Belles Heures* in which one finds *twenty* flaming seraphims. These are the twenty rubies, I am sure of that."

The room is silent. Outside the wind is howling and it has begun to rain.

"With no expertise in manuscripts, Chrissy, you have been able to see the parallels between the two illustrations. I think this is what the Duke of Berry wanted the de Limbourg brothers to do. He wanted them to hide the rubies, but also to create a code for the right persons to retrieve them. Those persons were probably his grandsons. The Duke, however, was aware that his grandchildren were not as erudite as he was, and they would not understand a very complicated coded message. So he chose instead an illustrated message that did not require much knowledge of Latin or of Christian liturgy."

"But why was the message split in two? Why was half in one Book of Hours and the other in the second?"

"My guess is that he planned to give each of his two favorite grandsons, Charles d'Orleans and the Count d'Eua, one Book of Hours. Each would have had half of the code and would have needed to work with the other to find the rubies."

"So what happened?" I ask.

Sister Felicity shrugs, "The two young men were killed in the battle of Agincourt in 1415. That's probably when the Duke of Berry decided to give the *Trés Riches Heures* to the Count of Provence for safekeeping."

"Did he tell the Count that the rubies were hidden in the Cathedral of Notre Dames des Fleurs?"

"I don't know. What is historically known is that the Count of Provence's mother, Yolande d'Aragon, bought the second manuscript when the Duke de Berry died."

"So the Count must have guessed that the rubies were hidden in Grasse?"

Sister Felicity removes her glasses and wipes them with her handkerchief.

"Perhaps. He probably knew that the two de Limbourg brothers had come to Grasse, and he had also heard the story of the two manuscripts."

"So how does this information help us find the manuscripts, Sister Felicity?" I ask impatiently. Don't feel like hearing any more about the counts of Provence or the codes of the de Limbourg brothers. Grand-mère sent me to try to find these manuscripts. Instead, I've spent three hours speculating about lost rubies.

Sister Felicity gets up and picks the history of Grasse and replaces it on the bookshelf.

"Once you have figured out the reason for the theft, you can start discarding a number of suspects," she says, walking back.

"How so?"

Resuming her seat and picking up a pencil, she continues,

"Well, it can't be a collector, because a collector would want to keep the manuscripts. He would not be searching for rubies."

"And it would not be someone who is trying to sell the manuscripts, either," I add.

"Exactly. But it is someone who knows Grasse well enough to know the legend of the rubies." Sister Felicity is ticking off the various possibilities on a sheet of paper that she has taken from the desk.

"And it is someone who is familiar enough with manuscripts to understand how those illustrations were made, and how secret messages could be encoded." Am getting into the game once again.

Sister Felicity suddenly stops writing and frowns. She looks worried.

"Chrissy, I think we need to go to the Cathedral right now. There's no time to lose."

XIX

Inside the Cathedral of Notre Dame des Fleurs it is cold and dark. Candles on the left, next to the statue of St. Francis of Assisi, create a halo at the foot of the statue. Looking down the nave, the altar seems far away and dimly lit. In the flickering candlelight, the huge gray columns appear old and unsteady, and about to tumble over us. Brown pews, aligned in neat rows, fill the cathedral on each side of the aisle. There's a smell of incense, damp walls, and burning wax.

Sister Felicity and I tiptoe inside the Cathedral, afraid to make noise.

"But there's no one here," I say at a low voice. "Why are we tiptoeing?"

Sister Felicity squeezes my arm. With her forefinger on her lips, she whispers, "Listen. Don't you hear something?"

Straining my ears, I do hear some kind of muffled sound.

"What is it?"

"I don't know," replies Sister Felicity. She turns and walks on to the right aisle. Moving ahead quickly and silently, she directs her steps towards the altar. I follow as quickly and noiselessly as I can. Sister Felicity suddenly stops, and I bump into her.

"Sorry, Sister, I didn't see you." Her black cape and hood make her almost invisible in the dark. Realize that I must look like a floating spirit in my white cashmere coat and cap.

Without a word, she points to the eighteenth-century baroque chapel on the east side of the Cathedral. It's the Chapel of the Sacred Sacrament. Behind the altar stands Fragonard's huge painting of Jesus washing the feet of his apostles.

"Look," she says in a voice that is barely audible.

I scan the altar and the painting, and see nothing unusual.

"What?" I signal with my palm turned upward.

She points her finger towards the floor.

Look down. The floor is dark. At first I see nothing. Slowly a dark shape begins to emerge. Not a recognizable object. Sprawled next to a pew.

"What is it?" I ask hoarsely.

Silently, Sister Felicity, bending low, seems to sprint towards the object. She crouches next to it, turning her back to me. I move quickly behind her.

"It's a coat," she whispers without lifting her head. She continues to examine it, looking through the pockets.

"A man's coat?"

She nods and continues to search the pockets.

"What are we looking for?" Am sitting on my heels next to Sister Felicity, and beginning to feel ridiculous crouching on the floor.

Looking over her shoulder, she says, "There is someone in the Cathedral." Fingers the label on the coat. It is a Balmain label.

She points to the label and raises her eyebrow in a question mark. I nod, "Yes, very expensive." The stone floor is cold and uncomfortable. Try to get up, but Sister Felicity pulls me down by my sleeve.

"He'll see you," she whispers.

"Who will see me?" This cloak and dagger behavior is becoming annoying. If Sister Felicity will not explain what we are doing, crouching, whispering, and looking at labels of coats that have been dumped on the floor, I am leaving.

"Sister Felicity, I'm cold and hungry. And frankly I don't have the least idea about what we're supposed to be looking for here.

All this hush-hush business is not getting us anywhere. I am going back to Grand-mère and perhaps tomorrow we can continue where we left off tonight."

As I stand up to go, I hear a loud bang. Then another, and a third in succession. It fills the silence and seems to come from the other side of the aisle. I drop back on the floor next to Sister Felicity, who is looking up and listening.

"What is that sound?" I ask alarmed.

"I think someone is hammering," she answers.

Then it starts again, followed by the cracking of stone.

"Chrissy, I am going across to see who is hammering," Sister Felicity whispers. "You stay here with the coat."

"No way, Sister. I'm coming with you." Tone brooks no disagreement.

She and I get up and move towards the entrance of the chapel. We reach the aisle and look in the direction of the sound. There is a small light that is moving in the chapel on the west side of the Cathedral, just across from the Chapel of the Sacred Sacrament in which we were just crouching.

"Are you sure you want to come with me, Chrissy?"

"Two people are better than one in case we need to call for help," I argue.

She bows her head in acquiescence and walks towards the pews. Silently, she glides through a row, sliding on the bench. I follow suit. The hammering starts again. Sister Felicity darts across the aisle to the row of pews on the west side of the nave. I do the same. We slide on the wooden bench until we reach the other end which faces the little chapel. Some light from a street lamp is filtering in through a stained glass window. An ornate brass candelabra with three candles casts a flickering light on the altar. The floor remains in the shadows. But someone is there, with a flashlight. Seems to be kneeling on the floor. But it's too dark to see who it is.

"Look!" I gasp suddenly, pointing at the stained glass.

Sister Felicity, who was straining to see who was hammering, raises her eyes to where I'm pointing.

"Heavens!" She exclaims under her breath.

Just then the hammer crashes down on the stone floor. I jump at the noise and kick the pew. Sister Felicity catches my arm, thinking I am going to fall. Shake my head to indicate I'm all right. We hold our breath. Hope the person has not heard. There's a momentary silence, followed by the sound of sand or gravel being thrown on the floor.

"He has started digging," Sister Felicity whispers.

"What do we do now?" I ask.

"We need to alert the police."

"I think I've got my cell phone with me. I'll call Inspector Bizzard."

She nods, "Go outside. I'm staying here. I'll keep an eye on him."

Open my purse to find my cell phone. As I pull it out, another crash shatters the silence. My cell phone drops with a loud clatter. Too scared to move, I stand paralyzed.

And then a familiar voice snarls out of the shadows.

"Who's there?"

"God! It's Uncle Xavier!" I murmur to Sister Felicity. "Hide! I'll speak to him."

She shakes her head.

"Be careful. He could be dangerous."

"Who's there?" The voice is threatening and getting closer.

"It's only me, Marie-Christine, Uncle Xavier," I call out.

My voice is shaking.

"What in the name of . . . are you doing here?" His voice is harsh. I can hear his footsteps coming toward me. Must move quickly so that he does not see Sister Felicity.

Silently, I push her towards the front end of the pew.

"Go and call Grand-mère!" I whisper as I pick up the phone from the floor and press it in her hand. I then walk up toward Uncle Xavier. Realize that he must have spotted me because of the white coat and cap.

Feel sick in my stomach, but must pretend that I know nothing.

"Hi, Uncle Xavier!" Try to sound cheery. "I came to find Monseigneur d'Epinay."

"Why?" He growls. I can see him more clearly now. He looks so much taller than at Grand-mère's house.

Try to improvise but I find that my mind has become a complete blank. Can't think. "Grand-mère wants him to come over for dinner tonight."

"Do you know what time it is?" He almost shouts at me.

I have completely lost sense of time. Feels as if I've been with Sister Felicity for three days. Don't know what to say.

"It's ten o'clock!" he yells. So why was he asking me about the time? "Your grandmother has sent you to the Cathedral at ten o'clock at night to ask the bishop to dinner?"

Oh God! I just said the first thing that came to my mind.

"I'm sorry, I didn't mean tonight. I meant she wanted him to come over tomorrow night."

Uncle Xavier is now standing in front of me. I can see him clearly. His face is white and distorted with rage.

"Liar! You were spying on me!"

"No, Uncle Xavier! Really! I—I just came to find Monseigneur d'Epinay!"

My heart is pounding wildly. I can't breathe very well.

"You little snake! You must have followed me all the way up here. Haven't you?" He gets hold of my left hand and squeezes it. His hand is so cold it feels like a metal vice. A sudden surge of anger flares up in me: how dare he hurt me?!

"Ouch! You're hurting me. Let go of my hand!" I yell. The fear is gone. I want to kick him.

"I'll hurt you much more if you don't tell what you were doing here tonight." His voice now is as cold as his hand.

My mind is suddenly very clear. It must be the pain. Sister Felicity is gone. She'll call Grand-mère, and Claude will come with Inspector Pasteur and his assistant Guerrier. Uncle Xavier does not know that. So I must play for time.

"I won't tell you anything, if you continue hurting me!"

He emits a cackling sound.

"Gutsy little thing, aren't you? Very well then, let's sit down here, and tell me what you've been up to."

We sit on the bench. He is so close I can feel his breath on my face. It smells of rotten eggs. I just can't look at him, so I stare straight ahead at the altar. It makes me feel stronger. How long will it be before Claude and the inspectors come? Need to waste time. I begin, "Well, you see it was when we were all seated at the dinner table that first night. . . . "

"Don't give me a long rigmarole. Just tell me what you know," he hisses.

"Let me tell you how I found out."

"What do you know?" he insists.

It is going to be more difficult than I thought. Uncle Xavier senses that I want to waste time and is getting nervous.

"There is the legend of the two manuscripts," I try again.

"What about it?" The smell of rotten eggs on his breath is getting overwhelming. I think I'm going to be sick if I don't move away from him. I slip sideways on the bench. His hand immediately closes on my wrist in a vice-like hold.

"Don't move!" he warns.

I try to pull my hand away, but he doesn't let go.

"Take your hand off me and I'll show you what I know." I stand up. He immediately jumps up and drops my hand. Feel the blood flowing back in my fingers.

"Where do you think you're going?" he shouts.

"To the chapel where you were hammering a few minutes ago." He stands in front of me blocking the way, unsure what to do next.

"Yes, I know what you were doing there," I continue, encouraged by his apparent confusion.

He grabs my arm and shoves me forward.

"Very well, if you're so clever, show me what you've figured out."

He pushes me towards the little chapel. Have no idea what I'll find there. What if all those stories Sister Felicity told me this afternoon were just silly legends? In that case what is Uncle Xavier doing here? And then there is the stained glass window. We reach the chapel. "The nativity scene," I say, pointing to the window.

"I can see that," he growls. "So?"

"It's like the one in the manuscript," am trying to keep my voice from shaking.

"What are you talking about?" He snarls, still holding my arm.

"Like the one in the *Belles Heures du Duc de Berry*." My arm is throbbing.

Uncle Xavier laughs, making a low, mirthless squawking sound.

214

"So you're an expert on manuscripts now, are you? Do you know how many thousand nativity scenes have been painted on prayer books and stained glass windows in the past five hundred years?"

"But none has four gargoyle-like creatures surrounding Jesus in the manger," I blurt out. He gasps and lets go of my arm. I start rubbing it vigorously.

"A spoiled brat like you could not possibly have figured that on her own, could she?" There is something cold and dangerous in his voice.

"Why not? I have a bachelor's degree in English Lit. from Yale."

"You little twit! Don't try to tell me that you have any understanding whatsoever of medieval manuscripts. Who has told you that story?"

"What story?" Where are Claude and Inspector Pasteur?

"The four gargoyles, dammit! Who? Is it that pimply librarian?"

"You mean Alain LeMoine?"

"Yes, LeMoine, a fool like his father!"

So he recognized Alain, after all. I wonder if I can pursue this line of conversation until Claude and the police arrive.

"Yes, Alain told me about you." I begin.

"Told you what about me?" It is working. Uncle Xavier sounds nervous.

"About the fire, and his father."

"He would not sell me the Pucelle manuscript that I wanted. 'That one's not for sale,' he told me. 'It's for my son.' Too bad. He got what he deserved."

Feel a sudden chill down my back. A terrible thought is dawning on me.

"Did you kill Alain's father?"

215

He shrugs but does not answer.

"And then you set fire to the house and stole the manuscript?"

"What else could I do? I made him a very good offer and he refused it."

Uncle Xavier is mad! Completely and totally mad! How could Tante Geneviève have married the man? Oh my God! If he killed Alain's father, then—then—he must also have killed Phillipe! What shall I do? Must speak to him calmly as if all this were quite natural.

"So, Uncle Xavier, why did you kill Phillipe?" I ask conversationally. What's happening to Sister Felicity? Where are the police? I can't go on like this much longer.

He cackles.

"What a fool, that poor Phillipe. Did you know that he fell for some little tramp in Paris and wanted to marry her?"

Let him talk. Time is passing.

"And of course he had no money. So he came to me for help. To me? What a joke! I was up to my ears in debt. It would have taken a hundred years to get out from under my debts. But just then, your grandmother, bless her soul, offered me a way out."

"The manuscripts."

"Yes, the manuscripts! Those fabulous manuscripts! Together for the first time after five hundred years! And she asked me— *me*—to find a way of insuring them because—hear this, they were going to be in her house for safekeeping!"

"I see. And that's when Phillipe came to see you to borrow some money?"

"Yes, the timing was perfect. So I told him that if he wanted to make some money all he had to do was show up at your grandmother's place, a couple of days before Christmas, with some trumped-up excuse. I would let him know where the manuscripts were; he would take them and hand them over to me. For his help I'd pay him fifty thousand euros and he could buy a diamond ring for his little tart!"

"And he fell for it?"

Uncle Xavier is enjoying himself. He seems to have forgotten why we're in the chapel.

"Hook, line, and sinker!" he chuckles.

"Then what happened?"

"Everything worked like a charm. I told him to meet me that night in the garden so that I would give him the money and pass on the manuscripts to a friend of mine who would be waiting there. This way, when the theft was discovered the next morning and the police searched our rooms they would find nothing. They would assume someone broke in from outside. He and I would be safe, and I would have the manuscripts and he would have the money."

"But you didn't have the money." Am encouraging him to talk. Hope he doesn't realize that we are not talking about what he brought me here for.

"Of course not. Where would I get that money from?"

"So how were you going to pay Phillipe?"

"You really are a twit, Marie-Christine. Just like your aunt Geneviève, who believes everything I tell her."

There's a faint creaking sound behind us. We are still standing at the entrance of the chapel. My heart skips a beat. Perhaps the police are here.

"What's that sound?" Uncle Xavier barks. He turns around and scans the empty pews. I too look behind me but can't see a thing in the darkness.

"It must be the rain outside." Don't sound convincing even to myself.

But the spell is broken. Uncle Xavier is once again cold and in control.

"Very clever, Marie-Christine. Very clever. You got me talking in hopes that someone will come and help you. Who? Monseigneur d'Epinay?" He chuckles. "I had him called on an emergency in Plascassier. He won't be back before midnight! Ha, ha, ha."

He slips his hand in his pocket and pulls out a small gun. I look at him in disbelief.

"You're going to shoot me?" Am so amazed that I am not even frightened.

"And why not, *ma chère,* Marie-Christine? You know a great deal too much already about my private affairs. And frankly, I never did care much about you, or your family, for that matter."

"But I'm your niece!" I protest.

"Correction! You are my wife's niece. We are not related by blood. But first, tell me who else knows about the nativity scene and the manuscripts?"

And suddenly out of the darkness, "I do," the voice of Sister Felicity.

XX

Feel an enormous sense of relief, followed immediately by one of misgiving. Why is Sister Felicity alone? Where are Claude, and Inspector Pascale, and Guerrier? Wasn't she able to contact them? Uncle Xavier is mad. He'll kill us both!

Uncle Xavier twirled around at the sound of her voice, his gun pointing towards the pews. I try to move, but his left hand is on my arm again. The man has a vicious hold!

"Let her go," says Sister Felicity, emerging from the pews. She stands in front of him yet out of his reach.

Uncle Xavier waves his gun at her.

"Come here and stand next to Marie-Christine!" he orders.

"Not until you release her," she answers defiantly.

"Come here, or I'll shoot you," he screams.

"No, you won't." She seems very sure of this. I don't share her confidence.

Her quiet tone has a calming effect on Uncle Xavier.

"Why do you think I won't shoot you?" he asks, curiosity getting the better of him.

"Because you have not found the rubies yet."

There is a silence. The hand on my arm loosens its grip. He starts to breathe heavily, as if he were running.

"What do you know about the rubies?" he asks, finally.

"I'll tell you, once you let Marie-Christine go. You can hold me instead if you want."

"Do you know where the rubies are?" His voice is filled with greed.

"I have figured out where they were hidden."

219

His narrow eyes are glistening. He passes his tongue over his dry lips.

"I can't let her go. She knows too much." Fear is triumphing over greed.

"If you kill her, you will have to kill me too. I know as much as she does. If you let her go, I'll show you where the jewels were concealed."

He hesitates, "But she'll call the police and they'll catch me. So what's the use of finding the rubies?"

"If you take me hostage, the police won't be able to get near you for fear you'll shoot me. So you'll be able to get out of here, unharmed, and escape by car."

What's all this business of hostage-taking and getaway cars? That's not the scenario I'd envisaged.

"Sister Felicity, don't! The man is a murderer!" I shout.

"Shut up, you idiot!" Uncle Xavier, enraged by my outburst, lets go of my arm and hits me across the face with his left hand.

Stunned by the blow, I slip and fall. Sister Felicity rushes forward to help me. He catches her arm, twists it behind her back, and points the gun to her head.

"Go, Chrissy! Run!" Sister Felicity shouts.

Not quite sure what to do, I scramble up and rush towards the door of the Cathedral. Hear Uncle Xavier's raspy voice, "Now, you'll tell me where those rubies are, *ma soeur*, won't you? If not I'll just pull that little trigger here. I've done that before, you know, and with that very same gun."

"You shot Phillipe Bousquet, didn't you?" Sister Felicity asks in her calm voice.

"Yes, I did, and I'll shoot you too if you don't start talking."

Have to call the police, Grand-mère, Claude, someone, before Uncle Xavier kills Sister Felicity! Stumble blindly down the main aisle of the Cathedral and bump into a dark form that emerges from one of the pews. Am about to scream when I'm almost stifled by a big hand placed on my mouth. A voice whispers, "Quiet, Marie-Christine. We're here."

It's Claude! Want to hug him and shake him at the same time. Relief, anger, fear, joy, frustration, overwhelm me. He takes his hand off my mouth, "Where have you been all this time?" I ask, trying to keep my voice down. "It's Uncle Xavier! Over there!" I point to the chapel. "He is going to kill Sister Felicity!"

"I know. We've been here all the time. Got him on tape." Claude points to something on the bench next to him. "Get out of the Cathedral," he commands. "We're going to arrest this man now, and there may be some shooting. I don't want you to be in the way. Understand? Go!"

The man is maddening! I've just spend an hour with my Uncle Xavier, with a gun pointed at me, getting him to admit to his crimes, while waiting for the police to show up. Now this idiot, who's been doing nothing but taping the ravings of my uncle, wants to send me home?! No way!

Claude pushes me aside, then flashes a light signal. Out of the shadows, from behind columns and pews, springs a whole battalion of men in black. Stealthily, they move forward, and I decide to follow silently. When the men reach the chapel, Claude pulls out his gun and points it towards the two people in the chapel. He thunders, "Monsieur de la Rochereau, you are under arrest!" His voice resonates on the ancient walls of the Cathedral. I almost expect to hear the organ erupt into a joyful *Gloria!*

The men in black have surrounded the entrance of the chapel and are all pointing their guns at Uncle Xavier. Standing behind Sister Felicity next to the altar, he is holding a gun to her head.

"Tell your men to lower their guns or I'll shoot her!" shouts Uncle Xavier, beside himself with rage. In the wavering candle-light, this is like a scene out of St. Catherine's torments illustrated in the *Belles Heures*. Sister Felicity's eyes are closed. She is very pale, but her face shows no sign of fear.

Silence follows. Between the men in black standing around the chapel I can see the glittering stained glass window of the nativity scene.

Claude calls out, "Lower your guns!" The men obey.

"Let's talk," he addresses Uncle Xavier.

"I have nothing to say. Get out of my way if you want this woman to live."

Claude waves to the men to move. They open a passageway for Uncle Xavier to exit the chapel. He walks out, using Sister Felicity as a shield, and holding the gun to the back of her head. Sticking out from the pocket of his jacket are the two manuscripts!

"Don't follow me, or I'll shoot her!" he shouts.

We all stand back as the figures of my uncle and Sister Felicity disappear like two ghosts into the darkness of the Cathedral. A minute later, we hear the doors of the Cathedral swing open and slam shut. Still no one moves. A car starts, and Claude jumps into action.

"Quick! Move! Follow their car at a safe distance!"

I get hold of Claude's sleeve. He jumps, "You're still here? I told you to go!"

"I want to come with you."

"No!" he snaps. "This is police business."

He turns toward one of his men and orders him, "Take Mademoiselle de Medici back to her grandmother's house." And with that he marches out of the Cathedral.

"*Bonsoir,* Mademoiselle," says a familiar voice. I peer into the shadows, and there beaming at me is Dupont, the gendarme who came to the house the night the manuscripts were stolen.

"You were very brave in there with Monsieur de la Rochereau," he says admiringly, pointing to the chapel.

Finally, some appreciation for my feat of derring-do!

"Thank you, Dupont. You too were courageous to come here."

My mind is racing ahead. Must follow Claude and his men and be there when they catch Uncle Xavier. After all I owe it to *Le Loup-Garou.* The scoop of an eyewitness account of this drama will put us in the black. I've got to find a way of getting Dupont to follow the other cars.

"Dupont, do you know how to get to my grandmother's house?"

Some hesitation and shuffling of feet.

"Not really, Mademoiselle. I am new here. I was transferred to Grasse last month from Marseilles."

The man is positively at my mercy.

"That's all right, Dupont. I'll show you a shortcut. The house is quite far from here. But we must hurry."

Don't want to lose track of the police cars. As I get into Dupont's car, which is parked in *Place du 24 Août* just behind the Cathedral, I look down the steep slope and can see the trail of cars following Uncle Xavier's Mercedes.

"Dupont, let me guide you. First, you must go down that road," I point in the direction of the cars.

Without a word he follows my directions, and very soon, we find ourselves trailing the other cars, which in turn are following my uncle Xavier.

"But don't we have to overtake the cars?" he asks innocently.

"We can't, Dupont. My uncle Xavier may see us, and then God knows what he will do to Sister Felicity."

"You're right," he agrees.

Wonder whether Uncle Xavier will drive down to Cannes? No, he's turning right, towards downtown Grasse. Why? It would be so much easier to escape through Cannes!

"Do we go straight or turn right?" asks Dupont when we reach the crossroads.

"Turn right, Dupont, it's much shorter through town."

We are in fact driving away from Grand-mère's house. Will have to explain everything later. Now I must not lose sight of the police cars.

"But, Mademoiselle, we are still behind the police cars," Dupont protests.

"Yes, Dupont, I am aware of that. But this is the road that will take us to Grand-mère's house in no time." My tone is peremptory.

He frowns but obeys. I suppose he learned to take orders in the army and the police force.

We drive slowly through town. Suddenly the police car in front of us stops. Dupont applies the brakes and just misses bumping into it. Within thirty-seconds all the unmarked police cars are parking, or moving discretely to side streets. I get out of Dupont's car and look around. Uncle Xavier has stopped at a gas station. He has run out of gas! Sister Felicity is still inside the Mercedes. As he is about to put gas in the tank, he looks up and sees me! His eyes dart around as he realizes that the police have surrounded him. He jumps back into his car and drags Sister Felicity out. Uncle Xavier looks quite frantic. He screams, "You won't get me! I'll kill her and shoot myself before you catch me!"

Rather melodramatic, if you ask me. He can't escape and he knows it.

The police officers come out of their cars, and stand by awaiting orders. Claude moves forward.

"Monsieur de la Rochereau," he calls out. "Drop your gun and give yourself up. Your car is out of gas! You can't escape this time."

"I'll walk all the way to Cannes, if I must!" Uncle Xavier shouts back. "Stand back or I'll shoot this woman."

Sister Felicity is offering no resistance whatsoever as she stands next to him. But what is she doing now? Watch in amazement as she starts whispering in Uncle Xavier's ear. He looks surprised but listens. She continues talking to him. He seems to be getting quieter and less frantic. This charade lasts for almost ten minutes. Finally, he nods.

"*La bonne soeur* and I are going to take a walk," he announces.

The gendarmes look at each other, then at Claude. He waves his hand in a sign that signifies "don't move." Sister Felicity murmurs something to her captor, and then speaking loudly and clearly, she says, "Please gentlemen, Monsieur de la Rochereau and I will walk to *La Place aux Aires*. We need to talk. If you wish to follow us, do so, but please keep your distance."

Without even a glance back, the two start walking slowly down the narrow *Rue de l'Oratoire*, talking like two old friends. Claude and his men stare in disbelief. Claude then signals the gendarmes to follow on foot. Cars cannot enter these medieval streets built only for men and horses.

I suddenly remember something. Dash across the street to the gas station where Uncle Xavier's Mercedes is still standing. The driver's door is opened. I peer inside, and sure enough, lying on the front seat are the two manuscripts! Uncle Xavier must have taken them out of his pocket when he went down to get gas. Most of the gendarmes have followed Uncle Xavier and Sister Felicity. Dupont is waiting for me next to his car.

"Dupont, take these two prayer books." I hand him the manuscripts. "And guard them with your life. French-American relations depend on their safety. You will become a hero in Grasse for protecting France's honor and her glorious patrimony. I'll be back very soon. Wait for me here."

Race behind the gendarmes, leaving Dupont behind holding the manuscripts. He is so overwhelmed by his great responsibility that he is unable to utter a single word.

Claude, his men, and I trailing behind, finally reach *La Place aux Aires*. It was only a few days ago when Tante Geneviève and I had come here to do our Christmas shopping. Grasse's main square then had been full of light and laughter, and bustling with people. It is now dark, cold, and deserted. The stores are closed, the stalls are covered with plastic sheets. Standing in the middle of the square is the carousel with the horses, giraffes, and the big black bear.

Suddenly the lights go on. The music begins to play. Slowly, the carousel starts to move. As Claude and his men, with their guns drawn, watch dumbfounded, the white carriage comes into view. Sister Felicity and Uncle Xavier are sitting companionably next to each other on the seat of the carriage pulled by a white horse and a yellow-striped tiger. He is talking and she is listening, her hand on his arm. The unicorn behind them is keeping guard, protecting them from gendarmes and anyone else who may wish to harm them. The surreal image is accompanied by the tune of "O Christmas Tree," blaring in the empty square.

For the next hour, the carousel continues turning and the music playing. Claude has given the order to his men to spread out around the square so that no one can enter or leave the place. The music wakes up people. Lights appear on the darkened facades of buildings. Windows are thrown open with a bang. Insults are hurled. A woman throws a pail of water that just misses Claude's head. Dogs start barking. And Uncle Xavier continues talking, gesticulating. Sister Felicity sits silently, nodding at times.

As the white carriage comes into view for the nth time, I see Uncle Xavier bowing his head, and—and—I believe he's sobbing! Sister Felicity pats him on the back as if to console him! The carriage moves on, followed by the unicorn, and the giraffe.

Just as the carriage reappears, I see Sister Felicity stand up and move toward the center of the carousel. Then everything stops as suddenly as it had started. The lights go off, the music ceases. Even the dogs stop barking. Claude gives a sign and the men in black advance towards the carousel. I'm standing, watching, stiff and half-frozen. The hallucinatory scene unfolds a stage further when Uncle Xavier alights from the carriage and holds out his hand to help Sister Felicity step down. His manner is that of a Louis XIV courtier accompanying a lady to a ball!

When they are both standing before the carousel, Uncle Xavier waves his hand towards Claude and bids him to come forward.

"Monsieur l'inspecteur," he calls out, "you may have my gun." He hands over his gun to Claude, who has come up to him. "I am giving myself up and take full responsibility for the two murders I have committed, namely, those of Phillipe Bousquet last week, and of Pierre LeMoine five years ago."

He then turns to Sister Felicity, bows, and takes her hand and kisses it.

"*Ma soeur*, although I will never again be a free man, I have found myself today, thanks to you. And for this I will forever be grateful. Good-bye and God bless you, Sister Felicity."

And with that, he walks up to Claude, his arms outstretched, his fists clenched. Claude turns to Assistant Inspector Guerrier, who is standing behind him, and tells him to take over. Guerrier handcuffs Uncle Xavier and walks him back through the cobbled *Rue de l'Oratoire* to a police car.

XXI

The next few days are a blur. Tante Geneviève appeared not the least bit surprised when told of her husband's arrest. In fact, she looked positively relieved. Although she said nothing to the police, I think she had figured things out long before anyone else. When I offered Tante Geneviève the one hundred thousand euros to tidy her over until she could straighten out her financial affairs, she refused. Said she was fine now that she was rid of her husband.

Tante Helène, on the other hand, created a scene. I mean major drama: with tears, and hysterics, and wild accusations of fratricide in the de Medici clan. No use pointing out to her that Phillipe and Xavier were not de Medicis and were not brothers but brothers-in-law (in fact ex-brothers-in-law). That did not change matters.

United by a new bond (having had both their fathers murdered by the same man), Gerard and Alain decided to drown their sorrows together. They disappeared for two days and two nights. From what little I could gather when they returned, they had visited every bar between Grasse and Nice. They had also met every uncommitted female between the ages of twenty and forty in the region of the Alpes Maritimes!

Monseigneur d'Epinay and Sister Felicity took the manuscripts back to the bishop's house and began preparing for the New Year's Day celebrations at the Cathedral and the visit of all the dignitaries, foreign and national. Claude left for Paris but promised to return for the New Year Day's celebrations and luncheon at the house.

But it was Grand-mère who was most affected by the discovery of Uncle Xavier's misdeeds. She took to her bed for two days and would see no one but Valérie. Her faithful companion climbed up and down the stairs many times a day, carrying steaming tisanes and bouillons on bed trays. Jean lugged wood for her fireplace. Every pillow and blanket in the large linen closet were brought to her room by Valérie to make her comfortable. As Valérie bustled around with those pillows, she asked me an odd question: "Mademoiselle, why was your down comforter in the sitting room the other day?" I could not remember, although there was something I had dreamt. . . .

Even the octogenarian *Docteur* LeBon was called to check on Grand-mère. He declared that she was fine, but that the Christmas celebrations must have been a bit too stressful for her. He prescribed rest and more tisanes and bouillons. Finally, Grand-mère asked to see Papa. He came up from Cannes and spent a couple of hours with her. When he finally emerged from her room, he said that she was all right physically, but that emotionally the events of the past two weeks had taken their toll. When I pressed him for an explanation (Grand-mère is not given to serious emotional upsets), he explained that the de Medici's honor and social standing in Grasse had been severely tested by the murder and the theft of the manuscript. He said that Grand-mère felt that the town would no longer look up to the de Medici family with the same respect that it had for over three hundred and fifty years.

I had to make sure that *Le Loup-Garou* got the whole story from the horse's mouth. The day after Uncle Xavier's arrest, I rushed to the office and sat with Leon, Vivianne, and Paul and dictated literally every juicy detail of the theft and the murders. Gave them also some old family photos to illustrate the story. On Saturday, January 31st, *Le Loup-Garou* sold out by 9 AM. We reprinted the paper three times that day and a great many readers became subscribers!

Valérie hid that issue from Grand-mère and scolded me for "washing the family's dirty linen in public." I could not convince her that had I not printed the true facts of the story in *Le Loup-Garou*, other papers would have exaggerated or even distorted the facts, and the scandal would have been much worse. Guess the way the media works remains a mystery for Valérie.

Mercifully, Mother has been in London visiting an old friend in the past two days. Although aware of the latest developments, she does not as yet know all the details. Am *really* not looking forward to having to tell her that one of her French brothers-in-law (her favorite, by the way) threatened to shoot me. Mother and Papa have talked on the phone, and she has promised to be here for the New Year celebrations.

◆

New Year's Day! From my bed I can hear the bells of the Cathedral pealing! Get up and open the shutters to let the sun in. Am humming to myself the names of the bells the way my father taught me, "Do for Sauveterre, Ré for Martin, Mi for Veran, Fa for Bernard, Sol for Thècle, La for Agathe, Si for Joseph, and Do for Honorat." The bells will continue ringing throughout the day to celebrate the New Year and the eight-hundredth anniversary of the Cathedral. And this morning all of Grasse will be attending these celebrations at the Cathedral!

Dress with care. Slip into my most conservative outfit: a soft wool and silk ensemble, a royal blue dress and coat from Givenchy (a gift from Mother). After all, the high and mighty will be gathered in the Cathedral, so my skirt needs to hover no higher than two inches above my knee caps. Small gold and diamond earrings and diamond pin, and my favorite silk scarf in

231

gold, blue, and red. Goes well with my long dark red hair which I've let loose on my shoulders.

After breakfast the family is gathered in the entrance hallway. Miraculously everyone seems to have pulled himself or herself together. Without a word exchanged we all know that it is important to be dressed up and ready to present a united de Medici front at the Cathedral today. Grand-mère, as usual in black and pearls, inspects us like a general inspecting the troops before a parade. It is a matter of de Medici honor, which has been somewhat tainted in the last few days. At a quarter to ten, Papa and Mother arrive in their car.

And once again, as on Christmas Eve, we drive in a caravan of cars to the Cathedral.

But this time the sun is shining and it is unseasonably warm. There is a sense that this is going to be a very special day, and that these celebrations will not happen again—not like this, not ever.

We park in *La Place du 24 Août* and walk to the Cathedral in silence. As we arrive, a crowd has gathered. People stare at us and then begin to whisper. Reporters and photographers are hopping around us, taking pictures, hurling questions, "How do you feel about your husband being a murderer?"

"What is it like to have a criminal in the family?"

We move silently towards the stairs of the Cathedral. Papa has given his arm to Grand-mère, who leans on him slightly but remains erect and impassive. We all follow suit, staring straight ahead and pretending not to hear the questions. Mother and I, in matching coat and dress (hers in burgundy), walk behind Grand-mère. Even Tante Helène's striped turban is sitting straight on her head. Gerard is holding his mother's arm ensuring her headgear's vertical position. In a winter white coat and navy hat, Tante Geneviève brings up the rear, accompanied by Alain in black, looking pale and impossibly handsome.

Monseigneur d'Epinay is waiting at the top of the stairs. He is standing in front of the massive Cathedral door to welcome us inside. In full regalia, he seems to have stepped right out of one of the eighteenth-century paintings in the Cathedral. As we gather around him at the top of the stairs, the foreign dignitaries begin arriving. The press and the public lose interest in us and turn their attention to the Minister of Foreign Affairs, who is accompanied by the U.S. Ambassador and his wife. The Mayor of Grasse and Madame Martel wearing a hat with a French and an American flag intertwined, hurry behind them, followed by lesser local dignitaries.

The *Grande Messe* is truly splendid: with the organ playing Bach's *Sanctus* and *Agnus Dei,* and the choir in full form. Towards the end of the Mass, Papa turns around, and facing the congregation from the front pew, he leads it with his powerful tenor in a magnificent *Gloria!* I too turn around and observe the people assembled in the Cathedral. They are smiling. Realize what my father is doing. He is re-establishing the social order that has been disturbed by the murders, and most important, re-establishing the position of the de Medicis in that order.

And so it is that, after the Mass, all the Grassois line up to view the two manuscripts, exhibited side by side in a glass case in the Chapel of the Sacred Sacrament. They also crowd around Father and Grand-mère to wish them Happy New Year! Grand-mère is beaming happily and greeting everyone serenely. The photographers look disappointed. They will only have photographs of smiling people for their news reports. Leon, Vivianne, and Paul are also here to take photos of the manuscripts for *Le Loup-Garou.* Papa has promised to give them an inside scoop on what the French foreign minister has said to the U.S. ambassador and to Monseigneur d'Epinay on this special occasion.

◆

Back at the house, Valérie has prepared a grand New Year's Day lunch. Sister Felicity and Monseigneur d'Epinay have been invited to join the de Medici clan, but only Sister Felicity can make it. The bishop has too many obligations. Sister Felicity and Claude Bizzard, who has returned from Paris early this morning, sat unassumingly at the back of the Cathedral throughout the Mass. But now they are here to celebrate with us not only New Year's Day, but also the end of this drama that almost wrecked our Christmas holidays.

Grand-mère is sitting at the head of the table. Her mood and health have much improved since the *Gloria* at the Cathedral this morning. Papa has settled at the other end, and we have all taken our seats around the table. Claude is seated next to me. Grand-mère signals to Jean, who brings two bottles of champagne in ice buckets and proceeds to fill our champagne flutes. Papa then raises his glass and wishes us, "Happy New Year, everybody!"

We all raise our glasses and shout, "Happy New Year!"

Father then stands up and says, "I want to propose a toast to Sister Felicity, for her courage and goodness! She has saved a man's soul and a woman's life! To Sister Felicity!"

We all stand up except for Grand-mère, who doesn't have her cane, and Sister Felicity. Pointing our glasses in her direction, we call out in unison, "To Sister Felicity!"

Jean then brings in a large tureen with the traditional Provençal *L'aigo boulido*, my favorite garlic soup with eggs, Gruyère cheese, sage and laurel leaves, served on a bed of dry bread.

"Reminds me of the French onion soup," remarks Mother to Sister Felicity.

Turn to Claude, "Why did you go to Paris?" I ask conversationally.

"Business," he answers laconically, eating his soup. "Had to do some background checking on your uncle."

"You mean, about the murder of Alain's father?" Lower my voice, because I don't want Alain to hear our conversation. He's gone through enough already.

Claude nods, "Yes, I have asked for an autopsy to verify Monsieur de la Rochereau's claim to have killed Monsieur LeMoine."

The smell of the soup is so appetizing, I start eating slowly.

"By the way, Claude, why did Uncle Xavier kill Phillipe?"

Claude is finishing his soup, while I have barely started mine. Jean moves quickly to Claude's side and serves him another portion.

"I asked him that. He said that Phillipe Bousquet wanted his money up front in exchange for the manuscript. He even threatened to reveal the theft to the police unless he got his money that night. Apparently Bousquet wanted to buy a diamond ring from Tiffany for his fiancée. But someone there, a Mr. Thompson, would not sell him the ring unless he could show that he had money in his account."

"But if Phillipe reported the theft of the manuscript to the police, wouldn't he have been arrested, as well, for his role in the theft?"

"Not necessarily, because Phillipe Bousquet would have denied everything. If the manuscripts were found in the possession of de la Rochereau, it would have been one man's word against another's. The man in possession of the stolen goods would have been the one arrested."

I inhale deeply the aroma of the fresh Provençal herbs in the soup. After a moment of silence in which I take a few more spoonfuls of the soup, I return to the subject:

"I gather my uncle Xavier did not have the money to pay Phillipe. But why did he have to kill him?"

"I believe your uncle never intended to pay Phillipe Bousquet. He lured him to the garden on some trumped-up excuse that they were going to meet some third party there. He then shot him and took the packet he was carrying. That packet, supposedly, contained the manuscript."

The soup plates are cleared and Jean brings in an earthenware dish with baked tuna.

"*Thon à la Chartreuse,*" announces Grand-mère.

She looks at Sister Felicity and smiles, "Since you live close to the ocean on Cape Cod, I thought you might enjoy this Provençal dish. We prepare it with anchovies, tomatoes, and steamed sorrel leaves. How do you prepare tuna in America?"

Sister Felicity shakes her head and looks embarrassed.

"Thank you, Madame de Medici, for thinking of me. And yes, I do love tuna, but I'm sorry I really can't cook."

Grand-mère lifts her eyebrows in surprise, "Really? But you have so many other talents. . . ."

I turn to Claude, who is savoring his tuna.

"So Uncle Xavier brought his gun to Grasse because he was planning to kill Phillipe?"

Claude dips his bread in the tomato sauce, "Yes, your uncle came up here to spend Christmas with his wife's family, armed, and planning to kill a man related to him by marriage."

Put this way, the crime seems even more cruel and calculated. Continue eating my fish, but it seems to have lost some of its taste.

Valérie and Jean roll in a serving table. On a big silver dish are woodcocks sliced in two with a white wine sauce. Stuffed onions with breadcrumbs and celery are arranged around them, while sauteed mushrooms with parsley have been placed in a luminous ceramic bowl. Jean begins serving.

"And how did the manuscript of the *Trés Riches Heures* end up among the Christmas gifts by the manger on Christmas Eve?"

Claude smiles and looks across the table to Tante Helène, "You should ask your aunt, one day, what happened in her bedroom that night. But it is clear that Bousquet took the manuscript from your grandmother's study and hid it among the gifts of your aunt Helène. He then went to the garden to meet your uncle Xavier with nothing more in his hands then wrapped up newspapers. He obviously did not trust de la Rochereau."

Swallow a mushroom, and begin coughing. He slaps me in the back, and I pick up my champagne glass and drink. "You mean my uncle Xavier killed my uncle Phillipe for nothing?"

"That's about the size of it. Because your uncle finally had to steal the manuscripts himself, without anyone's help."

Claude has finished his woodcock and looks up in the direction of the pantry door. But Jean is already at his side scooping more woodcocks, mushrooms, and stuffed onions.

Grand-mère turns to Sister Felicity, who is seated on her right at the place of honor, and asks, "Sister Felicity, I have a question for you, one I'm sure everyone around this table would like an answer to. What happened to the famous rubies? Did the manuscripts really have clues to their secret location? Or was this just another Grassois legend?"

Sister Felicity smiles and looks at me across the table.

"Chrissy and I spent a whole afternoon figuring out if the manuscripts really held a clue to the rubies. And Chrissy was very clever and figured out that in each of the two manuscripts there was an illustration that indicated that the rubies were indeed hidden in the Cathedral of Notre Dame des Fleurs."

"No, Sister Felicity," I interrupt. "It was *you* who figured that out and led me to the same conclusion."

"You're very modest, Chrissy. The point is that if Chrissy and I could guess where those rubies were hidden, so could others, and they must have long before we came along. I believe that in the early part of the fifteenth century, Louis d'Anjou, the Count of Provence to whom the Duke of Berry had given the *Trés Riches Heures*, and his mother Yolande d'Aragon, who had bought the *Belles Heures* after the duke's death, found the rubies. I did find the secret drawer under the altar where the rubies were once hidden. The nativity scene on the stained glass window just above the altar was very similar to that in the *Trés Riches Heures*. One of the rays descending from the image of God towards the infant Jesus pointed directly through the red seraphims to the hiding place of the rubies. But of course the drawer was empty."

Silence follows. We all realize that Uncle Xavier murdered Phillipe for nothing. He was about to snuff me out as well for a dream of rubies that had disappeared five hundred years ago! Feel like giving a big hug to Sister Felicity.

Mother looks around the table and declares very proudly, "Well, I'm glad that we had a no-nonsense American woman here to figure things out!"

For once Grand-mère does not respond to this direct challenge to her French pride.

Valérie helps Jean clear the dishes, then brings in a platter of cheese. Jean places a bowl of tangerines, apples, and pears in the middle of the table, and declares, "Dessert and coffee will be served in the sitting room."

"One moment, please, before you all move to the sitting room. I have an announcement to make." Grand-mère taps her glass with a knife. We all fall silent and turn towards her. She clears her throat and pats Sister Felicity's hand.

"On behalf of all of us gathered here today, I want to say thank you, Sister Felicity. You have done this family a great service, and we will always be in your debt." She beams at her.

"Madame de Medici, it was nothing really," answers Sister Felicity, bowing her head and blushing.

But Grand-mère has not finished what she wanted to say, "You saved my granddaughter's life. That is something that can never be repaid. To express this family's gratitude, I am establishing a special fund so that sisters from Scholastica Abbey can come to Grasse every year to study and work at the Cathedral and at the many churches big and small in the area. Your prioress at the Abbey will decide whom to send and the sisters will be most welcome to stay in this house for as long as they choose."

Everyone around the table claps! At a sign from Father, Jean brings in another champagne bottle and fills our glasses. Once again we drink to Sister Felicity. She thanks us all, and says something sweet about the sisters of Scholastica Abbey appreciating what Grand-mère and all of us are doing. And then we move to the sitting room to consume Valérie's delicious *Clafoutis,* a cherry pudding *nonpareil,* and an apple tart that just melts in your mouth.

XXII

Holding my *Clafoutis* in one hand and my glass of champagne in the other, I slip next to Sister Felicity on the sofa. There are still many unanswered questions.

"Sister Felicity, how did you do it?"

Her face is serious, almost sad. She does not look up from the slice of apple tart she is eating.

"You mean why did Xavier de la Rochereau give himself up and confess?"

I nod eagerly and add, "Is it all right to tell me what happened, Sister Felicity? I mean you wouldn't be violating his confidence, or something, would you?"

Sister Felicity puts her plate down on the side table, and wipes her eyeglasses with her napkin.

"I am going to have to testify at your uncle's trial, and have asked his permission to tell the court what he said to me on the carousel. He's agreed to this. In fact, he wants everyone to know what happened to him. 'Let people learn from my experience,' he said. 'So that they don't repeat the mistakes I've made.'"

"So what did he tell you?" I ask curling up on the sofa. Am really curious about what caused my uncle to turn into a murderer.

"Well, I think the realization of what he had done began dawning on him in the chapel of the Cathedral of Notre Dame des Fleurs. You see, when I told him I knew where the rubies had been hidden, he thought I knew where they actually were. He let you go and then at gunpoint asked me to locate the rubies. He had the two manuscripts with him, so I showed him the illustration of the nativity scene and the shaft of light that pointed

240

directly to the infant Christ lying in the straw. I then showed him the stained glass window in the chapel, where the exact image of the nativity scene had the shaft of light not only pointing to the manger, but allowing light from outside the Cathedral to filter through and fall directly on the altar. To make a long story short, I found a secret drawer under the altar, but when I pulled it open it was empty."

"Uncle Xavier must have been furious!"

Sister Felicity nods.

"He was stunned. Then the police showed up, and he had to think quickly about saving his own skin. So he used me as a shield. As for the rest, you witnessed the drama as it unfolded."

"But you planted the idea into his head of using you as a shield," I remark. Will never forget Sister Felicity popping out of the pews just as he was threatening to shoot me.

"Well, I really didn't want him to kill either of us. He had to be made to realize that we could be more useful to him alive than dead."

"Yes, of course. But later, after he was surrounded by police at the gas station, how did you get him on the carousel?"

Sister Felicity's eyes twinkle behind her glasses.

"It was his choice. He wanted to talk in private. But there was nowhere to sit, and the police had surrounded the *Place aux Aires*. The carriage on the carousel was a perfect confessional. The music also isolated us. No one could hear what he was saying except me, because I sat next to him."

Jean comes by with the coffee tray. We both help ourselves, and settle back comfortably on the sofa. Grand-mère is talking with Father about the state of the economy; Tante Helène is explaining to Alain and Tante Geneviève how turbans are worn in Bukhara; Mother and Pushkin are getting acquainted over a piece of apple tart; while the merits of French versus American cigarettes are being loudly debated by Claude and my cousin Gerard.

"What motivated my uncle Xavier to kill two men? Was it just greed?"

Sister Felicity takes a sip of her coffee, then resumes her story.

"No, it was not just greed. It was more a matter of pride. Pride comes before the fall, you know. Your uncle realized that your aunt Geneviève was becoming a very successful woman. She was making much more money than he was, and his pride was hurt. At first, he tried to compete with her and make more money by taking greater and greater risks. He bought works of art and antiques that he could ill afford, hoping to find a buyer and make a killing. But he is not a businessman. He fell into debt, and needed money quickly to pay off some of his loans. He did not want to go to his wife and admit his mistakes."

"But Sister Felicity, I know for a fact that he did go to her and borrow money," I interrupt.

"Only later, when he was quite desperate," answers Sister Felicity, shaking her head. "But at first, he thought he could manage on his own. When Alain's father called him and offered to sell him some rare books, he thought his luck had changed. He knew a collector who wanted a rare manuscript that Mr. LeMoine owned. The man was willing to pay your uncle Xavier a very large commission if he could obtain it. LeMoine, however, would not sell that specific manuscript. It was the crown jewel of his collection, and he wanted his son, Alain, to have it. So your uncle decided to kill LeMoine, set fire to his house, and steal the manuscript."

"But that crime did not solve his problems, did it?" I ask rhetorically.

"No, because he continued trying to outdo his wife and fell even deeper into debt."

"But how did you get Uncle Xavier to tell you all this?" Am really impressed by the depth of Sister Felicity's understanding of that rascal of an uncle of mine.

Sister Felicity hesitates for a moment, and then says, "When he dragged me out of the Cathedral and pushed me into his car, I began praying for him. I asked God to forgive him and to help him realize the evil he had done. I then felt very calm and at peace, and talked to him. At first, he would not listen. He kept repeating, 'Why were the rubies not there?' 'Who stole them?' By the time we got to the gas station and he realized that he would have to kill the whole police force of Grasse if he wanted to escape, he began to listen to me. 'Walk with me and tell me what happened to you,' I said. 'I'll try to help you.' He knew the game was up and he was frightened. He needed someone to talk to. I called out to Claude and his men to leave us alone while we walked to *Place aux Aires*."

Claude gets up, pulls a chair, and joins us.

"Did I hear my name spoken in vain?" he asks, smiling his crooked smile.

"Sister Felicity was about to tell me what happened on the carousel with Uncle Xavier."

Claude raises one bushy eyebrow.

"Is that so? May I listen too?"

Sister Felicity waves her hand toward him, "By all means. You'll hear the story again in court though. As I was saying, by the time we reached the carousel, the horror of what he had done was crashing down upon him in waves. He was realizing that he had killed Phillipe Bousquet for nothing, since there were no rubies, and that he had basically thrown his life away, because he was going to be arrested. At first, he talked incoherently about how your aunt Geneviève had become a very successful woman, and how she no longer needed him. He rambled on about how much he had loved your aunt Geneviève, how he had wanted to impress her, and how he had failed her miserably. The fact that she never mentioned her success, or asked anything of him, infuriated him. He said something about trying to make her jealous and taking a mistress, and how his love had turned to hate because his wife did not understand what he was trying to do. He felt ashamed and humiliated when he finally had to turn to her for help, and she gave him the money to pay his debts. His hate became all-consuming and he wanted to bring her down with him. As their financial situation deteriorated, so did their marriage, and your aunt finally asked him for a divorce.

"At that point your grandmother called her son-in-law about insuring those rare manuscripts, and you know the rest of the story. At first, he just wanted to steal the manuscripts and sell them to save his doomed auction house. To have an alibi, as he knew he would be a suspect in the theft, he thought of engaging the assistance of your uncle Phillipe, and then of getting rid of him. At the dinner at your grandmother's on the night of your family's arrival, the mayor talked of the rubies. Your uncle Xavier remembered the old Grassois legend, and decided there and then that in addition to stealing the manuscripts, he would also find the rubies."

Claude, who has been silent the whole time, scratches his head, and his hair begins sticking up on top of his head (I must speak to him about changing his barber).

"But Sister Felicity, you haven't told us yet how you got him not only to confide in you, but also to turn from a very angry man to one who had reconciled himself to his fate."

Sister Felicity stands up. She looks tired and drained.

"Inspector Bizzard, I *have* told you. I listened to the man. Not the elegant, witty, sophisticated expert in antiques, but the very troubled and frightened man. I also pointed out to him that there was something very important that he could still save from the shambles of his life. . . ."

Claude murmurs, "His soul?"

She smiles at him, "So you *have* been listening?"

◆

After coffee, Tante Geneviève announces that she is leaving. She has decided to sell what is left of her own consultancy business in Paris, to cover some outstanding debts. She then plans to take a long trip around the world to get over those devastating events that have "ruined" her life. Elegant in her silver fox, and looking not in the least bit devastated by the recent events, she kisses Grand-mère and Tante Helène good-bye. Her suitcases are packed and Jean has called a taxi. Turning to me, she says, "Marie-Christine, as I plan to be away for a long, long time, I can no longer keep Pushkin. I'm giving him to you because I know you will take good care of him. Perhaps one day he'll be of some help to you in one of your investigations."

And with this, she picks up Pushkin, drops a kiss on his left ear, and hands him over to me. He starts whimpering. He knows she is leaving. Turning his little head away from her he nuzzles into my sweater. Guess I'll be responsible for him from now on.

◆

Later this afternoon, Claude says he has to return to Paris. He bids everyone good-bye, and kisses Grand-mère on both cheeks. Few outside the family circle have dared, and yet Grand-mère takes it quite naturally. Extraordinary! Claude turns to me and asks casually if I would walk with him to the garden gate. Intrigued, I wrap myself in my pink *pashmina* shawl and step out of the house with him. The sun is setting and the wind is rising. But it is not cold yet. Staring straight ahead, Claude seems to be in a hurry to go.

"I'm sorry that Christmas in Grasse was not quite what you had expected," I say, trying to have a conversation. His silence is unnerving.

Claude does not seem to hear me.

"By the way, I brought you a little Christmas gift," he says as he starts looking in the pockets of his coat. "But with all that happened, I forgot to give it to you. Ah! There it is."

He pulls out a little square packet from his left pocket. It looks as if it's been there a while. The Christmas wrapping is all creased and the silver bow is askew.

"Thanks." Feel a pang of guilt, because I never got him a gift.

"Well, why don't you open it?" he asks brusquely.

"I will. Don't rush me!" I tug at the silver bow, and promptly drop it on the gravel. Finally I manage to open the box.

"Oh, how lovely!"

Nestled in a cotton ball are a pair of tiny ruby earrings!

"Since I could not find the fabled rubies of the Duke of Berry, I thought you should at least have a token to remind you of this very special Christmas—at least it was for me."

And with this, he kisses me lightly on the forehead. Before I'm able to say a word, he is out of the gate and into the street where Inspector Pascale is waiting for him in a police car.